THE WARRING STATES CONUNDRUM

BY

SEYMOUR GRUFFERMAN

The Warring States Conundrum

Interior Book Design and Layout by
www.integrativeink.com

ISBN: 978-0-692-09122-7

Acknowledgements

I wish to thank the many people who helped make this book possible. It began with the courses I took from Stanford's Online Writers Studio, their excellent teachers and my creative and helpful classmates. In particular, I thank Malena Watrous, my teacher and editor, for her encouragement and for converting me from scientific writing to fiction writing. I also thank my friends who read drafts of the novel and provided helpful suggestions. Above all, I thank my wife Sue for her steadfast support, inspiration and encouragement.

PART I

The Warring States Period: An epoch in Chinese history dating from about 475 BCE to 221 BCE. It was a time of great turmoil with strong regional states at war with each other to consolidate power, wealth and territory. It is believed that Sun Tzu wrote the "Art of War" during this period. It was also a time of great ideas with the "Hundred Schools of Thought" flowering. Among these Schools were Confucianism, Taoism and that of Yin-Yang and the Five Basic Elements of the Universe.

Conundrum: A puzzle or riddle the answer to which is a pun: a very challenging or complex puzzle or problem.

Chapter 1.

It was 8:20 P.M. and coal dark outside when Winston Sage got the phone call that would change his life. He was at his desk and had just poured himself a glass of the special 25-year-old calvados he'd been saving to celebrate his retirement when the damn phone rang. He took a slow sip of his drink before picking up.

A man's voice asked, "Is this Dr. Sage?"

"Yes."

"My name's Bill Harvey. I'm a neighbor. I hope I'm not interrupting anything."

Sage eyed the snifter of amber calvados in his hand. "No. Not really."

"I have a problem I was hoping you could help me with. I got your number from Sandy Greene."

Sage, an epidemiologist, and his wife Julia, had been in their new house barely two weeks. They had moved to Santa Fe without knowing a soul there, so it was nice when another neighbor, Sandy Greene, had a welcoming party for them. He couldn't remember having met Bill Harvey there, and he was surprised by what this stranger revealed next.

"You see, my wife's disappeared," the man went on. "About two weeks ago she just vanished. I've been to the police and gotten nowhere and I'm at the end of my rope. I wonder if I could talk to you about it."

"I'm not sure why you think I could help," Sage said, as he rubbed his forehead.

"I heard from Sandy that you're an expert on tracing people. Look, I'm desperate. Is it all right if I came over now? I won't stay long."

He took another sip of his drink, sighed, and said, "Sure. Do you know where our house is? It's a new, contemporary house..."

Bill broke in, "Oh, I know it. Dr. Sage, I really appreciate your kindness. I'll be right over."

No sooner had Sage hung up than his wife Julia appeared in his study doorway wearing a cozy pink chenille robe and holding a Japanese tea mug. She found a pile of boxes to perch on. Win smiled and thought it was a pedestal hardly befitting his Korean-American princess. "Who was that Win?" she asked

"A neighbor named Bill Harvey. His wife disappeared a couple of weeks ago."

"So why on earth did he call you?"

"Remember the party last weekend at the Greenes? I told Sandy about my research and how I was able to find cancer patients years after their treatment. She told him that I'm good at tracing people. We're new here and I wanted to be a good neighbor, so he's going to stop over."

"What! Is he coming over now? The house is a God-awful mess," she said, pointing to the piles of books on the floor.

Win shrugged. "I'll just bring him here to my study. I've always fancied myself a medical detective. Remember how I used to joke with my research assistants that I could always open up a detective agency if we lost our research funding?" Win grinned and went on, "This could be my big chance to play real detective. Who knows, maybe I can help him."

Julia rolled her eyes. She surveyed the wood-paneled room and said, "You don't look like a pot, Win."

Win looked down at his belly. "I hope not."

He'd asked their architect to design this study to look like the pale wooden boxes that hold precious pieces of Japanese pottery. By default, that made him the pot.

He smiled at his wife's joke. Win was still smitten by Julia some thirty years after meeting her on their first day of classes at Harvard's School of Public Health. He had proposed to her on their first date. Her response was that she would need at least a five-carat engagement ring to even consider marrying him. So Win trudged off to the supermarket and the next day presented her with five carrots tied together in a ring, in a plain brown paper bag of course. That was in September and they were married in Harvard's Memorial Church two days before Christmas.

Julia got up, came over to Win and kissed him gently on the forehead. "Oh, Win; you're a hopeless softie, but that's one of the things I love about you".

Chapter 2.

The doorbell rang, setting off a chorus of barking dogs. The man in the doorway was fiftyish, tall and good-looking, with a tanned, leathery face that reminded Win of an old baseball glove. He was wearing a Santa Fe uniform -- fringed, brown suede jacket, black T-shirt, torn jeans, and embroidered cowboy boots. He smelled faintly of sandalwood.

"Come on in. I'm Win Sage and you must be Bill Harvey. Would you mind taking off your boots? We live Asian-style and don't wear shoes in the house. Help yourself to a pair of slippers over in the corner." Julia grew up in Asia where people automatically removed their shoes on entering a house. Win had acquired the habit when he served in the Air Force in Japan. He got so attached to the felt Japanese slippers he wore at home that on more than one occasion he absent-mindedly wore them to the hospital with his Air Force uniform.

Bill gave Win a strange look and slowly chose a pair. Win figured he was trying to remember whether he had any holes in his socks. He was wrong; Bill was barefoot.

"The house is still a mess after our move," Win said as he led the way. "Why don't you come back to my study, it's the least messy place."

"You don't know how much I appreciate your willingness to see me on such short notice."

Win ushered Bill to the study and to the only upholstered chair in the room. Bill sank into the red chair as if he were a balloon deflating.

"I was having a drink when you called. Can I get you something to drink?"

"No, thanks. I'm fine," Bill said, getting right down to the business at hand. "My wife and I have lived in our subdivision for about four years now. We own the East-West Gallery on Canyon Road."

"That's an interesting name."

"We sell Asian and Southwestern art. That's how we got the name. Jessica, that's my wife, handles the Asian side and I do the Western stuff. We developed our business interests before we met, so we just merged them when we got married. This is the second marriage for both of us."

"What sort of Asian things do you carry?"

"Jessie specializes in ancient Chinese ceramics. She's become quite expert on the subject."

Win pointed to one of the display cases built into the maple-paneled walls. "I have several pieces of antique Chinese ceramics over there."

Bill surveyed the room and its display cases. "Oh yeah; you have a lot of Chinese and Japanese pottery. It's nice stuff. You'd like Jessie. " His mood darkened. "Thirteen days ago Jessie left the Gallery and never came back. There's absolutely no trace of her. I went to the Santa Fe and State police and they've come up with nothing. I'm at wit's end over what to do."

"Jeez, that's alarming. Do you have any idea where she might have gone or if something could have happened to her?"

"None at all. Sandy Greene thought you might be able to help me trace Jessie."

"Well it sounds like you've taken the right steps to find her. The police are probably best for finding missing people nowadays with computerized data sources and access to hospital information and accident reports. When I was in the business of tracing cancer patients, I would first do death certificate searches. Depending on the person's occupation, I might use state registries of licensed occupations like nurses, beauticians, electricians, and the like, or search telephone directories. Nowadays, a lot of that can be done via the Internet. Unfortunately, sources like these don't list a person's whereabouts until they've been in a place for a while and your wife's been gone for only two weeks. So stick with the police."

Bill started to play with a glass paperweight on Win's desk. "I really don't think the police have taken Jessie's disappearance seriously. They checked hospitals and accidents, the usual stuff, and found no trace of her. Also, there's no sign of her car, so they think she might have driven off somewhere, unless someone did her harm and stole her car. I've been checking with her kids – they're from her first marriage – and her relatives. Nobody's heard from her and she's usually pretty good about keeping in touch with the kids."

Win hesitated before asking, "Could she have been involved with another man?"

Bill let out a nervous laugh. "Oh, no. We're pretty happily married, and this being a small, gossipy town, I would have heard if she were having an affair. Could she have developed amnesia and gotten lost? I know those things happen and it would explain her disappearance."

Win tried to recall what he knew about amnesia. "That type of amnesia, a fugue, in medical lingo, involves someone losing their identity or forming a new one and is darn rare. At this point, you should stick to more likely reasons."

Bill squirmed in his seat. "Jessie seemed upset and depressed for a couple of days before she disappeared. That's why I asked."

"Did she say what was bothering her?"

"No. She keeps her feelings pretty bottled up when she's down."

"Oh, did she suffer from depression?"

"She had a few bouts of depression over the years. Her doctor gave her some medication that helped her get over them though."

"Did she ever talk about suicide or attempt suicide?"

"No, never."

Win realized he was beginning to sound like a doctor and changed course. "Do you know whom she was going out to meet the day she vanished?"

"She never said -- which is typical. It could have been a client or a friend. I don't have a clue and neither do the police."

Win caught a whiff of apples from his drink and offered again, "Are you sure you wouldn't like something to drink?"

"No. I'm all right."

Win went on out of medical habit. "Bill, were you and your wife having any marital problems or disagreements?"

"No. Maybe we both learned something from our first marriages."

"Were you having any financial or legal problems? Was anyone angry with her?"

Bill was staring at the bright Kurdish rug on the floor. "No. She's pretty much liked by everyone. We're in a tough business and had some hard times, but just when we're doing well after years of struggling, Jessie disappears. It was her side of the business that helped us strike gold." With that, he deflated even more into the chair.

Win leaned back, stared out the picture window and shook his head slowly from side to side as he reflected on the situation. He surveyed the brown hillocks on his land that were sharply outlined by a full moon that had just risen. He remembered the first time he had visited New Mexico and how he had immediately been taken by the spectacular landscape painted mostly in shades of brown, and the night sky punctuated with more bright stars than he'd ever seen.

He sat up. "Bill, I really don't think I can help. If your wife was injured in an accident or something terrible like that, you'd have found out by now. If she ran off for some reason, sooner or later you'll find out. People need money to live on. She's going to have to write checks, use an ATM or charge cards. That should lead you to her."

"I check regularly; she didn't withdraw any money before she vanished and she hasn't spent any since. Win, would you just poke around and see if you come up with anything? You never know; coming at it from a different angle, maybe you'll find something."

Win threw Bill the "change-up-pitch" kind of question doctors often ask patients at the end of an exam if they sense there's something that might be too frightening or embarrassing for them to have brought up, "Bill, are you sure you told me everything about Jessica's disappearance? What you say will just be between the two of us."

Bill sank further into the chair. The chair wasn't terribly over-stuffed, so it was amazing how deeply he could sink into it. "No. There's nothing else."

"I don't want to raise false hope, but let me see what I can come up with. Are you in your Gallery tomorrow? "

"Yes."

"Well, I'm going to be downtown tomorrow afternoon and I could stop by to share my thoughts with you. Before you go, I'm going to need some information on Jessica."

"Sure," Bill said, as he perked up.

"What's Jessica's full name, her maiden name, and her previous married name?"

"Jessica Elise Carter was her maiden name. Her first husband is Harvey Anderson and she went by Jessica C. – as in Carter – Anderson until we were married. She now uses Jessica C. Harvey."

"What's her birth date?"

"She's 49 and was born on March 15, 1968, in Ohio: Youngstown, to be specific."

Win scribbled all this down on a pad and said, "Oh, there's one more thing I should know – her description."

Bill reached into his wallet and took out a picture that he passed to Win. "She's five foot, seven and weighs around 125 pounds. You can see she's very pretty. She doesn't have any scars or unusual birthmarks -- the police were big on those. Is that what you need?"

"Yeah; she's very attractive. Okay, let me show you out and get you home." Win passed the photo back to Bill.

"You don't know how much I appreciate your listening to me."

Win led Bill out and said, "Let's hope Jessica shows up soon."

After Bill left, Win went to the bedroom where Julia was reading in bed. "What did the neighbor have to say? Did he comment on our house?" she asked.

"He told me his wife had gone out to meet someone and never came back. He thinks I can help find her. He didn't mention the house. Maybe he's not a big fan of architecture."

"Why on earth do you want to get involved? We're supposed to be retired! I don't like the sound of this and my recommendation is to politely stay out of it."

"Yeah, but guess what? His wife is a dealer in early Chinese ceramics. You know how much I love ancient Chinese pottery, and I could use something to do now that I'm retired. Well, so much for my fantasy of opening a detective agency. After a few minutes with this guy, I realized my tracing methods are useless for a newly missing person, so I'll just go through some minimal searching motions and bow out. I'm going back to my study. I'd just poured myself some of the special calvados I was saving when this guy called and I had only two sips of it."

Win went back to his desk, sat down, picked up his drink and turned on the computer. He leaned back and stared out the window at the moonlit clumps of green junipers and piñons on the otherwise barren hills and took another sip of his drink before beginning an Internet search for the East-West Gallery. He found the Gallery web site and an article in the local newspaper. The article was about a show at the Gallery last year. The leader read: "Historic Chinese Ceramics on Canyon Road." He got only the first lines of the story without having to register, and so all he could read was: "Jessica Harvey of the East-West Gallery on Canyon Road has assembled an impressive exhibition of ancient Chinese ceramics dating back over two millennia. The new show features fascinating burial pieces from the Warring States period and ....." He searched under Jessica Harvey and gave up because it was a common name. Next he searched for fatal highway accidents, then missing women, then murdered woman in Santa Fe and got a few sites, none of which involved a woman fitting Jessica's description.

Before he quit, he tried an on-line telephone directory he liked because it gave people's ages. There they were with a listed phone number – Jessica C. Harvey, age 49 and William J. Harvey, age 56. It was a bit of an age difference, but was it enough to make her wander? At least he learned that the media hadn't picked up on Jessica's disappearance and that she didn't have much of an Internet trail.

Well, he tried.

Chapter 3.

Next morning, Win was at his desk methodically wrapping green chenille thread around the shank of a fishhook in his fly-tying vise. Learning fly-tying was high on his list of "mañana projects."

He had telephoned the Emergency Room at the Community Hospital earlier to inquire about any unidentified patients or DOAs. At least they were polite when they informed him that under new Federal laws they couldn't divulge anything to him, doctor or not. He also called the State Medical Investigator, whom he had met as a result of his new, part-time faculty appointment at the University of New Mexico School of Medicine. Win was able to learn there had been no reported deaths of unidentified women in the last two weeks. Win, in turn, gave him a heads-up about the possibility of Jessica Harvey turning up in his bailiwick.

The doorbell rang, setting off the dogs again. Win shouted, "Julia, could you get the door? I'm tied up now, literally. It's probably Herky." Herky was one of their new neighbors, a retired investment banker who lived next door. Herky wasn't short for Hercules, although Win was sure he would like to think of himself as a Greek god; it was a childhood-acquired nickname for Charles Herkimer. He was a wannabe, elder super-jock, a frenetic marathoner, weight lifter, skier, golfer, tennis player, hunter -- you name it. The two had hit it off when they met at the Greene's welcoming party and decided on a program of Tuesday lunches in town.

"OK, tie-boy," she shouted back.

Julia showed Herky where to go and he padded into the study, startling Win. He had borrowed an oversized pair of Japanese felt slippers that made his approach stealthy and his appearance ridiculous. He inspected the study carefully, and eyed the display cases while swiveling his bald head slowly like a buzzard. "Hmm. What are you tying?"

"A green weenie."

"What the hell is a green weenie?"

"It's one of the two flies I know how to tie. It's dynamite on some Pennsylvania streams. When I was fishing on Spruce Creek, these were the only flies the trout were taking. I learned to tie it there and it's real easy. You can even tie it when you're dead drunk, which we were in the evenings."

Trying hard to keep the huge slippers on, Herky shuffled over to the desk to inspect Win's handiwork. "Win, I don't think it'll work here in New Mexico. Besides, that fly doesn't look well tied. Maybe you should tie it when you're drunk."

"Herky, it's very commendably tied, particularly when it's tied by a guy with ten thumbs." Win threw up his hands and said, "OK. I'll take some fly-tying lessons. It's an item that's already on my mañana list."

"What's a mañana list?"

"You know how we always put off things we want to do for mañana? Well, as I started thinking about my retirement, I put together a list of all those things I never got around to doing. So now that I'm easing into retirement, I'm very serious about this list. The big clock is running and I have a lot to do, fly-tying included. Shall we head into town? Are you driving?"

"Sure. I already drove over to your place. I've picked Tia Maria's for lunch. Have you been there before?" Herky asked.

"It's one of my favorites. I love their green chili stew and sopapillas, but I don't like the long wait for a table."

"That's only on weekends and we're in between breakfast and lunch. So we should be fine."

Herky's pick-up truck was dust-covered, dented and loaded with a bicycle rack, an oversized cooler and various chains, ropes and rusted tools. It was high Santa Fe chic, as was living on a dirt road, as they did. It was a cool, spring day with brilliant turquoise skies that made the drive into town exhilarating.

It was their lucky day. Herky cruised up to an empty parking spot right near the restaurant. They even got seated without a wait. Herky ordered the daily special – blue-corn tortilla, chicken enchiladas -- and Win ordered a bowl of green chili stew. Herky made sure his order would come with "Christmas" sauces -- both red and green chili sauces in the local vernacular. The choice of red or green was a matter of serious concern to New Mexicans, and Win always opted for both. After they were served, Win brought up Bill Harvey's visit.

"Herky, do you know Bill Harvey who lives in our subdivision? He and his wife own the East-West Gallery on Canyon Road."

"I think I met him a couple of times at the mailboxes and at parties. Seems like a pleasant fellow, but kind of nerdy."

"Did you ever meet his wife Jessica?"

"Yeah. I met her at a couple of parties. She's just the opposite of her husband – very outgoing; in fact, a big flirt and darn pretty."

Win wondered if Herky's mother ever taught him not to talk with food in his mouth. "Did you know she's been missing without a trace for two weeks?"

"No. I bet she ran off with another guy. She acted like a cat in heat," Herky quipped as he wiped a glob of melted cheese off his chin.

"Her husband seems to think otherwise; he's probably just denying the obvious. On the other hand, I don't think people usually run off with another guy without any communication whatsoever for two weeks. She hasn't touched her financial accounts either."

Herky ceased devouring the enchiladas to shake his head. "This doesn't sound good for the missing wife. How'd you get involved in this?" Before Win could answer, Herky went on. "You should go light with the honey on your sopas," referring to the local custom of putting honey on fried sweet bread. "It takes a lot of exercise to burn off those calories." Win, who loved sopapillas, noted that Herky was doling out dietary advice even as he mopped up his high-fat enchiladas.

Ignoring Herky's dig but returning to Herky's question, Win answered, "Bill came over to see me last night to find out if I could help trace her."

"I feel honored to be having lunch with Winston Sage, M.D., tracer of missing persons," Herky said with a toothy grin as he leaned forward in a mock bow. "But stick to tying green weenies and don't get involved. Marital problems and divorces are messy things. I should know; I'm on my third marriage. And you need your energy for getting physically fit."

Win didn't think he was out of shape. He finished up his sopapilla with less honey and a cup of coffee. "Herky, I'm going to walk over to Canyon Road. I was planning to do a gallery tour and promised to stop by Bill's gallery to give him a follow-up on my efforts. I found nothing, so it's time to bow out."

"I need to visit my barber and run some errands. When and where do you want to meet?" Herky asked.

"How about two and a half hours from now? I could be standing at the junction of Canyon Road and Paseo de Peralta." Win suddenly realized that Herky might not need much time at the barber; he was almost bald.

"That's about right and I can pick you up there. It's good you're getting some exercise by walking to Canyon Road

Chapter 4.

It was a long walk to Canyon Road. Win climbed San Francisco Street to the Plaza – a grassy square in the center of town that gives Santa Fe its old-world, European feeling. Once upon a time, it served as a grazing site for livestock. Nowadays, it was a place for tattooed and pierced teenage skateboarders to hang out, for moms to wheel their infant carriages, and for tourists to sip coffee from paper cups and munch croissants, looking as if they'd been transported to Paradise in this festive, laid-back ambiance.

He made a detour around the Plaza to the Palace of the Governors to look at the jewelry and pottery being sold there by American Indian artists. The Palace, one of the oldest buildings in America, was built in 1610 as the seat of the Spanish government for their colony of Nuevo Mexico. It had a covered sidewalk, a "portal" in the local vernacular where a daily lottery determined which Indian artists got to sell their wares under the portal, setting out blankets or tarps on the sidewalk on which they displayed their pieces for sale.

After inspecting the merchandise, Win turned south and continued on briskly. He wasn't acclimated to Santa Fe's 7,000-foot altitude yet and was short of breath before reaching Canyon Road. Most people don't know that the very small city of Santa Fe boasts one of the world's largest art markets. Who knows, but Canyon Road has door-to-door art galleries and shops, with even more packed down every alleyway off the Road. Mixed in with the kitsch and souvenirs was some very good art. The crowd of smiling, brightly dressed tourists walking up and down the Road added to the fiesta atmosphere of Santa Fe.

Win looked at his watch and decided to head directly to the East-West Gallery. It was tucked down a short, unpaved alley and looked pretty nondescript. It was in an old adobe house with a garden on the side and probably had been a residence before turning into a gallery. He went in triggering a loud chime. A beautiful young woman dressed in a starched white blouse and long, black skirt greeted him with forced enthusiasm. "Welcome to the East-West Gallery. Feel free to look around."

The Gallery had two sides, one with Asian and the other with Western things. Win headed to the Asian side, the pretty lady following. He was waiting for the usual gallery icebreaker line and wasn't surprised when it came. "Where are you from?"

Tired of hearing this from all of the art gallery salespeople in Santa Fe, he answered, "I'm from here."

"Oh, you mean you're like from Santa Fe?"

"I'm like actually a neighbor of Bill Harvey. I stopped in to see him. Is he like in?"

"He went down the street to get a sandwich and should be right back. He said he was expecting someone. Why don't you look around? He left his cell phone here and

I'd like go get him, except I can't leave the Gallery unattended."

Win ambled, noticing some exquisite and unusual Chinese ceramics labeled as being from the Warring States Era. There were yellowish earthenware bowls imitating ceremonial bronzes, gray jars with patterns of impressed linen, and an elaborate three-tiered incense burner -- all over 2,000 years old. He had always loved early Chinese pottery, although his academic income limited his collection. It started when he was a public health student in Boston. When the pressure-cooker environment got to be too much, he would disappear for a few hours to walk down Huntington Avenue to the Museum of Fine Arts. He would stroll through the Asian galleries and particularly loved their Chinese ceramics collection. Their Sung Dynasty tea bowls really talked to him. Maybe it was because scholars and poets used them in the tea ceremony in later years. He timed his visits so he could have afternoon tea served by volunteers in one of the galleries and head back to his drudgery rejuvenated. He'd been recalling a lot of distant memories recently and wondered if it was an early sign of senility. He was brought back from his reverie by the door chime.

Bill entered, noticed Win and made a beeline over. "Sorry to keep you waiting. I missed breakfast and needed to grab a bite before I keeled over. Come on into my office. Would you like something to drink?"

"No, thank you. I just had some coffee."

Bill, like many dealers in Western art, was in full drag – Western-style shirt, jeans, huge silver belt buckle, and scuffed boots -- and looked more relaxed than at their first meeting. He led Win back to a cozy office with brown leather chairs and earth-toned Indian rugs on the walls and floor.

"Were you able to come up with anything on Jessie?"

Win shook his head. "Unfortunately, no. As I expected, my methods for tracing people aren't worth much in this situation. The only thing I learned was that there haven't been any deaths of unidentified women in the State recently. I'm not sure I can do anything more for you Bill. The police have more access to information than I have."

"I spoke to the sergeant running the investigation three days ago and he just dismissed me with an, 'I'll call you if we learn anything more.' He always says that and he never calls back. But you just gave me the best piece of information I've gotten from anyone. At least Jessie hasn't turned up dead."

Win knew the absence of a death report to the State coroner's office was hardly proof she was alive. "Have you checked with the police about Jessica's car? It might be easier to trace a missing car than a missing person?"

"Yeah. The car seems to have disappeared with her. Not a trace of it."

"Have you thought about hiring a private investigator?"

"They do a lot of nosing around and probably can't do any more than the police."

"Maybe nosing around could turn up things the police might miss. What if Jessica had a boyfriend and ran off with him?"

"Like I told you, I don't think there was someone else in her life."

Win shrugged. "I'm just grasping at straws. My advice is to hire a private investigator."

"You're probably right," Bill said softly.

"I need to head on home. I enjoyed seeing your gallery and your early Chinese pottery. I'm a wannabe collector of that stuff and no expert, but those pieces look to be top-notch."

"They're really exceptional, and Jessie is the one who deals with them. She's getting to be an expert and has developed incredible sources for 'high end' pieces. She really blossomed out in the last two years and is gaining big-time status in the field and not just locally. That's why I can't understand why she'd just disappear. What she accomplished was incredibly hard to do, particularly for someone with no academic background in Asian art." His voice began to quiver. "When we first started, our business was very rocky financially. I'm not embarrassed to say that her side of the business has been our financial salvation."

"By the way, how did Jessie get involved in early Chinese ceramics? It's such an esoteric field."

"Well, she studied art in college and was always fascinated by East Asian art. Before we met, she started out selling low-end decorative Asian things -- new ceramic pieces, incense, lacquer rice bowls. Then she moved up to Korean chests, Japanese tonsu and hibachis, and blue and white Imari ware, while they were still available. When we met and planned this gallery, she wanted to try her hand at selling some serious stuff. We assembled a stock of old Chinese, Japanese and Korean ceramics and they sold reasonably well, but it wasn't profitable. Besides, they were mediocre pieces. Eventually, she was lucky to find a mentor who's an expert on early Chinese ceramics and she just blossomed under his tutelage. Things took off from there."

"Who's this mentor?"

"Oh, a local Chinese-American friend. He comes from a family of great collectors going back generations in pre-Communist Shanghai. He has a pretty incredible collection of Chinese ceramics and was willing to part with some pieces that we sold. He knows a lot of art dealers in Hong Kong, many of them relatives, and he helped Jessie to get great stock for the gallery. Jessie was incredibly lucky that our friend was willing to teach her everything he knows about the field."

"You don't think there was something going on between the two of them?"

"Oh, no way. He's elderly and like a grandfather to her."

Win smiled. "Watch out for dirty old men! By the way, how's your end of the business doing?"

"So-so. Buying and selling Indian art in Santa Fe is very competitive and prices have been escalating. We did so well on Jessie's side that we focused on buying the Chinese stuff since it's been so profitable."

Win stood up. "Well, I enjoyed talking with you. I'm sorry I couldn't do much. Let me know if you learn anything more about Jessica."

Win headed out and proceeded down Canyon Road, puzzled by why he remained fascinated by this mystery. Maybe it was because Bill seemed so pitiful or because Win still harbored his private detective fantasy. Maybe he was becoming obsessive in his old age. He shook his head as he walked on, probably looking like a dotty old codger, and stopped into several galleries before heading off to meet Herky.

* * *

Win waited at the designated pick-up point and before long, Herky pulled up in his noisy, beat-up truck, shouting at him to hop in.

"So how was your barber visit?"

"He always does a great job and I got all my errands done too."

Win couldn't detect any difference in Herky's hair (or lack thereof) although he did reek of cheap lavender barbershop cologne. Either Win was missing something or Herky's barber was a great con artist.

"How did your meeting with Bill go?"

"I told him I couldn't find anything about his wife. I suggested he hire a private detective. Maybe he just wants to delay finding out that his wife left him or something worse, so he enlisted an unqualified, burnt-out epidemiologist to help."

Herky flashed an impish toothy smile at Win. "Maybe it's because of your immense charm?

"Herk, he sought me out before he met me."

"Maybe news of your charm leaked out in the neighborhood?"

"I'm afraid something bad happened to his wife and he may be thinking the same. Maybe he and his wife are art thieves or fences, or they were selling counterfeit pieces and she got caught. He said she brings in most of the gallery's money, which makes her the more likely one to get done in. That reminds me; he said they were having hard times financially before Jessica started to hit it big with her part of the business. Herky, you used to be a banker. Can you still look up their financial status or business rating? I wonder if they didn't go bankrupt and then turn crooked to bail themselves out?"

Herky guffawed, reminding Win of a child with whooping cough. "Win, I think you're getting a little carried away with this amateur sleuth stuff, but just for the hell of it, I'm going to e-mail one of my buddies back at the bank to check the Gallery's credit ratings. Now let's get down to brass tacks, what are you doing to keep physically fit?"

Chapter 5.

Win and Julia were having an early "guacarita time" on their portal. Win came up with the guacarita name back in Pittsburgh, when they would sit outside in their lush green yard with guacamole, tortilla chips and margaritas and dream of doing the same thing in brown, desert Santa Fe during one of its spectacular sunsets. It was just after 4 p.m., way before sunset, but the drinks, the piney scent of junipers and piñons, the turquoise sky, and the snow-capped mountains in the background made it more than passable.

The dogs loved the event too -- either because the margaritas made Julia and Win mellow or because Julia always snuck them tortilla chips under the table and Win would furtively lower his empty glass for the dogs to lick the salt off the rim.

Julia brought up the Harvey business. "So Win, has our neighbor's wife shown up yet?"

Win shook his head. "I quickly realized that I couldn't help find a missing person, so I stopped by the gallery on Tuesday and bowed out. I told Bill to hire a private investigator if he thought the police weren't doing enough."

"So what's on tap for tonight with George?" Julia asked, as she passed one of the dogs a chip under the table. George was the friend with whom Win enjoyed the "gallery crawl," a Friday evening tradition in Santa Fe, where people ambled along from gallery to gallery with drinks in hand enjoying the festivities. Julia really didn't like the crawl scene; besides, modern art wasn't her thing. She was also convinced Win would get food poisoning from the canapés or slushed from the cheap champagne they usually served.

"George said there are a couple of openings of minimalist artists. One's a painter he likes a lot. I don't really care; it's the scene that I get such a kick out of. You know, George has a world-class minimalist art collection. His big ambition in life is to have a good enough collection so that he can donate it to a top museum."

Just then there was loud honking from a car outside. "Looks like George is a bit early," Julia said. "I hope he's driving because that was a mighty strong margarita you made."

"He offered to drive and I accepted gladly; it means I can enjoy the bubbly".

"Go light on the stuff. Remember the Greene's' party and its aftermath," she admonished, as Win patted the two dogs on the head and planted a kiss on her cheek.

George was outside waiting in his yellow Hummer. He sported a waxed, gray, handlebar mustache and wore a shocking-pink Western shirt. Win didn't have the heart to tell him his shirt and his Hummer really clashed. "Hi, George, ready to go?'

"Well I'm not sitting here in your driveway just for effect."

George was actually Jorge de Leon, a retired surgeon. After years of having his name mispronounced, he gave up and went by George. Win heaved himself into the oversized vehicle and stole a quick look down to see if George was wearing matching pink boots. They were boots all right, but black with appliquéd green saguaro cacti and a red dog-like creature that was probably a coyote. His pants were a sedate green. George sure knew how to mismatch his colors.

George drove with a lead foot on the gas and the radio blaring out country music. "Do you mind the music?" he asked

"Actually, I love the stuff. It's American opera."

"You think this stuff is opera?"

"I've been saying that for years George. Listen to the lyrics with their wrenching pathos; they're as good as any libretto. In fact, since I've been going to the Santa Fe Opera where they have the librettos translated into English, I realize how silly most are. If Puccini were alive today, I bet he'd love country music."

"Win, you're one very weird guy! And I don't think old Giacomo Puccini, or Giuseppe Verdi for that matter, would disagree with me. Puccini, huh!"

Win realized that if George found him weird, he was in trouble.

They arrived in town and George announced, "First stop, Palace Avenue. This should be a good show. I'm particularly interested in acquiring a piece from this artist for my collection."

Win went into the gallery first and was startled by huge canvases daubed exuberantly with bright primary colors -- mostly raucous reds, blues, and yellows – in complex patterns. "George, I don't think this is minimalist art," he quipped.

George looked befuddled by his misread of the opening announcement. "Yup, this ain't what I thought it would be," he mumbled as he wandered off to the least garish painting.

Win headed to the bar for a glass of champagne. It was the people at these openings that he enjoyed most. He was fascinated by the well-defined categories of uniform dressing in Santa Fe. Classifying people was an epidemiologist's thing. There was a group of outdoorsy-type dressers – faded green T-shirts, green or khaki short cargo pants, red bandanas, and oversized hiking boots. A lot of old guys with gray beards fell into this category. There was also the "non-conformist," Birkenstock-flower-printed-dirndl-skirt-dangling-silver-earrings crowd. It amazed Win that the uniform of non-conformism in his youth had persevered unchanged. Then there was the dressed-to-the-nines crowd, the affluent and wannabes who were about to dash off to a fancy dinner at an upscale restaurant or country club. They were deeply tanned, clothed in bright greens and pinks, and none of the men wore socks with their tasseled loafers. There was always the obvious Texans or Arizonans with overdressed women wearing voluminous skirts or dresses and covered everywhere with turquoise and silver jewelry, and men outfitted in cowboy garb -- high-heeled boots and all. Best of all, whatever the dress style, there was always a large number of beautiful women.

Win was drawn to a huge canvas by its piercing gaudiness. It was about six by eight feet and painted in harsh reds and yellows. He noticed a brightly dressed, middle-aged woman staring intently at the painting. She was full-figured, in her flower-printed, dirndl skirt and was totally bejeweled. She reminded him of his North Carolina days, when he'd learned that a well-dressed woman should put on all her jewelry, and then take one piece off for good taste.

Win couldn't resist asking. "Do you like this piece?"

The lady turned around and drawled, "Honey Chile, I think it's dreadful."

Win noticed she was quite good-looking. "I was wondering why you were staring at it."

"I was admiring the huge amount of paint the artist used. No wonder it's so expensive! Are you new to Santa Fe?"

"Yes."

"I'm Ann Boudreaux. My friends call me Honey Chile."

"I'm Win Sage."

Ann ogled Win, fixing on his wedding ring. "And what do you do, Mr. Win?"

"I'm in transition," Win said as he sucked in his gut.

"Hmm. Does that mean you're between jobs or reincarnations?"

Win thought that a very "Santa Fe" question and replied, "A little of both. I'm trying to ease into retirement and start a new life."

"What kind of work did you, do you, or will you do?" Ann went on.

"I'm a physician and an epidemiologist. I do research on the causes of cancer, actually."

"I see. So you're a skin doctor?"

"No," Win said through a smile.

"Well anyway you sound interesting."

It was Win's turn to pry. "And what do you do?"

"I'm in the gallery business, selling arts and crafts."

"What type of art do you sell?"

"Mostly Eastern-American folk art and antique country furniture. These aren't common in Santa Fe, so it gives me a special niche in this competitive market. I started in the folk art field when I was living in Charleston and when I moved here I just moved my business."

"So that's the origin of the 'Honey Chile' appellation. To quote W.C. Fields, a 'euphonious appellation' indeed."

"Oh no, I didn't pick up the name in Appalachia, I'm originally from New Orleans."

"Touché, Honey Chile! Where's your gallery located?"

"On Canyon Road. You should stop by and visit." She fished around in her voluminous handbag and retrieved a wallet. "Here's my card."

Win blushed as he said, "I don't have a card. I haven't decided yet what to put on my new personal card – this 'in transition' state takes a long time to figure out." He went on, "I have a neighbor who also has a gallery on Canyon Road, the East-West Gallery. Do you know it?"

She smiled. "Sure, it's a few doors down from my place. The husband's a bit of a nonentity. The wife runs with a fast crowd. They seem to have struck it rich recently, supposedly thanks to her. Maybe her sleeping around led to some business bonanza."

"What did she do to rub you the wrong way?"

"Nothing in particular. She's pretty and flaunts it."

Win leaned forward and lowered his voice. "Do you know she disappeared two weeks ago?"

"That's the first I've heard of it. She probably took off with one of her boyfriends."

"Is there a specific boyfriend that she might have gone off with?"

"No. I think she just plays the field -- a bunch of one-night stands. Although I heard that she was hot-and-heavy with the chef at Alphonso's."

"Her husband seems to think there wasn't another man and that she somehow got into trouble."

She threw her head back and laughed, "Let him dream on. I'm willing to bet she ran off with another guy, and probably a much younger guy now that she's in the money. While we're on the subject of men, I couldn't help but notice your wedding ring. Why are all the good men taken? You and I could make quite a pair. Come by and visit me at the gallery when you're on Canyon Road."

"I'll do that, Honey Chile. You take care now!"

Win went off to find George, who was engaged in an animated conversation with an elegantly dressed short guy with a full, gray beard, Panama hat, tan suit and white shoes. The contrast between the two men made Win chuckle.

Win got another glass of champagne and joined George and his dude friend. "Hi, George. Enjoying the show?"

George looked at Win glumly. "Win, this is Martin Cunningham, he's the art critic for the Santa Fe New Mexican. He actually likes this show."

"Hi, Martin! Nice to meet you. I'm sure that shows worse than this have gotten rave reviews."

Martin raised his bushy eyebrows affectedly. "Looks like our friend George has found himself a kindred spirit. George, you are a highly opinionated and unmitigated snob. See you next Friday. Ciao!"

"I see you two really like each other."

George replied, "Oh, we're really old buddies who enjoy disagreeing on art. He's not that bad a critic when he occasionally gets his reviews right. I saw that you made a new friend; I think she owns a gallery in town. She's got a bit of a reputation. Shall we head off for the next stop in our crawl? I suggest we go to the sculpture show next; this time I'm sure I know the artist and I can certainly vouch for the quality."

So, the dynamic duo headed off. On the way home, Win brought up the subject of Jessica Harvey's disappearance, letting him know that Bill had solicited his help but that he'd been unable to find out anything. George was squinting intently, and Win couldn't tell whether it was an expression of scorn or just the brilliant setting sun hitting him in his eyes. After a few minutes of silent squinting, George said, "I have a lot of friends still in medical practice, so let me nose around a bit about her for you." It dawned on Win that while he was disengaging from the Harvey affair, he had set two of his buddies off on the investigation.

Chapter 6.

It was Tuesday again, Win's day to go into town with Herky for lunch. As he awaited his friend, Win worked at his desk with a large sketchpad, a stretched out T-shirt and a ruler. He was humming and enjoying his task.

The dogs announced Herky's arrival. Today, he was dressed in very au courant, loud bicycle racing clothes. Coupled with the oversized felt slippers he always chose from the entry, he looked his usual, ridiculous, but dapper, self.

"So what's the good Doctor up to today?" Herky asked, as he spied the mess on Win's desk.

"Well, I'm working my way down my mañana list. Ever since I was a kid in college, I wanted to create this T-shirt. I found a place in Santa Fe that'll custom-print T-shirts. Unfortunately, the minimum order is a dozen. Which reminds me, Herk, would you like one of my first T-shirt creations?"

"What kind of design does it have?"

"Herk, there's no design. It has a short pithy saying on it, but I'm not sure about the style of lettering yet. What size do you wear?"

"A pithy saying, hmm. You think I'll like it?"

"Herky, it will suit you to a "P," I mean "T," Win corrected himself as he watched Herky's reaction to see whether he realized Win was pulling his leg.

"OK. I'd like a medium. Mind you, I really wear a small, but I like my T-shirts oversized."

"Which reminds me, what gives with the bicycle racing get-up?"

"Oh, I'm going out with my bicycling buddies after we get back. We're going to do a light 25-mile workout."

"That sounds like more than a light work-out to me."

"Remember, you asked me to do some financial nosing around on the Harveys and their gallery? Well, it turned out to be pretty interesting. They were in deep financial trouble until about six years ago -- on the verge of bankruptcy. Their Gallery was losing money and they defaulted on some loans. Then suddenly, their fortunes changed and they now they have a top credit rating and are really in the green. Did you ever see their house? It's a pretty fancy place that must have cost at least two million. I never knew the gallery business was that lucrative."

Win took all of this in. "I heard on the street that it's the missing wife that was making all the money. Maybe this whole disappearance is about money?"

"Most things in life are about money. You're starting to sound like a gossip columnist when you talk about 'hearing on the street'. People in a small town like to gossip, and sometimes they're not so nice about it. Anyhow, let's get going. Today we're going to have lunch at Estrella's."

"Herky, you always pick a place where everything they serve is high in fat and calories, and they don't take reservations. Maybe we should call our outings 'Mardi Gras'. My diet sure gets out of whack on Tuesdays."

"Very funny, Professor Sage. I never knew college professors were so childish."

"Herky, we can be more than a bit childish," Win said. "It's the low pay and the lack of diversity. Most faculty share herd opinions and silly jokes and have no contact with the real world, so they never grow up. It's not just the students who wear backpacks, hiking shorts and sandals."

"Win, you're a wacko, but I still like you. Let's go!"

"If you don't mind a quick stop at the T-shirt wallah before the restaurant, I might be able to get them made before we head home."

"No problem."

They bid adieu to Julia, went out and climbed into Herky's pickup truck. It was actually clean, with no mud for a change.

"Herky, did you actually clean your truck?"

"Yeah. The wife has been after me to junk it. So we compromised and I got it washed and waxed. I even got rid of all the junk in the back."

"I'm impressed, -- first, that you gave in, and second, with your Solomonic solution."

Herky gave Win a mock bow. "Now where is your T-shirt 'whatever it is'?"

Before long, they pulled into the parking lot in front of Sam's Tees on Old Santa Fe Trail. The sign outside proclaimed, "We make customized Tees, bowling shirts, award jackets and trophies."

"Herky, this is the place. I'll go in and finalize things; it should only take a few minutes since the T-shirt maker and I already discussed the design on the phone." Herky decided to wait in his almost-gleaming truck.

Morris, whom Win had deemed a true T-shirt wallah, was expecting Win and had an assortment of printed shirts spread out on the counter as samples. After a brief, animated discussion, Win chose a style and placed his order.

Morris, who was exuberantly pierced and tattooed, asked, "By the way, who's this Chaucer dude?"

"Oh, he's a DWEM. A famous English poet."

"What's a DWEM?"

"A dead, white, European male."

Morris raised his pierced eyebrows and said, "I went to college and never even heard of the guy or of DWEMs, but I majored in partying and skiing."

"Maybe, that's why you turned out to be so creative."

"Thanks dude. I'll try to have the shirts ready in a few hours."

Win went back to the truck looking very satisfied. "Herky, I just dealt with a mañana-list item of very long standing."

"I'm glad you're making progress. Now let's go eat!"

They parked in front of Estrella's and with Herky's good luck, got seated immediately. Herky ordered their Tuesday special: carne adovado with all the New Mexican fixings, and Win went with a tamale plate with red chili sauce.

"You know Herky, there's a basic principle in nutrition – if something tastes good, it's probably bad for your health, and vice versa. My tamales are mighty good."

"Everything in moderation except for wives and exercise," Herky said. "You need to exercise more."

"I do exercise regularly!" Win protested.

"But not enough. At our age, exercise is the Fountain of Youth."

Win changed the subject by looking at his watch and starting to lay out the game plan for where Herky would drop him off and meet him later. They decided that Win would get dropped off at the top of Canyon Road and they would meet in three hours at the foot of the Road. It was to be a day of gallery browsing for Win and they would swing by Sam's Tees on the way home.

"Are you planning to stop by Bill Harvey's gallery? You should stay out of this problem."

"I know Herky. But there's something odd about their sudden turn of fortune. His wife may have gotten done in by somebody they swindled or something like that."

"That's all the more reason to stay out of it."

"You're right, I guess. Maybe I'll just visit some of my favorite galleries.

Chapter 7.

Win was in "hog heaven" on Canyon Road. As much as he com-
plained about the junk in some galleries, he loved the American
Indian art, the modern pottery, the textiles, and the Asian art in
others. He also loved the holiday atmosphere generated by tourists thrilled to be in Santa Fe. Canyon Road was a place where you
could walk and tour art galleries for hours and later dine in some
of the country's best restaurants. So he strolled along with a big,
silly smile plastered on his face, especially enjoying the high-end
galleries where he felt transported by what he saw.

He noticed a quaint sign that read, "Ann's Antiques," which
he remembered was the name of Honey Chile Boudreaux's gallery.
He'd been planning to pay her a visit, so he headed off towards the
gallery tucked down an unpaved alleyway with hollyhocks growing
on both sides. It was what he expected, with high end, American
country quilts, furniture, paintings and bric-a-brac in the windows.
He went in, triggering one of the ubiquitous entry chimes. There to
greet him was a middle-aged lady in a white blouse and calico skirt.

"Welcome to Ann's! Feel free to look around. Call me if you
have any questions."

She followed a few paces behind Win. After about ten seconds,
he wheeled around, and before she could raise her question said.
"I'm from Santa Fe".

Her jaw dropped as she said:. "How did you know what I was about to ask?"

"It's a no-brainer, ma'am. I'm Win Sage. Is Ms. Boudreaux in?"

"I think she may be in back. Let me check for you." She walked away shaking her head.

After a few minutes, he heard an eruption from the rear of the gallery, "Win, Honey Chile, how are you? I was wondering whether you'd ever come see me. Come on back here."

Win walked back to her curtained-off office area where he was greeted with a theatrical hug and air kiss. "Dr. Win, how've you been? I haven't forgotten our lovely conversation at that incredible gallery opening. So how's your 'transition' coming along?"

"It's tough to figure out how to spend your time when all your life has been programmed for you. All those meetings and deadlines seem so remote and unimportant once you're away from the rat race. I'm actively working on my mañana list now. That's my list of all the things I always wanted to do -- you know, the 'round tuit' list."

"Honey Chile, if I had a mañana list, you would be at the top of it."

"Flattery will get you everywhere," Win retorted.

"That's what I'm hoping. So what's on this mañana list?"

"Things like learning fly-tying for trout fishing and writing a cook book with my favorite recipes."

"How about having a fling with another woman?"

"Meeting you makes me want to add that item. Right now I'm working on some T-shirt projects."

Ann scowled as she saw that Win was changing the subject. "So what are these T-shirts all about?"

"Oh, when I was a student in college I had these fantasies of making up humorous T-shirts for my courses, things like quotes from famous writers or organic chemistry formulae. Now that I'm entering my second childhood, I'm picking up on those old ideas. I'm having my first one made today. Would you like one? What size do you wear?"

"Honey Chile, don't you know that you never ask a woman about her size. You just politely estimate and on the small side at that. You're a very attractive man, but you need a bit more polish."

"Ann, you're a very attractive woman and a real temptation, but I'm married and pretty happily at that."

"Well, at least we've established that you find me attractive and tempting. That's a good start! I hope to become one of your 'round tuits' and I'm a patient woman. So what are you doing on Canyon Road today? Did you just come to see me or are you gallery hopping?"

"Actually, all of the above."

"Are you still interested in that Harvey girl's disappearance? You know, I still haven't heard a thing about it."

"I thought I'd drop it, but today I learned that they had a sudden major change in their financial status a few years ago. Like from near bankruptcy to big-time bucks almost overnight. So my curiosity is piqued again."

"I knew they were a bunch of deadbeats for a long time and then suddenly struck it rich. There's been a lot of gossip about where their money's been coming from."

"What sort of gossip?"

"A lot of people think they're fences, particularly for their Asian art. The wife was the one who dealt in Asian art and she seems a pretty ambitious type. It's quite possible she was up to something illegal and had to disappear or she could have run off with another guy."

"Unfortunately, her disappearance fascinates me. As an epidemiologist, I've always been a closet detective and this is my first chance to find a real missing person. You know, epidemiology involves a lot of medical detective work."

"Honey Chile, don't get too carried away with this detective stuff. I bumped into Bill Harvey recently and he looks like a different guy, still nerdy, but all shaken up. At the least you could provide some social support for him. He's a good candidate for a tranquilizer. Win, be a Good Samaritan and try to at least comfort the nerd."

Win suspected Ann was trying to get him to visit Canyon Road more often so he'd visit her. "Well, Honey Chile, I'd better head off. How about the offer of a T-shirt?"

"Okay, Win. I'll take up on your offer. At least that means I get to see you again. I'll do some nosing around about Jessica Harvey for you as an added inducement."

"Of course you'll see me again! Ciao, Honey Chile."

Before Win could leave she grabbed him and kissed him hard. Win unthinkingly dropped his hands to hold her by her ample, but shapely, butt. She whispered in Win's ear, "I'm yours if you want me," and playfully stuck her tongue in his ear. "To be continued, my future lover."

A very conflicted Win headed out and almost collided with the store manager. He winked at her and whispered, "You know, I can read your mind."

After he left, she shouted out to Ann, "That guy is really spooky."

Win continued his stroll on Canyon Road and when he neared the East-West Gallery wondered whether to go in. He weighed the pros and cons and finally decided to visit. The same pretty lady greeted him as at his first visit. "Welcome to the East-West Gallery!" she said as she clearly didn't recognize him.

Win was deliberating whether to wink at her again, but said instead, "Hi. I'm from here; you know, like from Santa Fe. Is Bill Harvey in?"

She looked at Win as if he had just emerged from a flying saucer. After all, this was New Mexico, the epicenter of UFO sightings. "Yes, he's like on the phone right now. I'll get him as soon as he gets off."

Win started to walk through the gallery studying the pieces on display, even more impressed than on his last visit. "Where do you people get your stock? It's very impressive," he said to the gallerina.

"Bill does a lot of traveling to the Four Corners and he buys from other dealers like all over the country."

"What about the Chinese stuff?"

"Jessie, Bill's wife, does that buying. She's like away right now. She gets most of it in Hong Kong and from a friend whose family has a so great collection of old pieces."

Win stopped in front of a glass cabinet containing a spectacular ceramic bowl from the Warring States Era. It was so classical in style; even Win could identify the piece. "Where did this one come from?" he asked

"Oh, that piece is on consignment from Jessie's collector friend in Los Alamos."

The conversation was interrupted when Bill came out to greet Win. "Hi Win! I'm glad you stopped in. Come on back to my office."

"Have you heard anything further about Jessica?" Win asked.

"No, I haven't heard a thing from the police or anyone. Her car hasn't been found and she hasn't used her bank account or charge cards. I'm starting to lose hope that I'll ever see her again." He shook his head and continued, "What on earth could have happened to her?"

Win sat down in one of the leather chairs. "Bill, I wish there was something I could do. You just have to hang in there and hope for the best. At least she hasn't turned up injured or dead. Not knowing what happened does let you hold out some hope at least." Win felt embarrassed by his dumb platitudes and abruptly changed the subject. "We were just talking about how you manage to keep up your supply of outstanding pieces."

"It's not easy. I have to travel a good part of the time to see my sources and dealers. When I'm not traveling I'm on the phone with suppliers. The Internet is another big source."

"How does Jessica get her stock? Those pieces outside are exceptional."

"Oh, she travels a lot to Hong Kong."

"Does she go by herself or do you go together?"

Bill frowned. "I don't like Hong Kong; it's too crowded and hectic for my taste. Besides, someone has to mind the store. She usually goes there with Dr. Wong. He has lots of family there and knows most of the top dealers."

"Could she be in Hong Kong now?"

"No. Her passport is at home. I also checked with Dr. Wong and he's here. He arranges most of her trips and he didn't set anything up for her recently."

"Who's Dr Wong?"

Bill lit up. "Oh, C.Y. Wong is Jessie's mentor. He's a physicist at LANL, that's the local name for the Los Alamos National Laboratories of atomic bomb fame, and a real big shot there. He lives near Los Alamos. His true love is Chinese ceramics, particularly ancient pieces. He's a sweet old guy and he's been like a father to Jessie. His kids never shared his love of Chinese art, and Jessie seemed to be the interested daughter he always wanted. He comes from a long line of Chinese scholars and collectors of Chinese art. His father had an incredibly large collection of Warring States ceramics. That's how Wong became such an expert on the period and he's taught Jessie everything he knows. We have an amazing Warring States piece of his on consignment outside. He inherited his collection from his father who escaped from Shanghai with the pieces just before the Communist takeover. They had to leave a lot behind in Shanghai. He and his family have never forgiven the Communist regime in China."

"How long has he been helping Jessie?"

"Let's see, about seven years, beginning about a year after we opened the Gallery."

"Has he been helping Jessie choose things? If so, he's got quite an eye."

"That's where he's been incredible. He seems to know all the best dealers in Hong Kong; many of them are his relatives. Jessie buys stuff from their private offices and homes. She could never have done that without his help. He's also been selling off part of his collection. He's getting old and he wants to lighten up. As I told you, his kids aren't interested in the stuff."

Win thought for a moment. "You know, Bill, I have a couple of Warring States pieces – a bowl and a small jar. It's one of my favorite periods of Chinese ceramics and I wish I had more from that era. My stuff isn't in the same league what you've got here, but Dr. Wong sounds like a person I'd like to meet. Do you think he might have some insight into Jessie's disappearance?"

"I don't know."

"Would it be okay if I talked to him? I'm going fishing in the Jemez Mountains, just above Los Alamos, this weekend with an old buddy. I could stop in to meet him if he's willing. I'd love to see his collection."

"It's worth a try, and his collection is definitely worth seeing. Maybe, he can remember something about Jessie that could be helpful. Let me get his phone number for you. I'll also give him a call to tell him you'll be contacting him. He's very nice, but shy." Bill scribbled Wong's name and number on a piece of paper and handed it to Win.

"Thanks, Bill. I'll let you know if I learn anything useful."

Win got up to leave and Bill thanked him profusely. On the way out, Win stopped to stare again at the Chinese pieces on display. The pretty lady re-appeared, standing discreetly behind him. As he was leaving, Win smiled and gave her another big wink, entertaining himself by playing the dirty old man that he knew she believed him to be, and she obligingly recoiled.

Chapter 8.

Win reached the bottom of Canyon Road early for his meeting with Herky, but it wasn't long before he was greeted by raucous honking from Herky's "restored" truck.

"Hi, Herk! You're a bit early. Anyway, it's good timing. Did you have a good outing?"

"Well, I got everything done and even had a chance to visit my dentist who had an unexpected opening." Herky flashed Win a smile to show off his newly polished teeth. "How was your day?"

"Not too bad. I saw some terrific things in the galleries and I got myself involved again in the Harvey disappearance."

"Don't you have more important things to do with your time than play two-bit detective?"

"I know, like using my time to exercise more."

"You're learning, Win."

Herky suggested they get going to the T-shirt wallah's place. He deftly used a series of side streets to reach the shop quickly.

Win went in by himself. "Hi, Morris! Were you able to finish the shirts?"

"Yup, and they're beauts! Wait till you see them."

Win unfolded one and smiled broadly. "Morris, you're a genius! Your idea about the slightly Gothic print is just the right touch."

"You must really dig this dude Chaucer."

"Not really, he's very hard to read. Actually, he dug me -- into a hole with a D grade for my English course."

"I thought you were a doctor. I didn't know you could become a doctor with bad college grades. I might have had a shot at medical school then."

"Morris, medicine is no place for creative people like you. Just keep up the good work here. You just helped an old man realize one of his lifetime dreams."

"You're putting me on Doc."

"No, Morris, I mean it sincerely."

"Well thanks. That's a mighty big compliment."

"You just made my day and I hope I made your day. I have some more ideas for T-shirts, so I'll be back for your creative input." Win paid Morris, gathered up the pile of Ts and set aside a medium-sized one for Herky. He gave Morris a bear hug before leaving.

The bright sun blinded Win as he came outside. He found Herky's truck, got in, and proudly announced, "Herky, I want you to be the first recipient of my new line of creative T-shirts. Ta da!"

Herky unfolded the presented shirt and stared hard at it. The shirt had printed on its front in "old English" type:

Chaucer

is a

pysser

"How do you pronounce p-y-s-s-e-r?"

"Like the 'y' is an 'i'."

'You're nuttier than a fruitcake, Win. You hung around universities a little too long for your mental health. Do you really expect me to wear this? It's obscene!"

"C'mon, Herk, you use language more obscene than this all the time. Pisser is a mainstream word nowadays. You could always wear it when you wash your truck, assuming you'll wash it again."

"You said it would have a pithy saying and you weren't kidding."

"I also said it would suit you to a 'P'."

"I don't know how Julia puts up with you! Outwardly, you appear normal, but you're a certifiable nut case. I have to make a quick stop at the supermarket on the way home, and no, I will not put on the T-shirt now."

They headed down Old Santa Fe Trail with Win in Nirvana due to his realized dream and Herky still wondering about Win's mental status

* * *

That evening, Win was pleasantly ensconced in his office wearing one of his new Chaucer shirts. He had successfully tackled the first item on his mañana list: a long-standing entry that could now be crossed off. He swiveled around and pulled his bottle of old calvados and a brandy snifter out of the cabinet behind his desk. He hadn't touched the stuff since the night Bill visited, and now he had something to celebrate. It was a small thing, but a symbolic accomplishment for Win. He poured some calvados into the glass, began swirling it around without thinking, and noticed his two Warring States pieces of pottery prominently displayed in one of the study's glass cabinets. He got up and brought them to his desk one at a time. One of the things Win loved about collecting is that you can touch the things you own. There was always a glass or human barrier between an item in a museum and the viewer. Win had a green Han Dynasty model of a granary; a piece buried with someone who died two millennia ago, that had in its baked clay discernible finger indentations of the potter who shaped the piece. He enjoyed putting his fingers in the indentations; it was like touching the fingertips of another person who left this world 2,000 years ago. Win wondered whether this is something archeologists also found themselves doing.

He began thinking of Jessica and the interesting Dr. Wong. Had she confided in him about plans to run off? Why did Wong adopt her and mentor her? How was he able to put her in touch with such good sources of Chinese ceramics and why didn't he buy and sell things himself? Was his collection really as spectacular as Bill implied? Probably, he was a busy scientist who had more important things on his mind and just wanted to pass his knowledge on to an interested daughter-surrogate.

Win welcomed the opportunity to meet Wong and see his collection, and he was going up there to fish anyway. He retrieved Wong's phone number that Bill had given him. It was 8:05 P.M., not a bad time to call. He dialed and after several rings a male voice answered, "Hello."

"Is this Dr. Wong?"

"Yes, this is he."

"This is Winston Sage; I'm a neighbor of Bill Harvey."

"Oh yes, Bill told me you might be calling. He said you were helping him in his search for Jessica."

"I wish I could be of some help. I'm a medical epidemiologist and I have a lot of experience in tracing people for research, but that's totally different from tracing missing persons. The police have come up with absolutely no leads on Jessica. Bill's desperate and thinks I might find something the authorities missed. I shouldn't get involved, but I feel sorry for him. He was hoping you might know something about Jessica that could be helpful."

"I really don't think I have any greater insight into what happened to her than Bill does. I spoke to her last about a week before she disappeared and she seemed her usual self."

"That's what I thought. Actually, I was also hoping to meet you to learn more about your interest in ancient Chinese ceramics. I have a couple of Warring States Era pieces, and some pieces from the Han, Tang and Sung Dynasties."

"Since you're a collector and a friend of the Harvey's, I'd be honored to show you my modest collection some time."

"Actually, I was hoping I could visit you when I drive up to Los Alamos on my way to go fishing in the Jemez this Saturday. Would it be possible for me to visit in the morning?"

"Fishermen go out very early I believe. I hope you don't mind visiting late in the morning."

"Actually, I fly-fish for trout and the fishing tends to be best later in the day when things warm up and the flies that trout feed on start to hatch."

"Saturday morning is my catch-up time in the laboratory, since no one is around then. I could meet with you around 11. Would that fit in with the schedule of your flies hatching?"

"Yes, that would be perfect. I hope I'm not imposing on you."

"No, not at all. Bill thinks very highly of you and we share a common interest in Chinese art."

"Do you live in Los Alamos?"

"No. We live in White Rock. Are you familiar with it?"

"I've never been there, but I can see it from our house."

"Let me give you directions."

Win wrote down Wong's meticulous instructions, thanked him profusely for his willingness to see him and said goodbye. Win wondered if he would he have been as accommodating if the situation was reversed? He shook his head and got back to enjoying his calvados. He needed to work harder at the 'drink' part of 'eat, drink and be merry', he decided. It occurred to him that he had better talk with his fishing partner, Chuck, the local expert who was taking him to the Shint River on Saturday. He would call him in the morning.

Chapter 9.

Chuck Orsini, duly forewarned, showed up at 10 o'clock on Saturday morning. Julia was really looking forward to seeing him again. They had shared an office many years ago, when they were Fellows in a Health and Society program at Harvard. Chuck a big bear of a guy and a professor at the UNM law school, had been the one to pique their interest in New Mexico. Later, Julia attended a medical meeting in Santa Fe, witnessing a sunset up at Chimayo that clinched the deal. She got Win to go out and take a look at Santa Fe and it was love at first sight for him too. So here they all were.

"Hi, Chuck. Great to see you!" Win said. In the years since they'd met him, Chuck had grown a magnificent full beard that was now largely white.

"Where's my old office-mate?" Chuck shouted.

Julia appeared and gave Chuck a big hug. "How're you doing big guy? I like your new beard. You can have a nice second career as a shopping mall Santa Claus with that growth. Your hair isn't white enough though. How are Evelyn and the kids?"

"They're fine. I'm about to become a grandpa again – did you hear?"

"Congrats! You wouldn't look old enough to be a grandfather without that beard. It's amazing how time flies."

Julia offered Chuck some coffee and doughnuts, which he suggested she pack up to enjoy on the road since it was getting late.

Chuck went over Win's equipment. He nixed Win's waders and suggested hip boots. He grumbled something about the Shint River being like most other New Mexico rivers -- shallow.

Julia pulled Win aside and whispered, "Remember, don't let him drive. He's a disaster on the road." Chuck was usually quite laconic, except when he was driving. He loved to expound loudly while driving, gesticulating with his hands and turning to face the person he was talking to. This was scary at 75 miles an hour, since he often forgot to turn back to look at the road.

Win walked over to Chuck who was checking out Win's fly rod. "Win, I think you'll be okay with a five-weight rod, but a four would be better. Do you have a four-weight?"

"Yeah, I have a 7 ½ footer, would that be all right?"

"That would be much better. Get the new stuff and we're ready to roll."

"I'll drive, Chuck, I have to show off my new car. Besides, I'd like to see how it handles on rough terrain."

"Are you sure? After all, you don't know the way."

"You can be my navigator."

So they shifted all of Chuck's gear and loaded the picnic lunch Julia had prepared into Win's car. Chuck could now safely gab away.

On the way to White Rock, Win told Chuck about the missing neighbor and how he had been drawn into investigating her disappearance. Chuck listened carefully and was silent for a long time. "You know, Win, when someone goes missing for more than a few days, leaving no money trail, it's a bad sign. But if something serious happened to her, where's her body? I can see why you're fascinated by the story. I would be too, in your position, but then, we're both leisure-class academics."

"Looks like White Rock's coming up. I need to make a turn onto Meadow Lane. Okay, there's my next turn coming up and then I have to go six more blocks. Here it is!" Win said, as he cruised up to a medium-sized, "Pueblo Revival" style house in a settled, upper-middle-class neighborhood.

"Chuck, do you want to come in?"

"If you don't mind, I'll take a nap in the back seat and leave the detective work to you. Chinese art is not my cup of tea, no pun intended."

Win walked up to the door and rang the bell. A neat-looking, trim, sixtyish, Asian gentleman wearing a white shirt, maroon cardigan, and gray pants answered the door. "You must be Dr. Sage. Come in please."

"And you must be Dr. Wong. It's a pleasure to meet you. Should I remove my shoes?" Win asked as he noticed that Wong was wearing slippers.

"Oh, it's all right to wear street shoes; our kids always do. So you're familiar with Asian household customs?"

"I lived in Japan for three years when I was in the Air Force, and my wife is Korean-American."

"I greatly admire Korean art. It's been heavily influenced by Chinese art, but the Koreans have evolved their own unique interpretations. I particularly like celadon ceramics of the Koryo period."

"Me too. I was able to collect a few pieces when I was in the Air Force, but I could never afford high-end stuff."

"Can I get you some tea?"

"Thank you; that would be nice," Win answered, understanding that the offering of tea was an important part of good hospitality. Dr. Wong seemed a refined, traditional Asian scholar.

"Please come into the living room and sit down." He showed Win the way and disappeared for several minutes to prepare tea, Win assumed. Win looked around at what appeared to be a comfortable, middle-class living room. Then he noticed the large number of glass display cabinets with ceramic pieces from floor to ceiling. As he focused more closely on the display cases, he realized that they held some incredibly fine examples of early Chinese ceramics. These were world-class works, good enough for top museums.

Wong reappeared carrying an elegant lacquer tray on which were two beautiful multicolored porcelain teacups. He offered the tray to Win, who was careful to use two hands to accept a cup. He assumed that good manners were the same in Japan and China.

Wong sat down across from Win and took a sip of tea before asking, "So how may I be of help in your investigation?"

Win was surprised by Wong's directness, which seemed out of character. "I'm not really conducting an investigation. Bill asked me to try to help as an epidemiologist and there isn't much I can contribute. I felt sorry for him, so I went along with him. My interest in meeting you and seeing your collection is probably my main reason for this visit."

Wong nodded. "I'm honored. But first, let me tell you what I know about Jessica's disappearance. I had no inkling that anything was wrong with her or that she had any reason to disappear. She seemed her usual cheerful self the last time we spoke. She's becoming successful as a dealer, and is increasingly being recognized as an authority on early Chinese ceramics. So I was as surprised as everyone else when she disappeared."

"Do you think she was involved with another man and ran off with him?"

"I've heard that she was involved briefly with the chef at Alphonso's, but that was a while back. I don't think it was serious, and I believe it's over now."

"So she did share some of her personal secrets with you" Win replied.

"Yes, that's her style, at least with me. She's very open."

"Did Jessica ever tell you of difficulties she was having with suppliers or customers? Was anybody upset with her?"

"She never said anything about such problems. She's an honest, straightforward person; it would be unusual for her to have upset anyone."

"Did you notice any health problems that Jessica might have had, like depression?"

"No. She seemed a happy person in the prime of life."

Win shook his head. "These are the same answers I get from others. That's why her disappearance is so puzzling. It sounds like you and Jessica had a close relationship."

Wong lit up. "She's the daughter I never had. My children could care less about art and collecting. Jessica just loves to learn about Chinese art. She has very little background in the field but she has a hidden talent. She's like a sponge for knowledge about early Chinese ceramics. This brought us close and then I was able to help her develop her trade in them. She's become quite an expert on the subject."

"How did you two meet?"

"I was touring galleries on Canyon Road and wandered into the new gallery that she and her husband had opened. She had a few Chinese ceramic pieces on display and we began talking about them. She was hungry for knowledge about Chinese art. One thing led to another and we eventually became friends."

"Did you join her in their business?"

Wong shook his head emphatically. "Oh, no, I don't have time for business ventures. I enjoyed watching her build her own business."

"Bill said you were able to help Jessica in finding good pieces for the gallery."

"Yes. I come from a family of collectors and art dealers, so it was easy for me to connect Jessica with good sources. Many of my relatives are gallery owners in Hong Kong and my father was an accomplished collector in Shanghai in the old days."

"Did your father specialize in early Chinese ceramics?"

Wong looked wistful as he went on. "He loved early works, from prehistoric to the Han Dynasty. He was particularly fond of pieces from the Warring States Era and Spring and Autumn Annals period. Just before the Communist takeover, he was able to escape to Hong Kong with most of his collection. For years he mourned the loss of his furniture collection and some of his large ceramic pieces and, of course, the loss of his country to the Communists. He was very bitter over those events. He was an executive with an American company in Shanghai before the fall, and in those days he had access to wonderful pieces. He continued collecting in Hong Kong, but the loss of some cherished pieces dampened his enthusiasm. When I was a child he used to take me around with him from gallery to gallery in Hong Kong, so he was able to transfer his interest on to me."

"Are these pieces part of his collection?" Win asked, pointing to the display cases.

Wong sighed. "Yes, what's left. After he passed away, the collection was divided among his children. I've lightened up considerably on my collection, as have my siblings. It's beautiful but burdensome; the pieces are fragile, one has to worry about theft, and insurance is expensive. My children and those of my relatives don't care for the pieces and would rather have the money from their sale. So we've been gradually selling off my father's collection, heart breaking as it is. I've enjoyed having these things for many years and now I'm getting old. It's time to lighten up and simplify our lives."

"So has your father's collection been a source of Chinese art for Jessica?"

"Yes. I've also helped her to meet some important collector-dealers in Hong Kong and she bought some great pieces. She was doing so well that it's hard to imagine she would suddenly disappear."

"Yes, Jessica's disappearance is an odd mystery. I'm curious as to how you ended up as a scientist."

Wong gesticulated with his hands as if he was giving a lecture. "It was really by accident. My father was a great admirer of the U.S. and insisted that all his sons get educated in the States. His admiration for America was only exceeded by his hatred of the Chinese Communists. So I ended up at Cal-Berkeley for my undergraduate degree. I started out as a liberal arts major and then found, to my surprise, that I didn't like the arts and preferred the hard sciences. I took a beginning course in physics under a brilliant teacher and fell in love with the field. He became my mentor and I went on to get a Ph.D. in high-energy physics at Cal Tech. I did a post-doc at Cal Tech with a famous physicist and then got a terrific job at Los

Alamos. America is such a great country; where else in the world could a foreigner come and get such an incredible education and career opportunity? Working at the Los Alamos National Laboratories was my first and only job and I still love it. So I never had time to become a serious collector."

Win smiled hearing Wong's history, so much like Julia's, and said, "It's stories like yours that make this country so great. How long have you been at LANL?"

"It's been 36 years. I'll be retiring soon."

"That's a long time! In my area of research, most people move from university to university every five to ten years. What sort of work do you do?"

"I work in high energy physics – basically, particle physics. I can't say more than

that; it's classified. The best thing is that I still love my work after all these years."

"You're a blessed man. I've really digressed and I'm taking up too much of your time."

"Would you like to see some of my collection before you go?"

"I'd be delighted. I have a particular interest in Warring States period pottery."

It was 45 minutes later that Win said goodbye and left, dazzled by what was only a small part of the collection. Wong suggested he return when he next passed through White Rock. He could see why Wong would be a great mentor, having learned so much from him during the brief visit.

Win found that Chuck had wisely rolled down all the windows and was fast asleep in the back seat. "Okay, big fellah, it's time to go fishing. Wake up and lead us on to the great Shint River!"

Chapter 10.

It was dusk when Win and Chuck returned to Santa Fe after a great day of fly-fishing, that is, of fly-casting. The trout were not very cooperative and they had caught (and released) just one 8-inch cutthroat between the two of them.

Julia greeted them at the garage. "How did your fishing go?"

"Well, it was nice to be out fishing, but the fish weren't too active today," Chuck responded.

Julia made sure that Chuck had a cold drink for the road. They all said their goodbyes and Julia planted a big kiss on Chuck's cheek. He had a long drive ahead to Rio Rancho, where he lived.

"Did you have a good time?" she asked Win.

"You know I'm always happy when I'm out fishing, and being with Chuck is even more fun. It's very different from fishing back east. There's some greenery along the river, but not like in Pennsylvania. Also, the water had an odd yellow color to it. But there are definitely less biting bugs here."

"How was your visit to the guy in Los Alamos?"

"He's very interesting and a throwback to another era – very refined and Asian --yet fully Americanized and savvy. He had an impressive education and is probably a star physicist. He has an amazing collection of early Chinese ceramics with a few knockout pieces. There's one Warring States bowl that imitates an elaborate bronze piece – I've never seen anything like it. It's probably good enough to be in the Freer or the Metropolitan. He inherited it from his father, who was a big collector and some sort of taipan for an American company in Shanghai before the takeover."

"Win, the term taipan is usually reserved for a Western big shot in China. Anyway, I bet his father was a friend of Mae's dad, and of Mr. Lam of the Great Wall Gallery."

"That's right; I should ask him. I was thinking of e-mailing Michael in Hong Kong and I could ask him if his dad knew Wong's dad. That would be something. What a small world!"

"I've got supper waiting, so why don't you clean up because you smell."

"It was a hot day."

Win cleaned up and they had a nice dinner with a little too much wine. Julia always joked that she was a "cheap date" since she couldn't handle more than one drink without getting tipsy. Like many Asians, she was probably deficient in the enzymes that detoxify alcohol in the body. Win didn't have the same problem; he just drank a little too much. Feeling mellow, Win decided he'd go to his study and e-mail his friends in Hong Kong. It would be an amazing coincidence if his friends in Hong Kong knew the Wong family. He drafted an e-mail to Michael Lam, manager of the Great Wall Gallery in Hong Kong's Central District.

"Dear Michael,
It's been a while since we were last in touch. Our house in Santa Fe has been completed – it took forever – and we finally moved in three weeks ago. Moving was an incredible hassle and fortunately, nothing was damaged. We've unpacked some of the pieces we got at your gallery and they look spectacular in the new house. There are two built-in display cabinets in one of the cast concrete walls of the living room. The concrete has been colored reddish-tan and looks ancient, so our pieces from the Han, Tang and Sung periods look fantastic against it. I'm looking forward to our financial

recovery from house building so we can obtain some more pieces from the Gallery, as we now have more display space. I love my last purchases -- the two Warring States pieces. I hope you can help us to find more on our next HK visit.

Speaking of Warring States Era ceramics, I met a very interesting Chinese-American physicist here who has an amazing collection of early Chinese ceramics. He has some of the most extraordinary Warring States pieces I've ever seen. Not only is the quality of these pieces outstanding, he has a large number of them. He has one large Warring States ceramic bowl on tripod legs that has incredible animal-mask handles – it's a knockout. The local physicist, C.Y. Wong, inherited them from his late father, who escaped with them from Shanghai just before the Communist take-over. His father must have purchased a truckload of these pieces. The family name is Wong and I don't know his given name or the Chinese character(s) for it. Most of his family is in the antiques business in Hong Kong. The interesting thing is that his father was an executive with some American company in Shanghai before the takeover, just like Mae's father. I suspect your dad will know him from the "good old days." It's such a small world! I trust your Dad is doing well and enjoying his retirement. Please give him my (and Julia's) best regards.

Now that we are settling in here, I'll try to keep in touch on a more regular basis and we should start traveling overseas again shortly.

Warm regards,

Win

P.S. Julia sends her love!"

Win next found Mae Lai's e-mail address. Julia and Mae had been classmates at Bryn Mawr years ago and somehow managed to stay in touch despite leading hectic lives on opposite sides of the globe. He sent Mae an e-mail message similar to the one he had sent Michael. Mae's dad used to take her from gallery to gallery in Hong Kong, just like Wong and his father. They might even know each other.

Win shut the computer and decided to have some calvados. It had been an interesting day, he reflected, as he settled back and enjoyed the nightcap. The fishing was lousy, but Wong's collection was spectacular, and a real privilege to have seen.

Chapter 11.

It was Friday and Win was looking forward to another round of new show openings at the art galleries. He'd had a productive, but tedious, day of unpacking and finding places to put things. Minimalist houses are great to look at, but they limit what you can display. He was hoping to hear from his friends in Hong Kong, but with the time zone difference and his friends' busy schedules, he'd have to wait. He and Julia were about to start their Friday "guacarita time" when it suddenly grew dark and began to rain heavily. You don't have to live very long in Santa Fe to appreciate the value of a good rain in the desert. It cheered them up to watch the rain come down and to see the dogs reveling in the puddles outside. Even dogs seemed to sense the importance of rain in Santa Fe.

"Have you heard back from Mae or Michael?" Julia asked.

"No. It'll probably be a while with their hectic lives in Hong Kong."

"I can't wait to get back to traveling overseas again. Win, would you let the dogs in? They've finally noticed it's guacarita time."

He let in two thoroughly soaked dogs that smelled of "eau de wet dog." Win gave them some tortilla chips far from where he and Julia were sitting, which kept them away for all of about 30 seconds.

"So where are you and George going tonight?" Julia asked while holding her nose.

"George selected an opening of pre-Columbian and other ancient ceramics to start and then two shows of sculptors -- one of whom works in stone and one who does bronzes. Then we'll walk around and see which galleries are still open."

"Sounds pretty boring to me. Remember to go lightly on the drinks and don't eat the food; it's a set-up for food poisoning."

"Julia, it's not a Bar Mitzvah with chopped chicken liver or potato salad sitting around at room temperature for hours. Your public health knowledge is dated."

"Is George a good driver? His car is built like a tank."

"Yes, he's a very good driver and he doesn't drink at these openings. He probably only drinks when he buys his clothes,"

At that, there was noisy honking outside announcing George's arrival.

Win got up, kissed Julia on top of her head, and carefully avoided the two smelly dogs.

Win went out and greeted George. From outside the Hummer, he could see that he was wearing a chartreuse band-collar shirt. Climbing into the passenger seat, he saw that the shirt was paired with hot pink trousers and chartreuse boots.

"That's quite an outfit you have on," he commented.

"Thanks; it's one of my favorite gallery outfits." George sniffed. "Win have you been around any wet animals or are you wearing some new-fangled after-shave cologne?"

"Our dogs were out in the rain and they must have brushed up against me. A word of advice George, be careful with band-collar shirts in Italy, particularly black ones."

"Who would wear a black band-collar shirt other than a priest?"

"That's precisely the point. I once wore a black band-collar shirt when I was working at a cancer institute in Milan. I knew I was in trouble when I got out of the taxi at the front of the hospital and encountered a group of nuns consoling a family. They all gave me respectful curtsies and called me 'Padre'. When I went to the hospital cafeteria, the workers piled my plate high, bowing slightly and referring to me as Padre. It was 'Padre' all day long, even at the bar back at the hotel, with refills on the house. I felt like a fashionable imposter."

"You know, Win, maybe I should get a black one for my next trip to Europe."

It was a pleasant drive into town and George found a great parking space near their first stop. The first gallery was very spare with ancient clay and stone pieces on pedestals perfectly lit by spotlights. The backdrop of the adobe walls with occasional hangings of Nazca weavings added to a very spiffy show. Win inspected a large pre-Columbian piece whose price tag made him whistle, and headed to the drinks. Armed with a flute of champagne, he made his way around the gallery.

He found some ancient Chinese and Korean ceramic pieces over in a corner. While he was carefully examining them, one of the gallery staff came over. "Are you enjoying the show?"

"Yes. This is quite a collection! I don't know much about pre-Columbian pottery, but your stuff looks quite exceptional. My interests lie more in these Asian pieces."

"You know, it's a lot easier for us to get Asian pieces than the pre-Columbian ones. You don't have the provenance issues."

"Why's the provenance so important?" Win asked.

"Buyers of serious pieces like these want assurance that their purchases are safe from being seized or repatriated. We guarantee all our pieces against such loss. It's not as bad, at least not yet, with the Asian stuff. It's hard to get old pieces out of Korea. They were plundered during the Japanese occupation, so they're fanatic about letting significant pieces out. China is another matter. The government tries to control new excavations, but there are a lot of corrupt officials there who have either commissioned new excavations or gotten a percentage of the loot. A lot ends up in their private collections or in the hands of local collectors. The rest goes out the Hong Kong back door and find its way to the U.S., export and import bans notwithstanding. There's also the resale market -- a lot of good Chinese art has been coming into the U.S. for well over a hundred years and people always want to sell off collections. So far, we haven't had any problems with Korean or Chinese old pieces."

"Would ceramics taken out of China in 1949, when the Communist took over, be safe for resale?" Win asked.

"Generally, objects taken out of China before1970 are readily sold if they have good documentation. By the way, I didn't catch your name. Mine's Jim Hardy."

"I'm Win Sage. By any chance, have you met Dr. Wong from Los Alamos? He has an outstanding collection of ancient Chinese ceramics. His father got them out of China just after the Revolution."

Jim thought for a moment. "The name doesn't ring a bell. I thought I knew all the major collectors in the area. I'll have to ask around about him. How do you spell the name?"

"C.Y. W-o-n-g."

"Hmm. Well nice to have you visit our gallery. Holler if you have any questions."

Win walked on, mulling over what he had learned about trade in Chinese art and reflecting upon Wong's anonymity as a collector. He resumed checking out each piece on display and caught up with George. "Hi, George. Have you been enjoying the show?"

"Yup, and I think we need to get going to the next show on our list. It's time for some modern sculpture."

So George and Win walked down the street to another minimalist design gallery. This one had stark white walls, light colored wooden floors and a plethora of spotlights playing on massive abstract stone sculptures. These monumental pieces wouldn't fit into many homes, let alone anyone's backyard. It was a wonder they could get them into the gallery.

"This looks like my kind of stuff and I see my sparring partner Martin Cunningham is already here. We should have great fun disagreeing over this show!" George commented.

"George, you have yourself a ball. I'm heading over to the drinks."

George had a lively argument with his art critic friend. Win ogled some pretty women, the third opening was also great, and the ride home was at the time of a glorious, multi-hued Santa Fe sunset.

On the way home, George brought up the subject of Jessica Harvey. "You know

Win, I got curious about the Harvey disappearance so I called some medical buddies here, in Albuquerque, and in Los Alamos. No one heard of any unidentified women showing up in their hospitals and none of my friends knew her as a patient. It looks like she just vanished; it's strange."

"I agree; it's very strange," Win responded. "She was tutored in Chinese ceramics by an interesting guy who works at LANL. He's got an amazing, large collection of Chinese ceramics. The reason I bring this up is that tonight I mentioned his name to the gallery manager at that ancient ceramics show and he'd never heard of the guy. It probably means nothing since the physicist isn't buying anything, but he is selling off his collection. I have no idea what you could find out, but maybe you could ask your Los Alamos buddies if they've ever heard of him. His name is C.Y. Wong, I forgot what the initials stand for; he's a high-ranking physicist at LANL. I know, I have an overactive imagination, but I'm curious about Wong."

George said, "Win, I think you're nuts, but since I have nothing to do now that I'm retired, I'll ask around for you."

"Thanks George." Win was outsourcing his non-investigation nicely.

Chapter 12

George dropped off a tipsy Win at his house. Win found Julia fast asleep, curled up on the living room couch. She must have bathed the dogs, who smelled significantly better. He walked back lightly to his study to see if he had any reply from Hong Kong. He turned on his computer, checked his e-mail and was surprised to have heard from both Mae and Michael. He opened Mae's e-mail first and it read:

"Dear Win and Julia,
   Great to hear you survived the move to Santa Fe. I would dread having to move all my junk, so I understand how hard it must have been. It's probably good at our age to be forced to winnow our possessions. We accumulate too much of the detritus of life over the years. I found the question about your friend Dr. Wong's father curious. I had never heard of his father, and I thought that through my own late father, I knew the whole collector crowd from Shanghai. I asked some of my dad's surviving friends and they too never heard of any Wong who was a serious collector, and the name doesn't fit with any of the dealer families here in HK. Could you have gotten the name wrong? Is it an Americanized version of another Chinese name? In any event, I'd love to meet

Dr. Wong and see his collection when I visit you. I'm sure I know his family.

All the kids are back in HK on holiday and it's great fun, but I'm exhausted. Let me know when you're unpacked and fit to receive guests. I'll make a beeline over as I miss you both and would love to visit mythical Santa Fe. I love the opera there and the restaurants! Tell Julia that I saw Amanda recently. She's one of our old Bryn Mawr friends who lived in Radnor Hall.

Much love,
Mae

Win was glad to hear from Mae again, but her not having heard of. Wong and his family was a disappointment. On the other hand, maybe the world of émigré Chinese antique collectors from Shanghai was bigger than he assumed. So he opened Michael's mail with interest, only to find a similar response. Neither Michael nor his father knew or had heard of the Wongs and they were major dealers in Hong Kong. So two knowledgeable people, particularly with regard to the old Shanghai collecting group and Hong Kong collectors, came up with the same results – zip! Win was sure Wong's name had gotten Anglicized.

He turned off the computer and walked back to the living room where Julia was now awake.

"Hi, Babe! Did you have a good nap?

Julia yawned. "Yeah. When did you get home?"

"About 15 minutes ago. I tiptoed past you and went to check my e-mail. He recapped what he'd heard from Michael and Mae, and told her that she hoped to visit soon.

"I'm glad that the house construction and moving are over so we can get back to traveling and seeing our friends again. I miss Mae. I think we're both ready to settle down and have fun in our new life."

Chapter 13

It was Tuesday again, Win's day in town with Herky. Win was putting the final touches on his second T-shirt design. His first shirt met with mixed reviews and he still had eight left. It was amazing to him that you couldn't give away a T-shirt if it even hinted of obscenity. Maybe it was his selection of friends – all aging, affluent prudes. They lacked the cultured immaturity of his academic buddies who would probably love them. This new shirt he thought would do better -- with no obscenity and with potential appeal to his fishing buddies. He packed his drawings carefully before Herky arrived and decided to wait outside. It must be the years in banking that made Herky so reliably on time, although Win couldn't think of any reason why bankers would be any more punctual than anyone else. As expected, Herky pulled up on time. His truck was still clean, almost shining, and the bed was empty except for a large cooler.

"Hi, Herk. Looks like you've been sticking to your clean truck commitment."

"Well, 'Wife Number 3' is pretty serious about my truck and I'm not aiming for 'Number 4'."

"Where've you picked for our Mardi Gras dining today?"

"Today, I thought we'd try our one and only bagel factory and restaurant in town.""Herk, that means we aren't locked in to a high-fat lunch, for a change."

"It depends on what you order. There are a few items on the menu for fat-conscious oldsters like you."

"Herky, is the restaurant near my T-shirt wallah's store? I have a new design and they can do it today if I drop it off before noon."

"Unfortunately, it's across town, but at this time of day we can zip over there. You know, I've been wearing your Chaucer T-shirt when I wash the truck. It's quite appropriate."

"I 'm delighted you've put it to such good use."

It was a nice day with little traffic. Herky navigated through town expertly and pulled up in front of Sam's Tees. Win went in alone and found his soul mate Morris, the Grand Wallah of T-shirts.

"Hi, Doc! I'm ready for your new shirt. Whatcha got this time?"

Win unfurled his drawings for Morris. Morris smiled, nodded, and said "Real neat, Doc; the General Prologue to the Canterbury Tales, and cleverly modified."

"Morris, how'd you know that? You didn't know Chaucer from Adam at my last visit. I thought you majored in partying and skiing at college."

Morris got all animated. "You know, your 'pysser T', got me thinking that I might be missing something in life. There you were all excited about this long dead white European dude and it got my curiosity up. So I stopped by the SF Public Library, it's on my way home, and looked up this Chaucer dude. His stuff is like written in Middle English and it threw me for a loop. Now I get the 'y' in pisser. A nice librarian saw me having trouble and came up with a great idea. She told me all the college students, like at St Johns, use ponies like CliffsNotes to understand Chaucer. So I went home with Chaucer and a pony and had a ball! This is really neat stuff and he lived in the Fourteenth Century. He's one cool stud and a true pysser to boot! Thanks, Doc."

Win was flabbergasted. "Morris, that's incredible! You actually went and looked up Chaucer, read his stuff and enjoyed it. I knew you were a genius, but I never expected this."

"Doc, you really influenced me. Maybe we need some teachers wearing 'Chaucer is a pysser' T-shirts in the classroom. I never had a teacher that had enough imagination or enthusiasm to turn me on to anything."

"Morris, once again you've made my day!" Win changed the subject since he was getting all choked up. "So what should we do with this design?"

"I don't think the pseudo-Gothic will work. There're too many words, so we need

to keep the print small and Gothic type would be hard to read from far away. Let me fiddle around with some modern fonts. Do you trust me to choose one?"

"Absolutely, Morris. I'll go with a dozen again."

"I can have them for you in about three hours."

Win went out to the truck and jumped in. "Herky, I just had one of the most gratifying experiences of my teaching career. My pysser T-shirt has gotten Morris the Grand Wallah of Ts to start reading and actually enjoying Chaucer. Can you imagine that?"

"I thought your teaching career was over. I remember reading Chaucer in college. That's a major accomplishment; who ever enjoyed reading Chaucer? Okay, we're off to Bagel Heaven for lunch."

Bagel Heaven turned out to be quite good. Win had tuna salad on a bagel. Herky had lox and heaps of cream cheese on his bagel.

"Win, it looks like you're finally learning to eat a healthy diet. So what are you planning to do this afternoon before our next T-shirt unveiling?"

"I was going to do my usual gallery tour on Canyon Road. There's a new show

I've been meaning to see of Indonesian textiles. I love to mosey along looking at different galleries. I may stop in and see Harvey to find out what's happening with the search for his wife."

"I thought you were dropping your two-bit investigation. Win, you're no Sam Spade!"

"I know I should drop it, but I love solving puzzles and I feel sorry for Bill."

Herky shook his finger at Win. "Win, stick to cross-word puzzles, they don't get messy."

Win nodded. "Thank you for your wisdom. I still think I'll pay Bill another visit."

"You're hopeless. Shall we meet at the usual place at say, four o'clock?"

"Sounds good to me. Don't forget that I have to pick up my new T-shirts."

"I can't wait to see what they look like."

Chapter 14

Herky dropped Win off at his usual starting point on Canyon Road, just above Alphonso's Restaurant, and as Win passed the restaurant, he remembered what he'd heard about Jessica and the chef at Alphonso's. He looked at his watch; it was 1:35 P.M.; probably not a good time to try to talk to the chef, but after hesitating for a moment he went in.

The woman in black at the small desk in the entry greeted him and asked, "Do you have a reservation?"

"No. I'm from out of town and heard about your restaurant from a friend, Jessica Harvey. She owns the East-West Gallery, just down Canyon Road. You might know her

"Sorry, I don't."

"Well anyway, I was thinking of making a reservation for tomorrow night. I heard you have a really great chef. I hope he's here and working tomorrow."

"Oh, our chef Bill Knox is here and working tomorrow night. He's very famous, you know."

"So I've heard. Let me check with my wife back at the hotel and I'll call to book dinner when we decide on a time. It's a nice-looking restaurant."

"Thank you. Try to book either early or late as we're already filled for the 8 o'clock slots."

"See you tomorrow," Win said as he headed out. Win thought it was interesting that the name Jessica Harvey elicited no response from the receptionist, but given the high turnover rate of restaurant staff, she could be new in her job. The chef was in town, so he hadn't run off with Jessica. However, Wong had said that Jessie's dalliance with Alphonso's chef was past history. Win wondered how Sam Spade would have handled this. He was still smarting from Herky's jab.

Win stopped in to see the show of Indonesian textiles he had read about. It was in a beautiful, totally white, modern gallery at the end of one of the many alleys off Canyon Road. He took in the show and left to continue his gallery hopping. Without thinking, he passed by several interesting galleries and found himself at the East-West Gallery. He triggered the entry chime as he went inside and was greeted by his old friend the gatekeeper in her usual black and white costume. She suddenly recognized Win and before he could say anything, she hurried towards the rear of the gallery and said over her shoulder, "I'll see if Bill's here."

Bill came out to greet Win and looked glum. "Win, I just had a terrible experience. The police found the body of a woman and they asked me to come see if it was Jessie. I had to go to the county morgue – a very grim place. The body they showed me was badly decomposed, but it definitely wasn't Jessie. I vomited after seeing the poor woman. What if something like that happened to Jessie?"

"Bill, let's hope not. Decomposed bodies are pretty gruesome even to doctors."

"It was horrible, but at least the police still seem to be looking for Jessie. It's been a month now that she's been gone!"

"I visited Dr. Wong," Win said. "He didn't have any significant insights into Jessica's disappearance, but he seemed to think that Jessica was playing the field with other men." Win paused, hoping he wasn't crossing a line here. "Could she have possibly gone off with another guy?"

"I told you that I didn't think she was being unfaithful. She would have told me if she was; we had that kind of a relationship."

Win shook his head and said, "Bill, I suggested to you earlier that you get a private investigator to pursue the possibility that her disappearance is related to a boyfriend of hers."

"Win, couldn't you do that sort of investigation for me?"

"I have no experience or training in being a private detective and you probably need a license. Also, I don't have the time; I'm still working part-time at the University in Albuquerque. I think you need an expert to do it as a full-time job."

"I guess I do." He sighed sadly. "I've got nothing left to lose."

Win nodded in agreement. "Bill, how do you spell Dr. Wong's name?"

"W-o-n-g".

Have you or Jessica seen it spelled differently; like H-u-a-n-g?"

"No, we've known him for a long time and it's always been W-o-n-g. His first name is Chung-Yi. We always call him CY or Dr. Wong. Why do you ask?"

"I was just curious, since I thought some friends of ours in Hong Kong might have known his father."

"His father died quite a while ago."

"My friends' parents could have known him. Anyway, it doesn't matter. Bill, why don't you take the day off? You had a pretty horrible experience this morning."

"You know, that's a good idea. Jessie's daughter is visiting to see if she could help. I should go home and spend some time with her. She's as upset as I am."

Win got up to leave and said, "Bill, you're under a lot of stress. Have you talked to your doctor about it?"

"No. But I am falling apart a bit."

"Bill, it's a lot. Get some help."

"Thanks, Win."

Chapter 15

Win continued down the road to visit more galleries. His first stop was Honey Chile Boudreaux's gallery; he thought that would be the most diverting.

He walked in and was greeted by the same attractive lady as at his last visit. She recognized him and said, "Oh yes, the man from Santa Fe who can read peoples minds. Have you read anything good lately?"

"No. I seem to have lost my skill," he said.

"Too bad! Are you here to see Ann?"

"Yes, if she's available."

"She's been on the phone with a client for over an hour now. Let me see if she can use you as an excuse to get off the phone."

She headed back to Ann's office and was gone a few minutes so Win started to look around. He really didn't like country antiques anymore, although when he lived in a small saltbox house in Brookline, Massachusetts, ages ago, he loved them. He also used to love the colonial period-rooms at the Boston Museum of Fine Arts. But tastes change and after his Air Force assignment in Japan and marrying Julia, he was now hooked on Asian art. He was awakened from his ruminating by Honey Chile greeting him and giving him a big hug.

"Well if it isn't Dr. Win! I'm so glad to see you again. At your last visit we got to your finding me attractive and tempting, so where are we heading today?" She took Win by the hand and led him back to her office.

"Honey Chile, you're incorrigible -- and also very beautiful and tempting. How've you been?"

"I've been fine and having a good spell of business for a change. I'm still looking for a fine man like you though."

"Honey Chile, I'm spoken for and not ready for another relationship -- although if I were, you'd be at the top of my list."

"Talking of lists, how's your mañana list coming along? I found your T-shirt very quaint."

"Thank you for being one of the few to appreciate my creation I'm having my second T-shirt made up today."

"Well, it sounds like you're making good progress in your quest. I'm waiting for the item on your list titled, 'Have an affair with a beautiful and mysterious lady'. It's so much less mundane than making T-shirts."

"I didn't realize you were mysterious."

"My dear Win, try me and find out," she drawled theatrically.

"Honey Chile, you are fast becoming the Siren of Canyon Road. I may have to seal my ears with wax and tie myself to the mast of my ship when I pass through the Road."

"Win, you're pedantic, and silly. You also don't know mythology. When Ulysses passed the coast of the Sirens, he followed Circe's advice and put wax in the ears of his sailors, not himself. His ears were not sealed, so he could hear the Sirens' beautiful song. He had his sailors tie him to the ship's mast so he wouldn't be drawn to crash into the rocks."

"Honey Chile, you amaze me."

"You're forgiven, Win. Are you still pursuing the Harvey girl's disappearance?"

"Unfortunately, it's become an obsession. Everybody but Bill Harvey thinks her disappearance is related to her having a relationship with another man."

"I always thought she was mighty loose."

"Maybe she had a fling with some rough guy who did her in?"

"I doubt that. I'd guess it's related to how she got so rich all of a sudden. That sort of overnight success story isn't common in the gallery business."

"Well, Honey Chile, there seems to be a good explanation for that observation. She lucked out and found a very knowledgeable mentor who taught her a lot about Chinese ceramics and connected her with the right dealers in Hong Kong."

"Why would anybody want to mentor her rather than start his or her own business? I bet this mentor was another boyfriend."

"No, he's an elderly Chinese-American physicist who treated her like a daughter. His own children have no interest in Chinese art and he wanted to pass his knowledge on."

"I don't believe it, Win; it's too farfetched."

Win wondered if she might be right. "By the way, Bill Harvey got a mighty big scare today. The police called him in to identify the decomposed body of a woman, thinking it might be Jessica. Fortunately, it wasn't her."

She grimaced and said, "How gory! Do you think she might be dead?"

"Unfortunately, yes."

"Then I think it's the police that you should be sounding out and not me. This is getting out of your league. You'd do much better having a fling with a mature, beautiful and understanding woman."

Honey Chile went over to the entry to her office and closed the door behind the curtain. "Win," she said, "you're a doctor and I'm scared about a lump I found in my breast." With this, she began unbuttoning her blouse and then unhooked and raised her bra. She went over to Win and placed his hand on her huge, but shapely, right breast. "This is where I felt a lump. Can you examine me Win?"

Win stuttered, "I believe that's called a nipple. Honey Chile, my clinical training was in pediatrics. I haven't done a breast exam in years."

Honey Chile shook her head and said, "Win, are you dumb? I'm offering myself to you. Feel my breasts." She pulled him onto the couch in her office. "Come on Win, kiss my breasts."

Win muttered, "Oh no! No, I've got to leave," as he extricated himself and stood up.

Honey Chile said through clenched lips, "What kind of man are you? I'm giving myself to you!"

"I can't. I'm married and I've always been faithful to my wife. I'm sorry."

Honey Chile was red-faced and hauled off and smacked Win's face very hard. "You led me on and then punked out on me. You are a despicable, nasty cad. Get out of here!"

Win turned and hurried out of the gallery trying to avoid the gallery-minder. Win couldn't believe what had just happened and he walked down the road, shaking his head from side to side like a dotty old geezer. He stopped to look at his reflection in a gallery window. The left side of his face was an angry red. He hoped he wouldn't have a bruise; it would be hard to explain to Julia. This was his fault. He didn't know why he had led Chile on. What on earth was his motivation? He continued on in a fog to meet Herky. He really was a cad!

Chapter 16.

Herky was within two minutes of their meeting time, as always. Win jumped on board.

"Hi Herk, did you have a good afternoon?"

"Yup, I got a lot done – even got the truck's oil changed – and visited my favorite sporting goods shop. What were you up to today?"

Win didn't feel like talking, but grimaced and said, "I visited Bill Harvey and we had a sad conversation."

"Win, leave poor Bill Harvey alone. You should have dropped your 'amateur night' investigation long ago. Hey, what happened to your face? Your left side is all red and swollen."

"I tripped and fell on Canyon Road. You know, the pavement is all broken up there."

"I hope you didn't get a concussion. You need to put some ice on it. Do you still want to go to your T-shirt guy on the way home?"

"Oh definitely; Morris would be very disappointed, and so would I, if we didn't pick up the shirts," Win said as he felt depressed.

"Let's go for it then!" Herky muttered as he turned his truck around. He masterfully wended his way through Santa Fe's back streets to get to the T-shirt shop in record time.

"Well done, Herk! I'll go in by myself, the better to surprise you."

Win went inside and blinked hard. "Hi, Morris! You need to brighten up your shop.""Hi, Doc! A blinded customer is a less critical customer." Morris craned his neck and said, "Hey Doc, what happened to your face; it looks like somebody hit you?"

"I fell on Canyon Road."

"Your face is pretty red. Are you all right?"

"I'm fine, thank you. Let's see today's creation." Win looked down in reaction to everyone piling on the guilt for him.

Okay, wait till you see today's new shirt; it's a knockout. Old Geoffrey would just love it." He shouted loudly, "ta da!" as he proudly unfurled a navy T-shirt with bright red lettering that read:

Whan that Aprill with
his shoures sote
The droghte of Marche
hath perced to the rote
Than longen folk to goon
fishynge for the troute

(With apologies to G. Chaucer)

"Morris, it's beautiful!"

"Doc, I'm glad you like it.

"Morris, thank you again for helping me with these mañana projects. You're a true talent and very creative."

"So where are we going next with your T-shirt projects?"

"That's a good question. I shot my wad on the Chaucer motif. Right now I'm concentrating on playing amateur detective."

"That's cool. Whatcha investigating?"

"The wife of one of my neighbors disappeared. They own a gallery on Canyon Road. I've been looking into what might have happened to her."

You know Doc, I might be able to help. You probably have a lot of friends in high places. I have a lot of friends in low places who can find out interesting things. What's the woman's name and the name of her gallery?"

Win gave him the details, which Morris wrote down on a psychedelic patterned pad. Win said, "While you're at it, see what your friends can find out about Dr. C.Y. Wong, he's a scientist at LANL and a big-time collector of Chinese art."

"Sounds like this could be fun. I always wanted to play detective, Doc."

"I've gotta get going, but I'll be back with more designs soon. I shall return!" Win said with a clumsy, MacArthur-like military salute. He had never learned to salute properly in the Air Force. He paid Morris and gave him a bear hug before leaving.

Win went out into the blinding sunshine and blinked his way over to Herky's truck. As he climbed in, Herky impatiently asked, "So what's today's creation?"

Win drew out a T-shirt for Herky and unfurled it ceremoniously. "What do you think of it, Herk?"

"Well, it's Chaucer again with no hint of obscenity. This is the start of the thing they had us read in college English. Oh, I get it; it's about the spring and the opening of trout season. I could wear this when I go trout fishing and be a real literary-type fisherman. This is much better than the first one. Do I get to keep it?"

"It's all yours!"

"Thanks. I can show this one to the wife. She'll be impressed."

They headed home with Herky in a lively mood talking about how trout fishing can be good exercise if done right. It sounded to Win like Herky's methods would spook the fish. Win kept up his chatter while growing increasingly depressed.

Luckily, Julia was out when Win got home. He headed to a mirror to check his face; it was red but not bruised. He put some ice cubes in a plastic bag and applied it to his face as he muttered to himself, "What the hell did I just do? Why did I lead her on? I must be losing my marbles!"

Chapter 17.

Over the weekend, Win unpacked more of the endless number of boxes from their move. It was work that allowed him to keep from sitting around feeling guilty and depressed over his encounter with Honey Chile. He also tried to distract himself by ruminating over what he'd learned of Jessica, but that didn't help much either. He felt he needed to touch base with Harvey and Wong again, but he wasn't sure about what.

On Monday, Win drove down to the University in Albuquerque to check on his research and to attend pathology grand rounds. He met with his study coordinator and spent a couple of hours dealing with problems in collecting their research data. He loved doing epidemiologic research and dreaded the day when he would finally retire fully.

Win remembered that he needed to hike quickly over to the auditorium for grand rounds or he'd miss it. It was on the newer classification systems for lymphomas and of great interest to him, but probably of little interest to most docs. Win paid close attention to the lecture, took copious notes and felt he learned a lot. As he was leaving the auditorium, he spotted Jim Abel, who headed the State's Office of Medical Investigation and their training program in forensic pathology. He caught up with Jim to say hello. "Jim, do you remember my call to you several weeks ago about a missing woman in Santa Fe?"

"Yeah, sorry I couldn't be of much help."

"Well, the woman's still missing. No one's seen her, her car is gone and she hasn't touched any of her bank or credit accounts. According to the police she hasn't shown up in any emergency rooms or turned up as an unidentified corpse."

"How long has she been gone?"

"About five weeks."

"That really raises the odds of something bad having happened or her committing suicide; but with most suicides, the victim doesn't try to hide his or her body."

"So far the police have come up with nothing and her husband doesn't think she was suicidal or would've run away."

Jim grimaced and said, "That's an odd story, Win! I'll certainly keep an eye out for any unidentified woman that gets reported to us. How old is she?"

"She's 48. If it's of any help, she's white, about five feet seven inches, of medium build and has brown hair and hazel eyes."

"I've got the picture. This could turn out to be an unusual one. Thanks for the heads up. See you."

At least Jim could keep an eye out for Jessica, should she turn up as an unidentified corpse. This exchange and his guilty feelings dampened his spirits on the ride back to Santa Fe, despite its being a beautiful day

Chapter 18.

It was Tuesday and Win was preparing for his trip to town with Herky. He carefully arranged the flies he had tied on the weekend to show Herky his improving skills. Julia let Herky in and he duly padded back to Win's study wearing his preferred, oversized, felt slippers. Herky was dressed in a black, velvet Western-style shirt with a remarkably worn and holey pair of jeans. Nevertheless, he always looked dapper and today was no exception.

"Well, well, Dr. Sage, what's that I see on your desk?"

"That's the latest batch of flies I tied. What do you think of them?"

Herky picked one up and studied it carefully. "They're getting a bit better, but they look like they'll come apart after a few casts. I don't think you applied enough tension when you wrapped your thread. Win, you ought to take some lessons and stop wasting your tying materials."

"I thought I was finally getting the hang of it. Okay, so where are we going for lunch today?"

"I thought I'd introduce you to the Elk Café in the De Vargas Center. It's a local favorite not frequented by tourists. They have very good New Mexican food and there's lots of parking."

"Sounds good to me," Win responded.

"Are you doing another T-shirt project today?"

"No, I'm not ready yet. I used up my ideas on the Chaucer shirts and I need to find a subject that might get Morris interested in learning some new literary things. So, I'm cogitating, Herky, just cogitating."

"That's too bad; I was expecting a new one. You know, I really like the first two, particularly the one about April and his showers sweet."

"It's not so easy to come up with new ideas. I cogitated over the first two for decades."

"Win, you're a very slow cogitator. At our age, the clock is running and you have to cogitate quicker."

"You're right. I do have an idea that I'm working on, though."

"Good! Let's get going."

They went out to Herky's truck that was still sporting a waxed shine. He also was keeping the truck bed clean and unlittered. Wife Number Three must have put the fear of God into him.

On the way out Herky asked, "Where are you planning to go today?"

"The usual, a visit to the galleries on Canyon Road."

"Win, you're like a character out of the movie Groundhog Day. Don't you get bored with the same routine? You know, there are some nice galleries and shops on Palace Avenue too."

"I know, and I'll eventually make Palace Avenue part of my Tuesday routine, but I need to talk to Bill Harvey again."

"Are you still playing detective?"

"Herk, I'm on the verge of giving it up, but I had some new thoughts that I want to explore."

"Please don't bore me with the details, Win. I suspect you're all wet on your new ideas just like your others. You're a stubborn guy and won't take my advice to just drop the detective stuff."

"I know! I just need to pursue these new ideas and if they don't pan out, I'll retire as a 'private eye'."

Herky pulled into the Mall's parking lot and announced, "Let me introduce you to one of Santa Fe's culinary secrets." So they marched off to the Elk Café.

It was a pleasant surprise. "Herky, this looks like a nice place. These are real locals, not the leisure-class, costumed characters that you see in the fancy restaurants. I hope the food is good too."

"Just try it Win."

Herky ordered carne adovado burritos and Win the chili rellenos, both of which were daily specials. Win's stuffed green chilis came with a sopaipilla, which made him uncomfortable because he knew Herky was sure to nag about the calories when he doused them in honey. Nevertheless, Win indulged, eliciting only a frown from Herky today.

"What are you going to do this afternoon, Herky?"

"I was thinking of looking for a new truck. You know, just a preliminary look at what's available."

"Herk, I thought you and the wife had reached an accommodation on your trusty old chariot."

"We did, but I'm getting tired of having to keep my truck clean and waxed. It's not easy with a rusting old jalopy."

"Have you negotiated a policy for a new truck? I mean, will you have to keep it clean and waxed as well?"

"Not yet. But the wife's gripe about the old truck was that it was rusting, dirty and filled with junk. So with a new one, I'll just have to keep it from getting loaded up with junk and wash it occasionally."

"I see, but aren't you really attached to the old jalopy?"

"Not any more, after trying to keep it presentable."

They paid their bill and went out. "Herky, how about dropping me off at the Plaza? I could use a walk to Canyon Road today."

"I'm proud of you Win; you're learning."

Chapter 19.

It was another typical Santa Fe day, crisp and sunny, so Win found the brisk walk exhilarating. As he walked, he began framing what he would say to Harvey. He needed to bounce some ideas off Bill and share his hunch that the disappearance was somehow related to Jessica's Chinese ceramics business. On his way to the East-West Gallery, Win stopped into a pair of galleries that specialized in high-end Indian crafts. He was taken in by the incredibly striking Navajo blankets in one of the shops and their similarly incredibly high prices. Before long, Win found himself in front of the East-West Gallery. He studied the window display before entering and noticed they had some new Chinese pieces. The beautiful greeter was on duty and was elegantly dressed as usual.

"Welcome to the East-West Gallery…" she began. She noticed it was Win and said, "Yes. Yes. I'll go see if Bill is like free", and took off in a rush. Win sighed and shook his head as she left.

Bill came out to greet Win and ushered him back to the office. "Hi, Win. Have you come up with any leads?"

"No, just some thoughts. By the way, I chatted with the State Medical Investigator yesterday down at UNM. There haven't been any unidentified women reported to his office recently. He thinks that Jessica's disappearance is starting to look suspicious of foul play and I'm also worried that something bad has happened to her.

I think it has to do with her business in ancient Chinese ceramics and her financial success. Is it possible that one of her customers had a grievance with her?"

"No. She never had any problems with her customers. They were all very pleased and most were repeat buyers."

"Bill, could she have been selling fakes? There are a lot of very well done counterfeit Asian ceramics on the market from what I've read."

"Oh, no way." Bill frowned and waved Win off. "Her friend, CY, knows a lot about authenticating ceramics and he helped her to buy our Chinese stuff. Besides, her customers are very knowledgeable and they certainly wouldn't buy anything that was a fake; they know the field too well."

"Bill, did you or Jessica have any loans from friends or associates, or are there any silent partners in your business?"

"No, we don't have any loans from friends or banks these days. We've been doing very well financially for the last few years, and we don't have any partners, silent or otherwise."

"Are you sure the stuff Jessica was buying in Hong Kong was authentic and not stolen? I've been bothered by the story of her buying from private sources in their homes and not from galleries."

"I'm sure the pieces are the 'real McCoy' and they certainly weren't stolen. As to buying from private sources, she was dealing in very rare, esoteric items and she was buying them from highly specialized collectors and dealers. At least, that's how Jessie and CY explained it to me."

Win squirmed, feeling like he was being a relentless interrogator, but went on. "Was Jessie still in touch with her first husband? Also, how did they get along after their divorce?"

"She has some contact with him, particularly about their kids. But it always seemed civil. Their divorce wasn't acrimonious; they'd been drifting apart for years before the break-up and they didn't have a lot of assets to divide. Are you implying that he may have something to do with Jessie's disappearance?"

"You never know what a jealous ex-husband might do."

Bill scowled. "That's far-fetched. He's not that kind of guy."

"How are Jessica's relationships with her children and family? Were they having any problems?"

"Jessie is very close to her kids and family. They've never had any major disagreements or problems that I know of."

"How was Jessica getting along with Wong? Was there any change in their relationship?"

"As I told you, Jessie was like his daughter. He's so proud of her and she adores him like she would a doting father. Nothing's changed there."

"Did Jessica ever have a stalker or some other crackpot bothering her?"

"Not that I'm aware of."

"I'm sorry to ask these questions; I should have asked them before. In a situation like this, where Jessica's been gone for so long, we need to consider all possibilities. I also was thinking that I should be asking some more questions of Dr. Wong. I hesitate to call him because it's an imposition to have an amateur detective like me asking him a bunch of dumb questions. Do you think you could get him to meet with me again?"

"Sure. He's as concerned about Jessie as I am. He's even been helping me run her side of the business while she's gone. I'll give him a call this evening and then get back to you."

"That's great. I'd also like to see more of his collection. By the way, do you have his business card?"

"I think we have his card somewhere in the office. Let me look." Bill rummaged through his desk and then through a business card file with no success. "I should be looking through Jessie's desk, not mine." He went out to Jessica's office and returned after a few minutes, waving the card. "I found it." He passed it to Win who examined it carefully. It read, "C.Y. Wong, Ph.D., Senior Research Scientist, Department of High Energy Physics, Los Alamos National Laboratory, Professor of Physics, University of California at Berkeley, …" Win idly turned the card over and noticed it had Chinese characters on the back. It was like the meishi, or business card, Win used to carry when he was in the Air Force in Japan that had his name and title in English on one side and in Japanese on the other.

"Bill, could I get a copy of both sides of this card?"

"Oh, sure."

Bill walked over to a copy machine, copied both sides, and passed the copies to Win.

As Win got up to leave, Bill, said "I still haven't given up hope that we can find Jessie alive and well."

"I hope so."

Win headed out and was seen by the hostess who artfully ducked out of sight. "I'm sorry," Win said to her general area of hiding as he left the gallery.

Win didn't learn much from the meeting with Bill, but he did get Wong's name in Chinese characters from his business card. He had spent a lot of time, so he decided to reverse course and walk down the Road to his usual meeting place on the Paseo. He also wanted to stay far away from Honey Chile's gallery. Win decided that if he learned nothing more after his next visit to Wong, he would drop the whole business, and this time he meant it

Herky was right on time, driving his old, beat-up truck; so at least he hadn't succumbed to buying a new one on the spot. Win realized he would miss the jalopy if Herky got rid of it. After getting in, Win had a sudden idea and asked, "Herk, could you do another credit check for me, this time on Jessica Harvey's mentor?" Win pulled put the copy of Wong's business card and gave Herky the details.

"You're hopeless, Win. I'll humor you and see what I can find out about Wong."

Herky was in high spirits and they had a pleasant chat on the way home. It turned out that the new model trucks available didn't conform to Herky's specialized needs as well as his old model did, so he'd scrapped his plans to buy a new one. He was clearly relieved by not having to part with his trusty old jalopy.

Chapter 20.

Win and Julia had a pleasant dinner that evening, with a nice bottle of wine that made them both a bit tipsy. Win noticed the wine's effect when he took the two dogs for their evening walk and found he was stumbling. Charlie, the terrier, sensed that Win was unsteady, so he stayed close by Win's side while Lucy just took off after some rabbit's scent. It was getting to be well into spring but it was still nippy outside after sunset. The cool air helped Win clear his head. Win was still shaken by his experience with Honey Chile and it cast a pall over his walk. He thought about his crazy involvement in the Harvey business and how he was out of his league in trying to play detective. He muttered, "Charlie, you're poppa is making a fool of himself by trying to play detective and he needs to drop this obsession." Charlie just looked up at him with a cocked head as Dandies frequently do. It looked to Win as if Charlie was agreeing with him.

After they got back and Win settled the dogs in their sleeping area, he headed to his study. He checked his E-mail and found a message waiting from Bill Harvey. Bill had been able to reach Wong, who could meet with Win on Saturday morning. He asked Win to call Wong to confirm the meeting.

Win felt conflicted over what to do. His curiosity urged him to meet with Wong again, but his common sense told him he was wasting his time and playing the fool. Being slightly drunk and depressed didn't help either. His idea that Jessica was peddling fake merchandise, and met with harm as a result, now seemed highly implausible. He was tempted to pour himself a bit of calvados, but he had already had too much alcohol for the night. He looked at his display cases and noticed his two Warring States' ceramic pieces. It seemed quite a coincidence that he loved ancient Chinese ceramics, particularly Warring States period pieces, and these arcane ceramics could be at the center of this strange disappearance. Maybe it was his Karma to become involved in this affair.

Win retrieved Wong's phone number and sat for a while thinking. Should he back out or go forward, at least for one more step? He looked at his watch; the time was 8:18 p.m. If he was going to call, this was a good time.

He caved in and dialed Wong's number. He recognized the answering voice as Wong's and said, "Good evening, Dr. Wong. This is Win Sage, Bill Harvey's neighbor. He told me he had spoken with you about my visiting again to get your advice on some ideas I have about Jessica's disappearance."

"Yes, he did. I certainly would like to be of any help to you that I can. Perhaps, I can answer your questions over the phone and spare you a visit?"

"I would love to see some more of your collection and I was planning to go fishing out your way this coming Saturday. I also was hoping to show you a couple of Warring States ceramic pieces that I bought in Hong Kong several years ago, to get your expert opinion on them."

"I see. Well, I guess I can make some time late Saturday morning to meet with you. This is a busy time in my lab as we have to write our annual report for the Government."

"I'll try not to take up much of your time."

"Okay; would 11:00 a.m. be good? I should be back from the lab by then."

"Yes, that would be fine. I look forward to seeing you on Saturday. Have a good night."

Win puzzled over why he wanted to see Wong rather than talk to him over the phone. He had this gut feeling that he'd learn more from an actual meeting. At least, Win could mooch a free appraisal of his Warring States pieces and see more of Wong's incredible collection. He decided to have a nip of calvados after all.

Chapter 21.

It wasn't long before Saturday rolled around and it was time for Win's visit to Wong. On the previous night's gallery crawl with George, Win had learned that Wong was a pretty healthy guy. George's Los Alamos Medical Center buddy, who was Wong's primary care physician, thought Wong was a nice old guy, very personable and very healthy. He couldn't legally tell George any more.

Win had carefully packed his two pieces of Warring States pottery in bubble-wrap and a sturdy cardboard box the night before. The pieces were already nestled in their custom-made boxes with padded satin liners that rare pieces typically came in. An extra level of cushioning was good insurance against accidents, he thought. He loaded the pottery and then his fishing gear into the car.

Julia came out to bring Win a special lunch she'd prepared for him. "Win, I made you some sandwiches. Don't you stop along the way and buy any more food. Knowing you, you'll probably eat the sandwiches before you even get fishing."

"I won't and besides there are no places to buy food up near the Shint River."

"Maybe you should take one of the dogs along?"

"No thanks! They'll get in the stream with me and spook the fish. We've never had any dog disciplined enough to sit quietly on a stream bank. Don't worry about my fishing alone. Also, remember that cell phone reception is very spotty up in the Jemez, but I'll try to reach you from time to time."

"Okay, just drive carefully and stay out of deep water. When you're done, call me and I'll get dinner started."

Win gave Julia a kiss on the cheek and got underway. He winced as he thought of his episode with Honey Chile. It was sunny with a brilliant turquoise sky and occasional fluffy white clouds, but it didn't cheer him up. Win reviewed the points he wanted to touch upon and wondered how much time Wong would be able to spend with him. He really wanted to see more of Wong's collection and get Wong's opinions on his own two pieces.

Win pulled up to Wong's house. There were other cars parked in front, so he parked further up the street. He carefully got his precious pottery out of the back seat and walked up to the door. The house was on a very attractive street with nice old trees. It seemed like a pleasant place to live and raise a family. Win wondered how many of Wong's neighbors also worked at LANL. He suspected it was a bit of an "atomic ghetto." He rang the doorbell and Wong answered.

"Hello, Dr. Sage. Come on in." Wong was dressed up today in a navy blazer and tie.

"Thank you for seeing me today. I know you're quite busy right now."

"Unfortunately, this is our annual review time at the Lab. I just came from a high-level budget meeting. Come on in and sit in the living room while I fix some tea."

Win welcomed this opportunity to examine the large display of ceramics in the living room. He walked around and peered into several cabinets containing some very beautiful and rare pieces of early Chinese ceramics. The ones he could identify as Warring States Period pieces were particularly spectacular, at least to Win's amateur eyes.

Wong entered the room silently and said, "I see you really appreciate early Chinese ceramics. Those in the case you're looking at are particularly exceptional pieces from the Warring States Period.

You said that you have a strong interest in that epoch of ceramics. That period with its incredible history was my father's special love. So he became a minor scholar on the subject."

"I can understand why. Did your father do any writing on the subject?"

"Unfortunately, no. He was a businessman and never seemed to have enough time. He was finally ready to start writing when he died suddenly."

"It's a shame he couldn't pass his knowledge on to the public."

"Well, at least he tried to pass some of it on to his sons. I wish I'd learned more from him. So many children fail to appreciate their parents' attempts to educate them until it's too late. My children are the same, which is why I found tutoring Jessica so rewarding."

Win sat down on the couch. "How did your father get interested in collecting early ceramics?"

"It must be something in our family's genes. My grandfather was an avid collector of Ming Dynasty ceramics, but my father developed his own interest in earlier ceramics."

"Did your father do most of his collecting in Shanghai?

"Yes. It was a golden time for collectors in the 30s and 40s in Shanghai, despite the war. By the time of the Communist takeover he had amassed a large collection of ceramics and furniture. He got a lot of his ceramics out to Hong Kong but lost most of his furniture collection."

"How sad!" Win said, as he began his planned questioning. "What sort of business was your father in?"

"He was an executive with a large, international trading company based in Shanghai. It was great for him because it gave him the means to build his collection."

"My wife has a dear friend from college whose father was an executive with Standard Oil in Shanghai just before the Communist takeover. He was a collector of Chinese art and he too escaped to Hong Kong without much of his collection. Mae Lai, my wife's friend, became a collector like you. I wonder if you've ever met her, since collecting circles tend to be so small?"

"No, the name doesn't ring a bell. Hong Kong is a lot bigger city than most people think."

Win pressed on. "Did your father go into the antiques business in Hong Kong?"

"No. He frequented the galleries and auctions and towards the end began selling some of his lesser pieces privately. He was a broken man after the Communist takeover, but at least he had enough money to live comfortably."

"That's a tragic story. What was his name?"

Wong looked down and sighed. "His English name was Samuel and that's the name he went by in Hong Kong." Wong fidgeted and went on, "It makes me feel sad, so let me change the subject. Let's have some tea."

After ceremoniously pouring tea into two elegant, overglazed-enamel Chinese cups, Wong asked, "So what have you come up with regarding Jessica's disappearance? Bill told me you have some new ideas about the mystery."

"Well, actually I'm a bit embarrassed by my latest ideas and I'm probably all wet. I was wondering whether Jessica might have gotten a buyer so upset with her that he did her harm. Is it possible that Jessica was buying counterfeits and selling them as authentic pieces? I've read several articles about the increasingly good quality of reproductions being made; some of them have been good enough to fool experts. Or could she have been selling stolen merchandise?"

Wong smiled and said, "Oh, I don't think either of the possibilities you raise is true. I helped Jessica buy almost all of her pieces in Hong Kong and they were all authentic. She only bought from reputable and scholarly sources and I think I know enough to spot fakes. These dealers definitely don't traffic in stolen goods and they know which major pieces have been stolen around the world. Also, Jessica's clientele is highly sophisticated and knowledgeable, many from museums, and they would certainly be able to detect fakes. So I don't think your theories are valid."

"Do you know if she was buying things from other sources that could have been disreputable?"

"I don't think so. I didn't see anything in the gallery that she bought on her own other than some lesser items she got from auction houses. The big houses are pretty good nowadays at authenticating items they put up for sale."

Win ran his hand over his head and said, "Well so much for my theories. I couldn't find other explanations for her disappearance and this was the only one remaining. One last question: Do you know if Bill and Jessica had another partner in their business? I wonder if they might have had a silent partner."

"I don't think so. I'm sure Jessica would have told me about such a person." Wong sighed. "Well, why don't you show me your Warring States pieces; that should cheer us up?"

Win carefully unwrapped his two pieces on the carpet and then he and Wong got down on their knees to examine them. Wong gingerly picked up the first piece, a small jar with two tubular ceramic handles on each side. He studied it carefully and said, "This is a nice piece! The cloth impressed pattern is classic for the period, as is the form. The tube handles, probably used for tying down a lid, are still intact and raise the pot to an above average level. Yes, this is from the Warring States Era and it's of pretty good quality." He next turned to the second piece, a medium-sized, shallow bowl with three small legs and animal-mask handles on each side. "Oh, this is a very nice piece. The rudimentary, yellow-green ash glaze is rare, as is the form. It's probably a ceramic reproduction of a bronze ceremonial piece. Notice the incised 'S on its side' pattern around the rim; it's typical of Warring States and earlier pieces. Yes, this too is authentic and an exceptional piece. You've done well with your purchases. Did you say you got them in Hong Kong?"

"Yes, I got them from the Great Wall Gallery. My friend Michael Lam who manages the Gallery helped me select them. Do you know him or his father?"

"I've heard of their gallery but haven't been there. They have a reputation for being high-priced. I have only a few more minutes to spare, unfortunately, so what would you like to see in my collection today?"

"Why don't we continue with Warring States Period ceramics."

"That's an excellent idea."

Wong and Win spent the next fifteen minutes rapt in the intricacies of Warring States ceramics. Win was again amazed by the range of Wong's knowledge and the quality of his collection.

Win thanked Wong profusely and felt a bit ashamed for having foisted himself on the good doctor about a lame-brained idea at an inconvenient time. He carefully re-wrapped his treasures that he valued even more now that they'd been deemed of good quality.

Wong was gracious and told Win, "I'm glad you're still trying to help poor Bill in finding Jessica. At least you're actively thinking about the case while the police don't seem to be doing much."

"Well, let's hope for the best, although I'm growing pessimistic about her safe return. Thank you again for seeing me and sharing your knowledge and your collection." Win walked carefully down the steps in front of the house and on to his car. It was time to do some fishing.

Chapter 22.

It was dark when Win returned home. The dogs started barking and Julia let them out to greet Win. "Hi, doggos, did you have a good day? You're poppa certainly did." They responded to Win by jumping all over him and lavishing him with wet kisses. Win methodically unpacked his fishing gear and put things away in the garage. He was tired, so he decided to unpack his precious pottery later. He went in and gave Julia a peck on the cheek.

"So how did your day turn out?" she asked.

"Well, I caught two very nice sized cutthroat trout, one 12 inches and the second 14 inches. I was able to release them unharmed to boot!"

"How was your visit with the Los Alamos physicist?"

"That went well too. He really added nothing about Jessica's disappearance, but while I was fishing I realized that the real reason I wanted to see him again was to learn more about his background, rather than ask him about Jessica. My gut instinct is telling me that he might be a factor behind her vanishing."

"Win, you've always had an over-rich imagination and you're getting carried away again. How many times do I need to tell you that this is none of your business and that you're a rank amateur as a detective? I give up! Why don't you clean up; you smell sweaty."

Win showered and got into a comfortable robe. They had an elegant dinner that Julia must have spent the whole day preparing. Win quipped, "Hey, maybe I should go fishing more often. It'll free you up to prepare more special dinners like this one. You know, I'm a very lucky guy to have such a multi-talented wife. How many successful doctors are also great cooks?"

"Probably a lot more than you think."

"Can't you just accept a compliment?"

"I certainly can when they're more direct!"

Win gave Julia a big kiss and apologized for his 'backhand' compliment. They cleared the dishes and Win fed the dogs and gave them another walk before heading back to his study.

Win settled into the chair at his desk. It was given to him as a gift when he finished his pediatric residency at the New York Hospital. It had the hospital seal and he particularly liked its motto, "Go and do thou likewise." It had held up remarkably well over the years because it spent most of its life in attics. Win had added some cushions recently so it was tolerably comfortable. But he felt relaxed when he sat in it; it was a tranquilizer for him. He had forgotten to drink any of the calvados in the pewter flask in his fishing vest this afternoon, so he turned around to get some from the credenza. He poured a nice measure and vacantly began sniffing the special calvados "nose."

Win reflected back on the day. Something about Wong's story didn't sound quite kosher. He now had a lot more information to run by Michael and Mae in Hong Kong about Wong. Win got out his copies of Wong's business card and decided it was time to learn how the scanner on his new printer-scanner-fax machine worked. He particularly wanted to send Wong's name in Chinese characters to his friends. He got out the instruction manual and in short order figured out how to scan the copies he had made. He was getting less intimidated by computer equipment as he aged; or maybe he simply had more time to read the instructions. He decided to e-mail his friends in Hong Kong, and attached the scanned business card to see whether this info helped to learn more about Wong and his family.

His first e-mail was to Michael Lam at the Great Wall Gallery.

"Dear Michael,

I hope this letter finds you and your family well. I had another meeting with Dr. C.Y. Wong today. He's the Hong Kong native and Los Alamos physicist that I had written to you about a few weeks ago. He's the one with the incredibly good – and extensive – collection of early Chinese ceramics. I showed him the two Warring States pieces I got at your Gallery, since he's a real expert on Warring States ceramics. He thought they were very good and he particularly liked the large tripod bowl. In my last e-mail to you, I thought you might know him or his family, since the collecting world for Chinese ceramics was probably small. You had raised the issue of whether I might have gotten the family name wrong or that it had gotten transliterated when Wong moved to the U.S. So, I've attached a copy of his business card in both English and Chinese characters. I learned that his father and grandfather were serious collectors in Shanghai. His father's English name was Samuel and he worked for a large trading company in Shanghai just before the Communist takeover. His father was never a dealer, but did sell some of his pieces privately. His father's particular love was Warring States ceramics, and judging from the amount that the son has, it must have been a huge collection since it was divided among several sons.

I'm curious as to whether you or your father know this family. Given the size and quality of the collection, I'm sure other collectors in Hong Kong know them.

Julia and I are settling into the Santa Fe lifestyle. It's a very different climate and culture here and takes some getting used to. How are things going in Hong Kong? I keep reading that the Beijing government wants to shut down the export trade in antiques and that they have tightened up their control of the HK government. I know that you already have a gallery in Toronto, but hope that you can continue the family business in HK, where you belong. We plan to visit HK and Asia again soon.

Warm regards,
Win

Win next turned to writing a similar message to Mae Lai who had an equally large, but slightly different, network of Hong Kong friends. He included the copied business card of Wong and an invitation for her to visit them soon.

Win was pleased to get these two e-mails off. He looked forward to seeing if Michael and Mae could shed any further light on Wong's family. He finished his Calvados and decided to call it a night. It had been a busy day, and he'd caught some nice trout.

Chapter 23.

The next day was gloriously cool and clear, with enough wind to carry the scent of junipers and piñons. What a change from cloudy, gray Pittsburgh. Win was sitting outside, reading a medical journal with a pair of sleeping dogs at his feet, when Julia opened the screen door to say, "Win, there's a guy in a black suit at the front door. He wants to talk to you."

Win was puzzled. "How did he get here without our being called by the gatekeeper? Are you kidding about the black suit? Does he look like a Mormon missionary? They usually work in pairs though."

"Win, I don't think so and he's also not a reincarnation of Johnny Cash – he has a white shirt on. He looks like a cop. He wouldn't say what it's about except that it's a law enforcement issue and it's important that he speak to you."

Win got up reluctantly and accidentally kicked Charlie, who grumbled and rolled over.

Sure enough, there was a guy in a black suit, white shirt and solid navy tie at the front door. This was definitely not Santa-Fe-style dressing. Win opened the glass front door and greeted the man. "I'm Winston Sage. I understand you want to talk with me."

"Yes. I'm Agent Tom Shaw with the New Mexico office of the F.B.I." he said as he produced a badge in a leather case, black of course, with a photo ID. "I'd like to talk with you. May I come in?"

"What's this about? I don't cheat on my income taxes and I haven't committed any crimes that I know of."

"No, it's about something different – perhaps serious."

"Are you going to read me my rights? Do I need a lawyer, not that I have one?"

"No, Dr. Sage, this will be an informal, confidential discussion. You're not being charged with anything. We're merely concerned about your curious behavior."

"Curious behavior; hmm. Well come on up to our portal. I was reading outside and it's a pleasant place to talk. Can I get you something to drink? I have some cold water, iced tea or coke."

"Iced tea would be nice, thank you."

Win went to the kitchen and whispered to Julia as he passed her "He's not a practicing Mormon, he drinks tea." He came back to the portal with two glasses and sat down while eyeing the F.B.I. agent.

Shaw began, "You're a very puzzling man, Dr. Sage; very puzzling indeed. Our

Bureau has had a long-standing interest in you and we could never figure you out."

"You guys haven't been too good at figuring anything out for quite a while now," Win said with a grin.

"To start, what were you and your wife doing in Ethiopia?"

"We were teaching public health at the Gondar Public Health College. That's what we were trained to do. We were young, adventurous and naïve."

"For whom were you working in Ethiopia?"

"For Haile Sellassie I University. You know, old Haile was also known as Ras Tafari of Rastafarian renown."

Shaw was getting red in the face. "Please cut the crap. Who were you really working for? We have a large file on you regarding dubious activities you engaged in while you were in Ethiopia. You were there just before the Revolution occurred and the country was a hotbed of spies. You also lived in the Province where the Revolution started. Let me give you some examples. You seemed to pal around with agents of the CIA, MI6 and the U.S. Army. Why did you have a photography lab and a short-wave radio with you? Why did the Ethiopian police interrogate you about your receiving documents in code? I could go on."

"You know, it occurred to my wife and me, after we left the country, that everybody probably thought we were spies for some mysterious government. There are simple answers to your questions. We always joked about the similarities between our stay in Ethiopia and Graham Greene's novel 'Our Man in Havana'; except we didn't have any diagrams of vacuum cleaners that we tried to pass off as state secrets. To answer your last question first, I remember the Gondar police interrogating me about a hard-to-decipher, document addressed to Major Sage that I had received by mail. I had served in the Air Force in Japan just before going to Ethiopia and the document that they thought was in code was a life insurance policy. Photography became my hobby while I was in the Air Force. The shortwave radio was so we could get some news broadcasts -- remember we were out in the boonies of Ethiopia. Probably, because everyone thought we were spies, we were befriended by some pretty high-up C.I.A. and MI6 people, although it never dawned on us who they really were until we left the country. We thought everyone was interested in us because we were so charming. We probably also had our fingers on the pulse of the growing unrest in our province better than they did.

Shaw was taking copious notes as Win went on. Win tried to get ahead of Shaw's note-taking with wordiness. "I wonder if this whole 'mystery spy' stuff didn't start with my Air Force hold-baggage getting shipped directly to Addis Ababa. I took care of the kids of one of the chief master sergeants in transportation. He pulled some strings and somehow my baggage showed up at a U.S. Air Force facility in Addis addressed to Major Sage. I think we were under suspicion from that time on. You know, sometimes the simplest explanation is the truth. Have you ever heard of Occam's razor; AKA, the law of parsimony? It's used a lot in science. Whenever there are many potential explanations for an observation, the most likely correct interpretation is the simplest. I looked it up recently in the dictionary; it comes right after ocarina."

Shaw looked like he was about to explode and said through clenched teeth, "Well thank you Dr. Sage for your wordiness and erudition. An equally simple explanation for your reported activity in Ethiopia is that you were an intelligence agent for some foreign entity. You also have a very interesting history of foreign travel, with a lot of it in Eastern Bloc countries. What's that all about?"

"There's another simple answer for that too. I was fortunate to do some teaching of cancer epidemiology for the International Agency for Research on Cancer – IARC for short. We taught where the needs for training in methods of cancer registration and research were greatest – Third World countries and the old Communist Bloc."

"Is that why you visited the USSR, East Germany, Poland and Pakistan?"

"Yeah. I was in East Germany, near the Czech border, at the time of the Chernobyl accident. I still glow in the dark."

Shaw took a deep breath and went on. "Okay, enough of your sophomoric humor. The point I'm making is that you have a very troubling record and I don't believe your explanations. Which brings me to the reason for my being here today. Why have you been visiting Dr. C.Y. Wong in White Rock? Also, there have been a lot of people suddenly asking around about Wong, doing credit checks on him and searching his medical records. Not only are gallery owners, a doctor who dresses like a clown, and a bank in New York making inquiries, but also a gang of hard-core criminals. I suspect you're behind this activity too."

Win winced and looked up at the sky. "I got involved with him by looking into the disappearance of my neighbors' wife. The neighbor sought me out because he'd heard that epidemiologists are medical detectives who can trace people. It turns out that Wong's been a mentor for the missing wife. He's quite an expert on early Chinese ceramics and owns an amazing collection. Apparently, he stopped into my neighbor's gallery on Canyon Road, saw his wife's early attempt to sell Chinese ceramics and struck up a friendship with her. He taught her a lot about Chinese ceramics over the past seven or eight years, introduced her to dealers in Hong Kong and even sold some of his family's collection through her gallery. It's an odd story, if you ask me."

Shaw squinted as Win went on. "Bill Harvey, that's the neighbor, suggested I meet Wong in case he might have some different insights into his wife's disappearance. I was also curious about Wong's collection. I've been a collector of early Chinese ceramics and I particularly love Warring States Era pottery, which is Wong's specialty. So, Bill arranged for me to meet Wong and I did so on my way to fishing in the Jemez Mountains. Again, this is a straightforward, but not so simple, answer. About the people asking around about Wong, it could be my buddies who were helping me with my investigation."

"Your approach to conducting an investigation is a joke. You've managed to broadcast your investigation over a loudspeaker." Shaw fixed Win with a stare and asked, "Okay, so how come you visited him a second time?"

"I went back because I had some more questions about Jessica Harvey. Also, quite frankly, I found his stories to be odd, maybe fishy. I also wanted to see more of his collection; he has some amazing Warring States pieces. I had him check out a couple of pieces of Warring State ceramics I own, too."

Shaw took a sip of his drink and leaned forward. "In what way were his stories fishy to you?"

"To begin, it seemed far-fetched that he would become a devoted mentor to Jessica Harvey. She was a rank amateur at dealing in Chinese ceramics. She and her husband were on the verge of bankruptcy. Additionally, the story of his father didn't wash with some of our friends in Hong Kong who'd be likely to have known him. To compound things, the way in which Wong helped her to buy things in Hong Kong sounded strange."

"Are you implying that Wong played a role in this woman's disappearance?"

"I don't know. It's more likely that she got into trouble with a disgruntled customer. But I keep coming back to this gnawing suspicion that Wong was using Jessica as a fence to unload some ill-gotten or counterfeit ceramic pieces. It also could just be that he was using her to help sell off his family collection. Maybe it was a way of avoiding taxes or auction commissions. I think he was using her and she was using him. You know, some sort of Faustian arrangement."

"You seem to have a hyperactive imagination. So, what did you learn at your second meeting with Wong?"

"I got more details about his father and his family collection to check with my friends in Hong Kong. I left with the same impression that he wasn't quite on the up-and-up."

"Did you check out the new details with your Hong Kong friends?"

"Yeah, but I haven't heard back from them yet."

"That's an interesting story you've concocted. I'm here today because we keep a close eye on our top scientists at Los Alamos. When a suspicious character like you, a possible foreign agent, turns up visiting a leading scientist at LANL, not once, but twice, the alarms go off. Then we have the simultaneous flurry of inquiries about Dr. Wong that concerns us. I still don't know whether to believe you. I'll do some checking on your story. What's the name of the missing woman and her gallery?"

Win gave him the info and Shaw entered it on his phone. "Are you going to look into her disappearance? The local and state police sure could use the F.B.I.'s help."

"What I do or don't do is none of your business! My strong advice to you, Sage, is to leave Wong alone and stay out of the missing persons business! You can get into trouble, particularly from our Bureau, and you're in way over your head. I urge you not to tell anyone about our meeting today or what we discussed. This is to protect you as well as the Bureau."

"I'm amazed that you guys have the LANL scientists under surveillance. Do you actually stake out their houses? You know, it's my turn to not believe you."

"That too is none of your business."

When Shaw got up, Win noticed he had a small recorder on his lap. Win ushered Shaw to the door and saw him out. Before Shaw got into his car, he reached into his jacket pocket to get a card. He scribbled something on the back of it and gave it to Win. "If you get into trouble with this investigation of yours, let me know right away. Use the number on the back and the code words there when asked for them."

"Aren't you being a little histrionic about this? What kind of emergency are you expecting?"

"It's always a possibility, so stay out of this business. Histrionic is a nice word. Have you been reading dictionaries lately or watching O'Reilly on Fox?"

"Neither."

"Sage, in my line of business you can never be too careful. Maybe I'm over-reacting, but hold on to that card. Capice? Thank you for your time."

Shaw got into a black sedan to round out his all-black gestalt. Win went back inside, lost in thought about this strange encounter.

"What was that about?" Julia asked.

"It seems the man in black is with the F.B.I. and they must be keeping some sort of surveillance on their top nuclear jocks at Los Alamos. Apparently I have a large file at the F.B.I. as a suspected foreign agent; can you imagine that! My two visits to Dr. Wong got them worrying that a foreign spy was meeting with one of their top scientists. And he thought that I have a rich imagination!"

"I bet it goes back to our Ethiopian days."

"That's right! And he's now joined the crowd telling me to stay out of the investigation business."

"Which brings me back to the point I've been making for several weeks; this is none of your damn business, Win! This whole affair is beginning to smell bad."

"You're right." Win sighed. "It's just I've always been a sucker for a good puzzle." "Win, stick to solving acrostics; they take less of your time and they keep your brain from rotting."

"Julia, your great wisdom has been heard.

Chapter 24.

Win went cold turkey on the Harvey business for two days before an e-mail reply from Michael in Hong Kong raised his interest again; it read:

"Dear Win,

I read your last e-mail and did some more checking about the Wong family. By the way, the name in Chinese characters jibes with the Anglicized "Wong," so you got his name right the first time. It's interesting that no one in my family or any of my collector friends has ever heard of anyone fitting the picture of Wong's father. From the description of his collection, he should be known to at least some of my friends.

It's unusual to have a large collection of fine Warring States Era ceramics, so I asked around about major collectors or dealers of this period's art. The only story I picked up was of a powerful Mainland army general who is an amateur archeologist and commissioned the excavation of two Warring States Period tombs about ten years ago. People are skeptical about this story because there was no increase in supply of Warring States pieces on the market following the supposed excavation. That's usually the case after a tomb excavation done by non-archaeologists. Maybe the general is a big collector himself. But I don't see how this would be related to your friend. To sum up, there are no known big-time Warring States collectors beyond this general, at least in Hong Kong.

No one has heard of the son, C.Y. Wong, either. Do you think your friend has made this story up to sound important? All of this makes me curious about how he amassed such a fine, large collection. I enjoyed doing a bit of detective work, but nothing turned up.

Best regards,
Michael"

So it was starting to look like Wong may have invented his family history – but why? Win wondered if the story about a Chinese general could somehow be related. The general's supposed excavation had occurred 10 years ago, and Wong began helping Jessica – and unloading Warring States pieces with the Harvey's gallery -- about eight years ago. Also, Wong couldn't have assembled such a large and important collection of Warring States and earlier pieces without registering on the HK dealers' radar screens; the same thing could be said of Samuel Wong. This was all intriguing, but Win had made up his mind to stay out of this business. So he went back to work, catching up on bill paying. He finished, and before leaving his study, checked his e-mail again. To his surprise, he had also received a reply from Mae. He opened the file and read it hurriedly. Mae too could find no one who knew Samuel or C.Y. Wong

Win got up and looked for Julia, who was in the den sewing. "Hey, Julia, I heard from Mae in Hong Kong. She won't be going to your class reunion at Bryn Mawr this May. Seems her calendar is full and the kids are coming home for a visit."

"That's good, because I really didn't want to go. Win, were you bugging our Hong Kong friends again about your Dr. Wong? I thought you dropped your detective game after the visit by the guy in the black suit."

"I did drop it, but I had e-mailed Mae and Michael before the Suit's visit. I had told you I was going to contact Mae and you asked me to find out if she was planning to go to your college reunion."

"You're right. I remember now, but please keep your resolve on the detective stuff."

"You know, neither Mae nor Michael could find out a thing about Wong or his collector-father. They think Wong's story is bogus and so do I. If his story is false, why would he spin it to me? Anyway, I decided to drop the Harvey business, particularly after the F.B.I. warning, and let the professionals sort things out."

"Good"

Chapter 25.

That evening, Win was busy at his desk, peer-reviewing a manuscript for a medical journal. Although review work was tedious, and unpaid, Win looked forward to it these days, as he believed it kept him mentally sharp. He was a great believer in the "use it or lose it" theory of senility development. He was deep in thought when the phone rang. He picked it up on the second ring.

"Win, I'm glad you're there. This is Michael in Hong Kong." Win had a hard time hearing him; there was a lot of noise in the background.

"Michael how's everything? Is there a problem?" Michael had never called before. "Yes, and big time!" Win thought he heard a car honking in the background.

"Where are you Michael?"

"I'm at an outdoor payphone. Listen carefully, Win: stay out of this business with Wong. It could be trouble. There's something strange going on. I continued asking around about Wong and his family, who nobody seems to know, and somehow, the Government learned of it. I received a very stern warning from them to stop making inquiries about him. They even threatened to take my import-export license away and close my business down. They wanted to know why I was making inquiries about the Wongs. I told them I'd heard rumors that the Wongs owned a fine Warring

States collection and I wanted to buy some pieces for our gallery. I didn't mention you or any American connection. That's why I'm calling from the street. Look, I can't talk any more. This is scary business. Please stay out of it and don't contact me about Wong any more. You're my friend and I worry about you. Give my love to Julia." Michael hung up abruptly.

Win hung up feeling worried by the fear in Michael's voice. He wondered where Michael could even find an outdoor pay phone these days.

He looked at his watch. It was 9:11 P.M., which made it 12:11 P.M. in Hong Kong. Michael had chosen lunchtime with its crowded streets to make his call.

Just then, Julia buzzed on the intercom. "Who was that, Winston? Is something wrong?"

"Yes. I just got a call from Hong Kong. Poor Michael has been making some inquiries for me about Jessica Harvey's friend from Los Alamos and his family. It seems the Hong Kong Government warned him off in no uncertain terms. Looks like I stepped on a hornet's nest!"

"Win, what the hell have you gotten yourself into, and our friend to boot? I don't like the sound of this! You've been warned by the F.B.I. and now indirectly by the Chinese Government. Stick to epidemiology."

"You're right."

Win tried to get back to work, but Michael's distress bothered him. This call put Jessica Harvey's disappearance in a new light. He looked over at his Chinese ceramics and realized that the answer to the puzzle now seemed to lie with Wong. The Chinese government clearly had a strong interest in protecting Wong from inquiry. They were hardly likely to protect an American nuclear scientist unless he was a PRC sympathizer or spy. "Holy cow!" he said out loud. How did Jessica fit in with a spy?

Win pulled out his calvados and brandy snifter and poured himself a hefty dose. He sat back and sniffed the brandy while thinking. There was a high probability that Wong was using Jessica and her gallery to convert ceramics into cash. He was possibly being paid off by the PRC with valuable Chinese ceramics in exchange for spying.

Michael had told him about a PRC general doing some personal excavations of Warring States tombs. Nothing from those digs had ever reached the market. If Win remembered correctly, the timing of the excavations fit with when Wong had started to sell pieces through the Harvey's gallery. Maybe that was why Wong's collection and the stuff Jessica was selling were so heavily weighted towards Warring States ceramics. Maybe Wong's story about his dad was a front for his having such a large collection of ill-gotten Chinese art? The fact that neither Michael nor Mae could confirm Wong's story would support that notion. Also, the story about Jessica buying pieces from dealers in their homes was far-fetched, and would further support this hypothesis. These "dealers" were possibly stooges acting on behalf of the PRC. The facts were starting to fall into place.

Win stared out the window at the stars. Could Jessica have been ignorant of how Wong was using her and her gallery and then suddenly figured out what was going on? Had someone felt compelled to get rid of her? Los Alamos was one of the country's most important nuclear development facilities, and Wong seemed to be a top gun there, and could have access to some pretty important secrets. So, if Jessica suddenly stumbled onto what Wong was doing and threatened to spill the beans on him, would nice old Dr. Wong do her harm -- or some Chinese Government agent? Where did Bill Harvey fit into all of this?

If Jessica got wise to Wong, she must have shared her suspicions with Bill, but he certainly hasn't shared that info with Win! He realized he was getting nowhere with his hypothetical questions, except to recognize that Wong was probably at the center of Jessica's disappearance and could be a spy for the Chinese. He finished his calvados and decided to call it a night. Things were beginning to smell bad – really bad.

Chapter 26.

Win was hopping mad the next day. He had gotten his friend Michael into trouble, possibly serious trouble, and he agonized over whether or not to e-mail Mae to warn her to stay out of the Wong business, then decided to let the matter drop.

He weighed the idea of visiting Bill Harvey again and confronting him with his suspicion that Wong was a spy who was using his wife as a fence. Maybe Bill would be more forthcoming then. Win had a hunch that a confrontation with Bill might be more productive than turning the matter over to the F.B.I. So he called the East-West Gallery to arrange to meet there at 3:00 p.m.

Win drove into town and up Canyon Road. Since it was a weekday, he was able to find a parking space close to the Gallery. He examined the window before going in noticing that there was still a large amount of Chinese ceramics in the window – some of them new pieces – even though Jessica had been gone several weeks. He found that curious, since Bill didn't do the buying for their Chinese antiques business. He went in, setting off the entry chime. The pretty lady that managed the gallery came to the door and recoiled when she saw Win.

Win threw her a big smile, and before he could say anything, she said, "I know, you're from Santa Fe. Bill's in his office and I'll like go see if he's off the phone."

"I'll like just look around, thanks." Win observed that they still had a good stock of Warring States Era and earlier ceramics, so either they weren't selling well or they'd managed to replenish their stock without Jessica.

Bill came out to greet Win and took him back to his messy office. He asked, "Have you turned up anything about Jessie?"

"No. I was about to ask you the same question."

"I haven't heard a thing from Jessie, the police, her family or her friends. My hope of finding her is fading, I'm afraid."

"I noticed that you still have a large stock of early Chinese pieces. Is the stuff not selling without Jessica, or are you doing the buying in that area now?"

"I'm still getting stock that Jessie bought before she disappeared. CY has been helping me get the stuff shipped here from Hong Kong. I never knew how much work it was to arrange international shipments of antiques."

"I'm glad you brought up Wong. I visited him again about a week ago. He does have a truly incredible collection and I appreciated it even more on the second visit. He told me his father was a famous collector in Shanghai before fleeing to Hong Kong and that his dad worked for a large trading company in Shanghai. My wife has a dear friend in Hong Kong whose father worked for Standard Oil in Shanghai at the same time and was also a big-league collector. I checked Wong's story with my wife's friend and a gallery-owner friend who owns one of the major Hong Kong antique galleries. His father too hails from pre-Communist Shanghai. They never heard of any one remotely like Wong's father in Shanghai or Hong Kong. I believe your friend CY may have told us a very tall story."

Bill frowned and shook his head. "That can't be true! Jessie heard all about his father when she was in Hong Kong. He and the whole family were well known collectors and dealers."

Win sneered. "Who did she hear that from?"

"All the people she met in Hong Kong and these were top dealers."

"Didn't you tell me that she bought a lot of her stuff from people's homes? That's not how the top dealers in Hong Kong that

I know operate. Wasn't Wong the one who introduced her to these top dealers? Did she ever shop in Hong Kong on her own and visit the galleries specializing in Chinese ceramics?"

"There was no need for her to do that. CY took such good care of her, and she was able to get all she needed through him. Also, the pieces he helped her buy were top quality. He taught her that to get the best pieces you had to shop this behind-the-scenes network of dealers. The galleries were for amateur collectors and tourists."

"That's odd, because the gallery people I buy from sell to top U.S. museums. Didn't Jessie's story seem strange to you?"

"Look, I know nothing about the antique trade in Hong Kong, and CY is a respected, honest man. Why would I have reason to doubt him?"

"Do you know what Wong does at Los Alamos?"

"He's some kind of physicist."

"Did he ever tell you about his specific work or whether his work was top secret?"

"No, he just told us physics was his life's work and that he loved it."

Win leaned forward and fixed Bill with a stare. "Did it ever occur to you or Jessica that he could be working for the Chinese, trading nuclear secrets for ceramic pieces that he could convert into cash – and through your gallery?"

Bill shook his head, looking incredulous, and Win went on: 'When I asked my dealer friend in Hong Kong about collectors or dealers who specialized in Warring States ceramics, the only one he could come up with was a Chinese general who was reputed to have done some excavation of Warring States tombs about ten years ago. This guy could be Wong's source. By the way, how've you been paying Wong and his dealer friends?"

"We always pay him by check in American dollars."

"How about his dealer friends and family in Hong Kong?"

"We also pay them by check."

"Do you pay them directly or through Wong?'

"We write the checks to CY and he handles the foreign currency issues for us. A lot of it goes to his family members and they have some sort of trust."

"Did you ever look at the back of the checks to see where they were cashed?"

"No. Wait a second; let me see if I can find some cancelled checks in the files."

Win waited impatiently while Bill rummaged through a pile of monthly bank statements. "Okay, here's one made out to Dr. Wong, and here's another one." He passed them to

Win, who flipped them over.

"Bill, both of these checks were deposited in a Cayman Islands' bank account. Don't you think that's a bit odd for a government-employed physicist?" Win took out his ancient PDA and recorded the name of the bank, the account number, and the date processed.

"I never noticed." Bill sounded bewildered. "He did tell us that he and his family are contributing to a trust for future generations. Maybe, because the family is scattered in several countries, the Cayman bank account makes good sense. I know this man well and I very much doubt he was up to no good."

"Bill, I've been involved in this situation for only a few weeks and it's readily apparent to me that Wong's a 'three-dollar bill.' You've been working with him for years now and you've noticed nothing unusual or worrisome about him? You must have had some inkling that all was not what it seemed to be. Did you and Jessica just look the other way because he was so important to your financial success?"

Bill shrugged. "I did always think he was too good to be true. But, he's such a kind and caring person that Jessie and I trusted him fully. I never thought to question his background or pay attention to where he deposited our checks."

"Bill, did Jessica ever express any doubts or concerns about him? Think hard."

"Come to think of it, there is one thing; I don't know why I forgot about it. About a week before Jessie disappeared she said that she was worried about her ceramics business. We were in bed and she was nervous and fidgety. She clammed up and never said anything more about it. I plumb forgot about it and never mentioned it to the police either. Do you think it was related to CY?"

Win slapped his forehead and said, "Why didn't you tell this to the police?"

"I thought she was talking about some financial deal she got into, rather than anything more serious. I guess I'm all screwed up in my thinking."

"Bill, call the police and share that last bit of information with them. I think I need to talk to the F.B.I. about this whole affair. There's something very wrong surrounding Jessica's disappearance. Don't share this full conversation with the police or with Wong. Just tell the police what Jessica told you. I think she was playing with fire and I sure hope she didn't get badly burnt."

"Now I'm really scared."

"Don't forget to call the police and don't mention this stuff about Wong. I need to go now. If you recall anything else about possible suspicions or worries Jessica had before her disappearance, you must let the police know, got it?"

Win stood up and headed out of the gallery, feeling amazed at Harvey's memory lapse. Win's hunches were starting to seem more likely. Could Jessica be alive and hiding to avoid harm from Wong or his compatriots?

Win had a lot to think about, especially whether to stay involved in this investigation or to call the F.B.I. The guy in black was certain to be ticked off with Win for not contacting him and for getting involved in the search again. He had some tough choices.

Chapter 27.

Next morning, Win was ensconced in his favorite easy chair in the den, engrossed in the newspaper and sipping a second cup of coffee when the doorbell rang. The dogs began barking and Julia shouted, "Win, would you get the door."

Win ambled to the door and could see a stranger through the tinted glass. He wondered how the guy had gotten into the sub-division, since Armando the gateman hadn't alerted him. Win opened the door and the man said, "Good morning Dr. Sage, I'm Sergeant Jim Ortiz with the Santa Fe Police Department. I'm a plainclothes detective in the missing persons office." He waved a wallet with a badge and photo ID. "I was visiting Bill Harvey down the road and he told me you were helping him in the investigation of his wife's disappearance. He thought it'd be worthwhile for me to stop by and see if you had any ideas that could help us. Can I talk to you for a few minutes?"

"Sure, come in, but I hope this won't take long. Come on back to my office."

Ortiz followed Win and said on the way, "Wow, what a neat house! Hey, is this designed by an architect? Because it's really different! Can I get a tour when we're done?"

"Sure; it was designed by Antoine Predock from Albuquerque."

Win ushered Ortiz into his study and pointed him to the red chair across from his desk. The Sergeant began, "So how come you got involved in this investigation? You're a doctor not a detective."

"I'm an epidemiologist. Bill Harvey got the idea I was some sort of medical detective. He came over and told me about his wife just going missing one day without a trace. I had to explain that I couldn't use my methods for someone who disappeared recently. In fact, I told him to go see you people. He seemed to think there might be some medical explanation for her vanishing and I advised him that it was highly unlikely, but he looked so pathetic that I felt sorry for him."

"So what did you do to help him?" Ortiz asked as he began stroking the small table next to the red chair.

"Well, I tried some Internet searches and came up with nothing. I called Community Hospital's Emergency Department and they couldn't tell me anything. I asked around about Jessica and got confusing and conflicting stories. A lot of people think she's in with a fast crowd and cheating on her husband. Some think she was doing something illegal, like being a fence for Asian ceramics, others seemed jealous of her recent success. The consensus seems to be that she ran off with some guy. Basically, my poking around came up with nothing." Win felt uncomfortable and didn't mention Wong.

"Did you ever talk to her mentor, the guy up at Los Alamos?" Ortiz reached into his jacket pocket and popped some sort of candy into his mouth.

Ortiz's hyperactivity was starting to grate on Win. "Yes, I visited him at his home in White Rock. I was more interested in seeing his collection of Chinese art than in asking him the same old questions I'd been asking on Canyon Road."

"Did he have any ideas about Ms. Harvey's disappearance?"

"Just the stuff about her playing around, although he didn't think she ran off with another guy."

"What did you think of the Los Alamos friend?" Ortiz was now stroking the underside of the small table and Win was getting distracted.

Win decided he wouldn't go into his ideas with Ortiz about Wong being a spy. He didn't think the F.B.I. dude would appreciate his spreading these suspicions around, so Win toned his answer down. "He seemed a nice, scholarly, old man who adopted Jessica as a surrogate daughter. The story of his mentoring of Jessica seemed far-fetched to me, but who knows, life is full of strange relationships. Don't get me wrong; I don't think he was having a love affair with her. All in all, I thought there was something interesting about him."

"In what way?" Ortiz asked.

"Well, he's probably a talented physicist," Win replied. "He's courtly in his behavior and a very knowledgeable collector of esoteric Chinese ceramics. Those are not common traits."

Ortiz went on, "Do you think he was somehow involved in Harvey's disappearance?"

"No. I don't think so." Win shuffled in his seat; he never felt comfortable lying.

"So what do you think happened to her?" Ortiz asked.

"I don't know. My gut feeling is there's some connection between her disappearance and her sudden success as a dealer in Asian art."

"What makes you think that?"

"It's just a hunch. The Harveys went from near bankruptcy to affluence in a short period of time, in large part due to the kind patronage of a stranger who's a nuclear physicist at Los Alamos. That's pretty unusual, if you ask me!"

"Well the whole thing has been strange to us in the police. People don't usually disappear without a trace. Now how about a tour of this great house? First, may I use your phone? My cell phone doesn't work out here?"

"Sure, it's over here on my desk."

Ortiz went behind Win's desk, dialed a number and said, "Hi Anna, this is Jim

- 121 -

Ortiz. Would you connect me with Captain Martinez please?" He covered the mouthpiece and asked Win if he wouldn't mind stepping out of the room since the call involved another investigation and was confidential. Win was getting exasperated and went to the kitchen.

After several minutes, Ortiz came out of the study and started exploring the house. Win found Ortiz in the living/dining room admiring the furnishings. He had the annoying mannerism of popping candy or something into his mouth and then chewing on it with his front teeth like he was taking the shells off nuts. He also fingered everything – chairs, lamps, pictures, tables -- he seemed a tactomaniac, if there's such a word. "Hey Doc, this is one neat house and you have some great stuff," he said as he walked over to the dining room table and began running his hands over the surface and underside of it. "Solid cherry I bet; that's real cool!"

Ortiz, without being invited, led himself on a tour of the house with a disbelieving Win trying to keep up with him. Ortiz fingered everything, interrupted only by his candy-popping. He finally led himself to the front door. "This is a very unusual house and I really enjoyed seeing it." He put his hand on Win's shoulder and said, "Look, I appreciate your information, but I think you should leave the investigation to us. Muchas gracias for your time and the house tour."

"Do you have a card, Sergeant, in case I need to reach you?"

Ortiz pulled out his wallet and rummaged about. "I guess I gave my last card to

Mr. Harvey. You can always call the main office and ask for me, but if you just stay out of this, you won't need to reach me."

After he left, Win felt tired. Sgt. Ortiz was one of the most hyperactive people he'd ever seen and Win had once practiced pediatrics. What a bizarro.

Chapter 28.

On Friday, Win had planned to go into town with George for a new round of show openings at the galleries as usual. Win was a creature of habit and always felt most comfortable in regular routines. Julia called it obsessive behavior and just plain old boring, but to Win, having a set of regular activities like his Tuesdays with Herky and his Fridays with George were anchoring events. He also enjoyed his Friday guacarita times with Julia and the dogs. He was gradually arranging his routines and environment to feel like home. The only thing he couldn't shake off was the Harvey disappearance. It was like a herpes virus infection -- once infected, the virus stayed with you for life.

Unfortunately, he learned late that week that George had to go out of town, so Win decided to skip the gallery openings and stay home with Julia. After this week's events, he was in no mood to make small talk with strangers.

It was windy, so Julia and Win decided to partake of their guacaritas inside. Win mixed up a batch of weak margaritas, to accommodate Julia, and a very spicy batch of guacamole to offset the drinks. He set things up on the dining room table and summoned Julia, quickly realizing it was a mistake when the dogs started yelping. They weren't allowed in the living-dining room and they felt cheated out of their snacks. Win, ever the indulgent dog father, solved the problem by putting a few handfuls of tortilla chips in each of their food dishes in the dog part of the house.

It was a magnificently bright day and the snow-capped mountains looked exceptionally sculptural. Julia and Win sat on one of the couches and enjoyed the scenery through the floor to ceiling windows. "Did you follow up and call the F.B.I. about Michael's call and your thoughts on the matter?" Julia asked,

"No, I was waiting to think things through more carefully. I'd be raising a very serious charge about Wong -- that he's possibly a spy for the Chinese. That's the only explanation that fits all the pieces together. The clincher is the call from Michael telling me that the Government in Hong Kong told him to keep out of further inquiry about the Wongs. That's pretty unequivocal evidence of some tie between Wong and the PRC, if you ask me. The arrangement between Wong and Jessica is a great cover for Wong. Rather than the Chinese giving him money directly, they could give him ceramics that he could pretend came from his father's collection. He then could sell the ceramics through Jessica with the excuse of lightening up on his inherited collection, since he was getting ready to retire and his kids had no interest in them. Jessica was also a cover for getting a lot more stuff into the States than the PRC could send to Wong without raising suspicions. If I'm right, it would be a pretty clever scheme to reward a spy handsomely for what may have been a lifetime of supplying nuclear secrets."

"You know, Win, a few weeks ago I would have said that you're totally out of your gourd, but I'm starting to think you may be right. If you are, this is really serious. Promise me that you'll call the guy in black first thing Monday morning."

"I'll do it first thing," he agreed. Tomorrow's fishing trip in the Jemez will give me some quiet time to think this whole thing through. Now how about a refill on your margarita? I made them pretty weak today."

"Okay, but just a short one and please pass the chips."

Chapter 29.

Today, Win and Chuck had planned a trip to a lesser-known tributary of the Shint River that was supposed to hold some large native trout. According to Chuck, this place was a "closely guarded secret." Win had given Chuck a gate-opener so he could let himself into the subdivision without waking up Julia. Win was up early, humming loudly as he loaded the car with his gear from the garage.

Chuck parked his car and got out slowly. He looked terrible and he sounded feeble as he told Win that he'd contracted food poisoning the night before. "We went to a party last night with lots of buffet food," he said. "I woke up in the middle of the night with the most awful stomach cramps, vomiting, and diarrhea. It occurred to me that I had loaded up on potato salad. I remember hearing that potato salad and chopped liver are major sources of food poisoning at buffets where the food stands around at room temperature. I feel terrible right now."

Win realized that he, Chuck and Julia had heard the same lecture when they were at Harvard. It must have been one helluva good lecture, since they all remembered it so well. "You got your public health info straight, but why on earth didn't you stay home in bed? You should have called and taken a rain check on the fishing."

"We've been planning the trip for a long time, and I had something like this before and it didn't last more than 12 hours. I should be okay by the time we get to the stream."

"I'm not so sure about that," Win said. "How long after eating did you start feeling sick?"

"We ate late, about 8:30 p.m. I got up from a deep sleep at about 2 a.m. I was in agony with cramps and nausea that woke me up."

"That sounds like classic staphylococcal food poisoning. You know, it's a true poisoning rather than an infection. When Staph gets into food that sits around for a long time at warm temperatures, it grows and produces a toxin. It's the toxin that causes the symptoms and there isn't any real infection. Did you take your temperature by any chance?"

"I did and it was slightly below normal: 98.2."

"That fits the staph poisoning picture too. You know, if it's staph food poisoning, you could be sick for a full day or two. Did you take anything for it?"

"I took some Imodium twice so far; I followed the directions on the package."

"Chuck, I think we ought to scrub the trip and you should come inside and lie down until you feel better. When you get home, you must call the Health Department and notify them of your story."

"I'm not going to get my friends in trouble. If it's just this staph type poisoning, anybody that got it would be better in short order."

"I still think you should report it. Someone who prepared the food could be a carrier of staph."

"I'll think about it. Win, I'm willing to chance going fishing. I know I'll be better in no time flat."

"Okay, if you say so. Do you want to use the John before we go?"

"No, I stopped at the rest stop on I-25. I'll just lie down on the back seat of your car and let you drive. You have the directions written out, I assume?"

"Yes I do, and we went over them the other day. I'll transfer your gear to my car. Do you want anything to drink before we go?"

"No, thanks. I'll just vomit."

"Great! Let's get going, although I have serious doubts about your sanity. Oops,

I nearly forgot my new walking stick. It's a gift from Julia to prevent her clumsy husband from tripping and breaking his neck. Unfortunately it weighs a ton."

"Win, that looks more like a shillelagh than a walking stick. We could use it if we run into bear or wildcats." With that, Chuck lay down on the seat and soon was out cold.

Win drove out of the subdivision looking like he was all by his lonesome, with Chuck zonked out on the rear seat. It took a little over an hour and a half to reach the fabled "secret" fishing site up in the Jemez Mountains. The branch from the main road was unpaved, but well graded, suggesting this place might not be a big secret after all. Win pulled up at the site pinpointed on his map and parked about 50 feet from the trees that probably surrounded the stream. He turned around and half-shouted, "Time to get up, Chuck. We're at the stream."

"That was fast, Win, or maybe I was just in a deep sleep. Uh-oh. I think I need to answer Nature's call, and in a hurry. I'll be right back," he said, as he dashed off to the cover of the trees.

Win got out and took his gear up to the crest of the hill and the clump of trees that he assumed surrounded the stream. Julia's new walking stick proved very useful for the rough, scrabbled terrain. He scanned the incredible moonscape-like vistas and decided this wasn't a bad place to fish at all.

He was surprised by the sound of another car below. This definitely was not a secret fishing place! Win saw that a gray SUV had pulled up right behind his car. He wondered if they were trespassing on someone's posted land and were about to be invited to leave as a tall, lean guy got out of the car and started to climb up towards Win. He looked Indian, was dressed in desert camouflage, and there was something weird about his gait. Win raised and waved his walking stick to greet him, but got no response. He noticed that the guy was walking as if he'd had a stroke. His right arm was held against his right side, suggesting a right-sided paralysis, but his right leg seemed totally unaffected. It was a long time since Win had even thought about neurology and his clinical training was in pediatrics, not geriatrics. Then Win noticed the guy had a long, black object in his right hand. He also was able to discern, as he approached, that the man was probably Asian and not an American Indian.

The man stopped near Win and asked, "You Dr. Winston Sage?" English was definitely not his native language.

"Yes; how do you know my name?"

The man, who was definitely Asian, came closer and raised his right arm towards Win. Win now realized that the long black object in the guy's right hand was a gun and a funny looking gun with something at the end of the barrel. It was pointing directly at his face. Just as the man said, "Goodbye, Dr. Sage," Chuck emerged from the trees shouting and waving, "Win, come here fast, I gotta show you something incredible."

The man with the gun was startled. As he turned his eyes towards Chuck, Win suddenly raised his walking stick high and brought it down hard. It struck with a sickening thud on the right side of the man's head, above his ear.

"Oh, my God, I think I killed him," Win said out loud. He put his hand over his forehead and shook his head.

Chuck came running over and looked down at the crumpled guy in camouflage. "Win, what happened?"

"Chuck, I was about to be shot by him. Can you believe that? You distracted him as you came out of the trees, so I tried to knock the gun out of his hand. But my aim was bad and I hit him on the skull. It was over his right tempero-parietal area. I'd better check his vital signs."

Win went over and felt the man's neck for a carotid pulse; he felt a strong, regular pulse. He next rolled him over to check his eyes. The pupils were small and equal in size and got smaller when Win flashed the miniature flashlight attached to his fishing vest on them. He next inspected the man's skull and right ear. There was no visible bleeding or apparent skull depression. His breathing seemed regular and wasn't labored. "So far, so good, Chuck; he's alive and in no distress and I don't believe there's any serious brain damage -- but I know beans about neurology." Win was shaking.

Chuck squatted down next to the unconscious man. "Win, this guy packs a serious weapon and the hammer's cocked. I think he really was about to shoot you. It's a large caliber gun and I think there's a silencer on it. He would have killed you from this range. I think we should get our butts out of here ASAP!"

"I'm going to take the gun out of his hand, in case he comes to. Chuck, do you know how to release the trigger without setting the gun off?"

"Yeah, I think so." Chuck unwrapped the unconscious guy's fingers from around the gun butt and carefully eased his finger off the trigger. He pulled the hammer back, released it slowly and let the gun fall to the ground. The gun didn't go off, to Win's relief.

"Be careful. Don't get too many fingerprints on it. I have a plastic zip-lock bag in the big pocket on the back of my vest, why don't you come around and get it out for me?" Win was a pure catch-and-release angler and only ate a fish when he accidentally took its life, keeping this bag for that eventuality. Win used the hemostat hanging from his vest to carefully lift the gun by the trigger guard and place it in the plastic bag. He next checked the unconscious guy's pockets for identification. He found a black canvas wallet in his jacket pocket and fished out a bunch of ID cards and a passport.

Win slumped as he said, "Chuck, we're in deep trouble! This guy has a Peoples' Republic of China diplomatic passport. He's based at the Houston consulate and has a Texas driver's license. I'm going to write his name down. Better yet, I've got my old sub-compact camera here in my vest and I'll take a picture of his papers." Win spread out the guy's passport, consular ID card, and driver's license on the ground, set his camera on a macro setting and took two shots. To be safe, Win also wrote Xiao Ping on the back of his hand with a ballpoint pen and under it the passport number. He also decided to take a mug shot of his assailant while he was at it. "Okay, now let's get out of here pronto! First, I'm going to tape his hands together to slow him down when he awakens, which I'm hoping he'll do." Win fished around in one of the many pockets in his vest to find a wad of duck tape that he carried for quick repairs of torn waders. "Chuck, I'm going to tape his hands in front of him so he'll be delayed, but only briefly. I never knew that a fishing vest with all the junk we carry around in it would prove so useful. I'm going to check his pulse and eyes to make sure there's been no change. I'm worried about an intracranial bleed with increasing pressure. You get going to the car; here are the keys. You're going to have to drive. My hands are still shaking. Get the car started and turned around and I'll join you."

Win checked the diplomat out; his clinical state seemed stable but he was still out cold. He repositioned him so that his head was uphill and elevated to minimize aspiration of saliva, or vomitus. Vomiting is one of the results of increasing intracranial pressure, he remembered. Win wondered how the hell he got himself into this unreal situation as he gathered up his gear, his walking stick and the encased gun and ran like the Dickens to the waiting car. Hardly the graceful gazelle, he twisted his ankle in the process but barely let it slow him down. He threw all the gear and stuff into the car, then stopped to fish around again in his vest for his mini-camera and snapped a shot of the Chinese guy's car and license plate. He finally lurched and fell into the passenger seat. Chuck floored the gas pedal and they hurtled away, strewing gravel behind.

"Win, I think we'd better call 911. I hope our cell phones work out here."

"Chuck, I'm going to call the FBI instead and let them do it. I don't think we want our phone numbers traced. I had a visit from an FBI agent a week ago. He was nosing around about why I had visited a scientist at Los Alamos – that's the collector guy in White Rock – since I had a very dubious FBI file, at least in his opinion. In any event, he told me to keep my nose out of the Los Alamos physicist's affairs and the business of the neighbor who disappeared. He and just about everyone else keeps telling me to keep out of this missing wife investigation. Unfortunately, after today, I think they were right. I'm going to have a shot of Calvados, do you want some?" Win fished around again in his vest and retrieved a small pewter flask whose cap he began to unscrew with shaking hands. "God bless fly fishing vests and their endless pockets."

"Win, if that's your usual apple rotgut, no thanks!"

Win took a slug of Calvados and started to rummage through his wallet. He pulled out the card that the F.B.I agent had given him, then got out his cell phone and dialed the number on the back of the card. They were within range of a cell tower fortunately. The phone rang for a very long time, but at least it didn't kick over to someone's voicemail. A man finally answered and asked, "What's your access code, please?"

Win read him the code words the "man in black" had written on the card: "Desert Fox." Is that ever trite, Win thought. Now he wondered why the agent had assumed there might be an emergency.

The man at the other end asked Win for his name and told him to hold for a moment. It proved to be a very long moment. Win took another swig of the Calvados and again asked Chuck if he would like some.

"Win, you know I don't like that stuff and besides, I'm driving."

After what seemed an interminable wait, there was a voice at the other end of the line. "This is Agent Shaw. Is this Dr. Sage?"

"Yes. I have a big-time problem, I believe." Win reported what had just transpired in careful detail.

After a short pause, there was a verbal explosion at the other end. Following an impressive recitation of expletives, Shaw shouted, "You have a very big problem indeed! You just stepped in very deep doo-doo, fellah. Why did you slug the guy?"

"Because if I didn't slug him, I would be in even deeper doo-doo – six feet deep to be exact. He was about to kill me."

"How do you know that?"

"Look, he followed me, knew my name, and then aimed a heavy-duty pistol with an attached silencer right at my nose. He wasn't exactly hunting elk. When he said 'Goodbye, Dr. Sage,' I knew he meant in the permanent sense, so I slugged him, but I aimed for his arm and missed."

"I probably would have done the same," the agent allowed. "Look, I want you and your buddy to head down towards Albuquerque. Work your way back towards I-25 and call me again in 10 minutes."

"My friend Chuck left his car at my house. Can we stop and get it on the way?"

"That's the least of your problems right now! Head south and keep driving. Don't stop for any reason and don't call anyone but me at the number you just used. We would like the two of you to stay alive, capice? Don't even think of calling 911, we'll take care of that."

"I got ya."

The man in black hung up abruptly.

"Chuck, the FBI guy thinks we are in very deep 'doo-doo' and he fears for our lives. He wants us to head south to Albuquerque as fast as possible. We're not to call anyone, stop, or pass 'Go' for any reason."

"What about my car? It's at your place."

"We're in serious danger. I'm sorry I got you into this. I don't think the gunman knew you were with me, since you startled him when you came out of the trees. That's when I tried to disarm him. I think I did the right thing -- only I hit him in the wrong place. You saved my life by distracting him. Are you sure you don't want some calvados?"

"No thanks, again. I really should call Evelyn and let her know what's happening."

"Chuck, my F.B.I. friend emphatically said we shouldn't call anyone but him." Win looked at his watch; it wasn't ten minutes yet.

Chuck turned towards Win and muttered, "You sure blew a nice day, Win, and I was finally getting over my gut problem."

Win noticed that Chuck was looking at him and wasn't watching the road.

"Chuck, I'm very sorry for what happened, but please keep you eyes on the road. The F.B.I. dude will come up with something, but we're not fishing today."

Chuck wasn't too happy-looking. "Shouldn't we call 911?"

"The agent said they would get help out to the diplomat. I'll try to reach him again."

Win dialed the emergency number with still trembling fingers and this time got connected to Shaw immediately. Shaw began, "I want both of you to drive down to Albuquerque. There are to be no stops and no telephone calls. You're to come right in, capice?"

"Yes. I may need some gas though."

"Look Sage, just keep driving. If you run out of gas, call me instantly, hear?"

"Yes, where should we go?"

"Do you know where the Hyatt Hotel is downtown?"

"Yeah, I stayed there while we were building our house. It's near our architect's studio."

"They have an underground parking garage that you enter on Copper Street." He gave Win precise directions for getting from I-25 to the parking garage. "When you get there, find a place to park underground in the hotel parking area. It's a multiuse garage. If nothing is free, park in one of the rental car slots or in the valet parking area. Park and stay in the car. What kind of car are you driving?"

"A 2010, silver, Subaru Forester."

"An agent will come up to your car. His name is Carlos and he'll show you his badge. Just get out of the car and leave the keys and garage ticket behind. Don't lock the doors and no conversations with him or your buddy. Follow him and don't take anything from the car. Now, drive fast. If you get stopped by the police have them call me at this number immediately."

"Okay. I'll take over the driving from Chuck; I'm more familiar with the garage."

"Don't you dare. I bet your hands are still shaking."

"How did you know?"

"Experience, Sage."

"I hope you contacted 911 about the diplomat. He was alive when we left him and I don't want a murder on my hands."

"That's been taken care of."

An hour and a half later they pulled into the Copper Street Garage, found a place to park, and turned off the engine. They hadn't run out of gas, but they were running on fumes.

Chuck sighed and said, "Whew, we made it in record time. What do we do now?"

"We wait."

Win sat with his head down.

Part II

"When elephants fight, it is the grass that suffers."
East African proverb

Chapter 30.

It wasn't more than 60 seconds before a husky man in dark glasses, a Padres baseball jacket and jeans came up to the car, flashed his badge, and knocked on the window. He said, "I'm Carlos. Follow me." Win and Chuck got out and silently followed him.

The agent led them to a nondescript black van whose rear doors were open and gestured for them to get in. They got in and as soon as the doors were shut the driver headed up the exit ramp. There were no windows in the rear compartment and it was dark. Carlos said, "No talking." The seats were uncomfortable and it seemed like a long time before they stopped. There was a series of thumps on the rear, and Carlos opened the doors and gestured for them to get out. They were in a large, dimly lit garage, probably underground. A character straight from Hollywood central casting asked them to follow him. This guy was all in black – black turtleneck, pants, gun holster and shoes – and was quite trim and fit. They got into an elevator and went to the fifth floor of what seemed to be an office building, which, judging by the drabness of the paint and carpets was probably some government facility. They were led to a large well-lit office with an oversized wooden conference table in the middle. Three grim-faced men sat at the table.

One got up and greeted them. "I'm glad you made it here without further incident. He went over to Chuck and said, "I'm Tom Shaw, and I'll try to get you out of here as quickly as possible. Please sit down. First, I need to see your IDs. Then we need to ask you some questions about the incident today up in the Jemez, and we'll be recording the conversation. I don't want any cute stuff about wanting a lawyer; this is not a criminal or other legal investigation. This is about your safety. There are two other Agents here who'll participate, Dave Loomis and Herb Orvis. There are some cold drinks and coffee on the credenza; help yourselves." Win and Chuck were parched from both the high altitude and the effects of anxiety and made a beeline for the drinks.

Shaw began as soon as they were settled. He looked at Chuck's driver's license and said, "Let's start with you Mr. Orsini. I want you to tell me about your day, beginning when you first got up this morning."

Chuck choked on his drink. "Well, I set the alarm for 5:30 and didn't have any trouble getting up since I was up most of the night with food poisoning. I got out of bed…."

"Hold it for a second. Tell me about this food poisoning."

"I woke up about 2 A.M. with terrible cramps and nausea. I vomited several times and then developed diarrhea. Is that what you want to know?"

"I'm more interested in how you think you got this food poisoning."

"I think I got it at a friend's house. We have a group of friends who get together once a month at one of our homes. This time we met at Dick and Laura's house. They had a buffet dinner and I assume I got sick from the potato salad. We ate late and the food might have been sitting around at room temperature for a while. Win thought the timing of my getting sick fits with staph poisoning."

"Did any of your friends there know you were going fishing today with Dr. Sage, and could they have known before last night?"

"I'm pretty sure nobody knew."

"Did any of the food come from an outside caterer?"

Chuck frowned; he was getting exasperated with Shaw. "No. Laura was bragging about how she made everything herself. She's a really good cook; that's why I pigged out on her potato salad. It's one of her specialties."

"Okay, let's get back to this morning. Why don't you continue?"

"Well, I wasn't feeling too perky when I got up, but I decided to go on the trip because I didn't think I'd be sick for too long. I had something like this before and it was over in ten to twelve hours. I skipped breakfast, had a shower, and then loaded up the car with my gear and the food my wife had prepared and headed up to Santa Fe. I was feeling a bit better and only had to make one pit stop on the way. I made it to Win's house in about an hour and he was outside ready to go."

"Dr. Sage lives in a gated subdivision. How did you get in? Did you buzz him on the intercom at the gate?"

"No. We had lunch together at the University a couple of days ago to plan the trip. He gave me a gate opener so I could let myself in without waking up Julia, his wife."

"Okay, what happened when you got to Dr. Sage's house?"

"I parked at his garage where he was loading gear into his car. I told him about my illness and he thought I shouldn't go on the trip. I felt I'd be okay by the time we got to the stream and he suggested I take a nap in the back seat while he drove. So I curled up in back and zonked out."

Agent Loomis interrupted. "Did anyone see you driving in to the Sages? Did you go into the Sage house to use any of the facilities? Did you talk to Dr. Sage's wife or use their telephone?"

"No to all those questions

Shaw went on, "Did you sit up during the trip so you might be visible to someone in another car?"

"No, I was out to the world until we got to the stream. Remember, I was up most of the night with my gut problems. In fact, Win had to wake me up when we got there."

"What happened next?"

"I woke up and had a sudden, bad attack of diarrhea, if you really want to know. I got out of the car and ran for the bushes to relieve myself."

"Did you notice another car behind you when you got out of your car?"

"I was in such a rush, I wouldn't have noticed anything except where I was heading."

"When you were in the bushes, did you hear another car pull up or any voices?"

"No. The only thing I noticed was a herd of five elk heading towards the river. In fact when I came out of the bushes, I shouted to get Win's attention so I could show him the elk. As soon as I did it, I realized I probably was scaring them off."

"When you came out of the bushes, what did you see?"

"I saw a guy in camouflage standing in front of Win, slightly below him on the hill. The guy had one arm straight out in front of himself and was bracing it with his other hand. They seemed to be talking."

"Okay, what happened next?"

"The guy in camouflage turned around to look my way, like he was surprised. Win then raised his walking stick and brought it down on the guy's head. I couldn't believe what I'd just seen. I never thought Win had homicidal tendencies, so I realized something was very wrong and ran towards them."

"What happened to the guy in camo?"

"He went down like a rag doll."

"Did you hear any shots, any scream or remark from the injured guy as he went down?"

"No. Nothing."

"So what happened next?"

Chuck described the aftermath of Win's clubbing of the diplomat with academic precision and excess.

Shaw put both his hands up and interrupted. "Okay, enough! Was the diplomat unconscious the whole time you were near him?"

"Yeah. I don't think he came to as we were leaving either."

"Did you notice anything unusual about the guy?"

"I didn't notice much; I was too scared. My eyes were mostly on the gun and his head."

"What kind of gun was it?"

"I think it was a large-caliber pistol with either a barrel extension on it, if there's such a thing, or a silencer. It was black and I don't know more about guns than that."

"Did you notice the man's car?"

"It was an SUV, I think, and probably silver-colored. Win took a picture of the license plate while I was getting ready to go."

"Did you take all your gear with you when you left?"

"I'm sure I did because I never took anything out of the car. I just ran to the bushes as soon as I woke up."

"Mr. Orsini, is there anything else you noticed that you think could be important?"

"No. Not really."

"I'm through with your questioning unless my colleagues have some questions."

The other two agents shook their heads.

"As you've witnessed, there's someone out there who'd like to do away with your friend. This is real hardball and you could place yourself and your family in serious danger. So my advice to you is to go home, forget about this whole affair and act like nothing has happened. Above all, keep your mouth shut about what you saw and heard today. Don't even mention it to your wife! Don't call or contact Dr. Sage. I suspect the wannabe assassin has no idea who you are. So let's keep it that way! Capice?"

"Yeah, I got you. What about Win?"

"That's our problem to deal with. Now we're going to drive you home or at least part way there. Your car is almost in Albuquerque and we'll take you to it so you can drive into your driveway as if nothing ever happened today."

"How did you do that? My car keys are here in my pocket."

"We have certain skills in the Bureau. I'm most grateful for your help. You probably saved your friend's life today. Oh, the glories of diarrhea!"

"You're a real poet, Shaw," Win quipped.

"That's enough from you, Sage. You've done enough harm today."

With that, Shaw got up and escorted Chuck out.

Loomis came over to Win and said "Dr. Sage, stay put; we aren't through with you. You won't be going anywhere for a while."

"Am I going to jail?"

"No; worse than that!"

Chapter 31.

Win helped himself to coffee while waiting for Shaw and his friends to return. He looked down at the cup and hoped they didn't notice how badly his hand was trembling.

Shaw came back into the room, sat down and sighed. "Sage, you screwed up big time today, but you probably saved your life. It's also likely that you did your country a great service by your clumsy, amateur detective work. Before I start a new line of questioning with you, is there anything you want to add to Mr. Orsini's account of the incident?"

"No. I told you what happened over the phone and Chuck's observations jibe with mine. You know, I never noticed anybody following me on the way."

"Had you ever seen the Chinese guy before – think hard?"

"No. He's very tall and that's not common in Asians – so that would have made him stand out."

"Okay Sage, let's change the subject. Where were you going in your investigation of the missing woman?"

"Well, I heard a lot about Jessica's boy friends and how she probably ran off with some other guy, but I didn't buy that story. Her husband seemed to think she had a sudden complete loss of memory that led to her disappearance. The medical explanation was far-fetched. I became intrigued by her sudden acquisition of knowledge about ancient Chinese ceramics and her ability to acquire some incredibly good pieces, as well as her sudden reversal of financial status. So, I made some inquiries and was either told to stay out of 'this', whatever 'this' was, or else I found big-time discrepancies in the stories I was told about her and her gallery."

"Who told you to stay out of 'this'?"

"My wife and several friends for starters. You and then Sergeant Ortiz from the Santa Fe police, when he visited me. Then my antique-dealer friend Michael called from a public phone in Hong Kong to say that the government had gotten wind of his digging and scared the daylights out of him."

"Okay, who's Sergeant Ortiz?"

"He's with the Santa Fe Police missing-persons branch. He visited me at home a few days after you visited me. He had come to our subdivision to meet with Bill Harvey. Bill told him about my looking into his wife's disappearance, so the Sergeant stopped over to see if I'd come up with anything useful. He's one heck of a weird guy."

"Coming from you, Sage, he must be really weird! What did he ask you?"

Win was feeling exhausted and slogged on. "He wanted to know what I had found out about Jessica Harvey and whether I had any theories about her disappearance. He's one of the most hyperactive people I've ever met. He just couldn't sit still. He wanted to see our new house and was all over the place and had to finger everything. He had this annoying habit of constantly popping some sort of candy from his jacket pocket into his mouth. He made some of my former ADHD patients look bush-league."

"So what did you tell him?"

"I told him I suspected Jessica's disappearance was related to her emergence as a very successful dealer in Asian art."

"Did you elaborate on this theory?"

"No. I was at an early phase in my thinking on this idea and there was something about him that I just didn't feel right about; don't ask me why."

"Did he ask you about any people you'd interviewed regarding the Harvey disappearance?"

"Yeah, he wanted to know whom I had talked to in Santa Fe and whether I had talked to Wong in Los Alamos."

"Had you talked to Wong in Los Alamos?"

"Yes; you asked me that when you paid me a visit. Remember, you were all in black and I thought you were an over-aged, Mormon missionary.

"What did the Sergeant ask you about Dr. Wong?"

"He wanted to know why I visited him and what I thought of his involvement in the disappearance."

"What did you say?"

Win sighed; he was getting very tired. "I told him I wanted to know if Wong had any fresh insights into the disappearance story and that I was anxious to see his collection. I think I was straight with him and told him that Wong seemed like a nice old guy with great ceramics, but the story of his relationship with Jessica didn't sit right with me."

"Did Sgt. Ortiz give you his card?"

"No. I asked for a card and he pulled his wallet out and found that he'd given his last card to Bill Harvey."

"Did he use your telephone?"

"Come to think of it, he did. He asked to use the phone in my office since his cell phone didn't work out our way. He asked me to step outside as the call involved another case and was confidential. It was odd, like everything else about him."

Shaw looked at Bill Orvis and gave him a slight nod. Orvis got up and left the room. "Okay, Dr. Sage, let's shift gears now and talk about your friend Michael in Hong Kong. What do you think made him call you and tell you to stay out of this?"

Win related the story of his bumbling investigation of Jessica's disappearance in full detail as Shaw took notes, even though he had a recording machine running.

"Dr. Sage, you stink as a detective, but you may just prove to be a star as a bumbling bird dog; you know, the type that flushes birds out of the grass. You may have flushed out the big bird we've been after for a long time with your 'bull in a china shop' finesse. Except you never waited for the command to flush the bird! You had your friends broadcast all over the antiques scene in Hong Kong that you had some suspicions about Wong and his collection and that attracted some serious, high-level attention. And then your nut-case buddies in Santa Fe created another ruckus."

Orvis came back into the room and came over to whisper something in Shaw's ear. Agent Shaw looked glum as he asked Win, "Are you sure you got the name right for Sergeant Ortiz?"

"Posolutely, as my grandmother used to say. He introduced himself to me as Ortiz and when he used my phone he started his conversation by saying 'This is Jim Ortiz.' I also wrote his name down after he left."

"Well, guess what, there isn't any Sergeant Jim Ortiz with the Santa Fe or State police. Let's take a break. Just stay here and take it easy. My colleagues and I have some work to do."

Win was puzzled and totally worn out. He realized he still had his fishing vest on and reached inside to retrieve his flask of calvados. He took a long swig and settled down to wait for more bad news. Boy, did he step into it this time!

Chapter 32.

It was a long time before Shaw and Orvis came back, unsettling for Win who couldn't stop thinking through all the implications of his assault on the homicidal Chinese diplomat.

When Shaw did return, he sat down and began, "Dr. Sage my colleagues and I, here and in Washington, have just spent a long time working out a preliminary plan for what to do. Unfortunately, the best strategy we came up with is to enlist you to work with us and for us to provide protective custody for you and your wife. As you learned today, this could be dangerous. Would you be willing to help us? I should add that it would be a great service to your country. Also, everything you hear and do, will have to be confidential and I mean top-secret. When this is over, it will never have occurred officially. Capice?"

"Yeah, I got you. What exactly does this 'work' involve?"

"I can't tell you until you sign on. Bill Orvis has prepared a document for you to read and sign. Take a few minutes." He handed Win what looked like a contract, which Win read carefully. It was an agreement that Win would work for the F.B.I. as a "Special Agent", with no pay of course, and would abide by the Bureau's confidentiality and state secrets policies at the threat of prosecution and imprisonment. He was to tell no one about what he would be doing – ever. At least the contract was explicit.

"If I sign this, does that mean I have to take orders from you?"

"Technically, yes, but I don't think you're capable of taking orders."

"I was pretty good at taking orders when I was in the Air Force. You know, I did have some problems with things like uniforms and saluting. I used to forget and wear my loafers or slippers when I went into the hospital."

"That's precisely what I mean."

"What happens if I don't sign?"

"Then you're on your own Sage."

"I see. If I don't sign up I get no protection from you."

"You got it."

Win sat for a few minutes thinking and then said glumly, "It looks like I don't have much choice, since what I did today puts me at big-time risk."

"You're right on the money!"

"Okay, I enlist."

"We'll need to get another witness to your signing."

It took only a minute for a drably dressed, middle-aged woman to come in and witness the grand event. Win signed two copies and was given one.

"Okay, my esteemed colleagues; what do you want me to do?"

"Sage, we can do without sarcasm. Let me give you the background. For a long time, we've suspected that someone at the Los Alamos National Laboratory has been leaking nuclear secrets to the People's Republic of China. I suspect you read the newspapers and are aware of the investigation a couple of years ago of a suspected LANL physicist, who is, very interestingly, Chinese-American, like our Dr. Wong. We thought the other guy, Chen, who was probably falsely accused, was our man. We ended up with egg on our face over that one. You probably also read about the very lax financial and security management of LANL. The place is a security nightmare. The scientists there act like they're university professors and forget they work for a top-secret, defense arm of the U.S. Government.

I think we may have underestimated how hard it is to deal with professor types."

"It's like trying to herd cats."

"May I go on without interruption?"

"Sorry, boss."

Shaw shook his head. "This brings me to you. By what appears to be sheer ineptitude, you've given us our best lead so far towards finding the LANL mole. I must say, your style is unique. You prove your theories by getting your friend in Hong Kong in big trouble with the PRC and then nearly getting yourself and your buddy Chuck killed. You may be one of the world's worst daredevil detectives and you're lucky to still be alive. The facts that your Hong Kong friend was directly warned away from inquiries about Wong by the PRC and then a PRC diplomat tried to kill you today makes a strong case for Wong being our LANL spy and our having a leak of much greater significance than we suspected. You know, you're a true agent provocateur."

"Well thanks for the compliment. You're right; I don't know what I'm doing as a detective. I stumbled onto this business by accident, and now I'm in trouble."

"So that brings me to our plans for you, which are sketchy at this time. We think you should go on with your life as if nothing happened and you never had any contact with us. Don't worry; we're going to smother you with protection. We need more time to gather information and hatch our strategy. Unfortunately, you're going to be our means for gathering information. Now, we have some immediate items to deal with such as the location and safety of your wife."

"Oh my God, I've been so wrapped up in feeling sorry for myself, I forgot about Julia!"

"Right now there are some agents watching your house closely, so don't worry."

"Can I call to let her know I'm all right and in Albuquerque?"

"Absolutely not! We suspect your phone's been tapped. We need to work out a means of your communicating with her via a written message or a neighbor getting her out of the house and into our hands for protection. In the meantime, we're going to go out to Kirtland Air Force Base for a meeting and we'll work out the details of our plan then."

"Am I now back in the Air Force too?"

"No way, Sage; once was enough for the Air Force! Help yourself to a drink before we go."

"Why don't you call me Win, now that I'm part of the gang?

"Okay, except that 'loss' might be a more appropriate name to call you."

"Bad pun, Shaw!"

Chapter 33.

Shaw led Win outside to a cubicle where Orvis and Loomis were going over some papers. "Okay Win, what ideas do you have for getting your wife out of your house without calling her? We want to get her into the care of Jim and Bill as soon as possible. Our current plan is to have them drive your car to your house to pick up your wife and then drive her to the Santa Fe airport where she'll join us. By the way, you were driving on fumes when you arrived at the garage. So how do you propose we get her out of the house without any verbal communication from them? We suspect your house has been thoroughly bugged by Sgt. Ortiz."

"Well, I could call one of my neighbors and have them go over and ask Julia to step outside, where I presume there are no bugs. The agents could then talk to her, but that brings another person into the game. You know, I could write a note to Julia that you could pass to her. She knows my handwriting and she would see our car; so that might work. Getting a note from two spooky-looking guys, badges and IDs notwithstanding, and asking her to go along with them in our car with no sight of me, is going to scare the living daylights out of her. I guess I can deal with that in my note to her. What about our dogs? Do we leave them behind?"

"Let's get you some paper and see what you come up with. Don't worry about the dogs. We plan to get you back home ASAP."

"Why don't you get me some F.B.I. letterhead stationery; it might have more impact. I could also show off my new status as 'Special Agent'."

"Using letterhead is a good idea; showing off your title is a bad one."

Jim gave Win some stationery and a pen, and showed him over to a desk. Win began writing:

Dear Julia,

Sorry that I can't call you. These F.B.I. agents will tell you why as soon as you step outside the house. Don't worry – everything is OK and I'm fine. I haven't been arrested by them or anything like that. Our house is probably bugged and that's why I can't call you and why you shouldn't talk to these guys until you're away from the house. Something strange has come up in my investigation of the disappearance of Jessica Harvey.

They have our car with my permission and the plan is for them to take you to the Santa Fe airport where you and I will join up for a meeting with the F.B.I. people. Don't bring the dogs or worry about them. We'll go home soon after the meeting. If you need to walk the dogs before you leave, keep them on leashes. I'll tell you why later.

Remember that there may be listening devices in the house so don't say anything to the agents inside the house.

Don't worry. I'm fine and will tell you the whole story later.

Love,

Win

"Okay guys, what do you think of this?"

The three of them pored over the letter carefully and it was Shaw who finally said, "This should do the trick. So now we need to deal with your trip over to the air base. We found a baseball cap and what appears to be a rain jacket in your car." He held them up and asked, "Are these yours?"

"Yup, they are. Do you want me to wear them?"

"Yes. You stand out like a sore thumb with that fishing vest." He handed Win a black, heavy vest and continued, "Also, we want you to wear this vest under your rain jacket for the trip out to Kirtland."

"Is this a bulletproof vest, and if it is, why on earth do I need it?"

"Yes; it's a bullet-resistant vest and we want to be super-cautious in protecting you, until we get you home where we can control the environment more fully."

"Are you just doing this for dramatic effect or am I still at risk for getting killed?"

"We don't know, but we aren't taking chances. We need you alive."

"I guess it's nice to be highly valued."

"Enough wise aleck talk, please! We're now going to head over to Kirtland to rendezvous with an airplane carrying one of our Deputy Bureau Chiefs who happened to be nearby at a meeting in Denver. Then we'll meet on board to develop plans for you more fully, and for Dan Tilikso, the Deputy, to be filled in on what happened today and what led up to today's events. We'll then fly up to Santa Fe where we'll brief your wife on what we expect of her and what our plans are, but we'll only brief her in generalities. We don't want too many people to be in on the specifics."

"That's not going to be easy. Julia isn't dumb and she's going to see through your attempts at wallpapering over whatever schemes you come up with."

"We'll worry about that when we get to it. We're also going to have to sweep your house for bugs and other surveillance gizmos. We're expecting a team of specialists to arrive at the airport in Santa Fe about the same time we arrive. These agents, we call them the 'Gs', will accompany you to your home to go over the sites where Ortiz wandered and fingered things. I don't know how long that'll take. We'll then bring you back out to the airport to finalize plans based on what the Gs find. After that's done, you and your wife will drive home in your car as if nothing happened today."

"As if nothing happened today!" Win repeated mockingly.

"That's right. You're going to become a great actor for the next few days and we'll coach you."

"Wow, I never considered a career as a thespian. I'd like to try my hand at 'method acting'. Who knows, I could become another Marlon Brando."

"Can't you ever be serious? You're in great danger and our Bureau needs to rely on you for solving a suspected espionage case of grave national importance.'

"That sounds like a line from a B-grade movie."

"Sure Sage, all our agents are trained by showing them every bad detective movie ever made."

"Hey Boss, I didn't know you had a sense of humor."

"That's enough! Let's get going to the Air Base."

Win put on his armored vest and rain jacket, grabbed his fishing vest, and they went out through a rabbit warren of cubicles down to an underground parking garage where another nondescript, windowless van was waiting with its motor running.

"Okay Win, you and I get in the back."

Win noticed there were several men and women standing around with rifles, wearing what he presumed were bulletproof vests.

Win commented, "Don't you think you're overdoing it a bit?"

"I told you this is serious business and some parties might like to see you very dead!"

"My problem is that this whole thing just doesn't seem real. All I did was poke around asking questions about a neighbor's wife. Now here I am, a survivor of a murder attempt, in an F.B.I. van, wearing a bulletproof vest and heading out to meet with some big shot in a plane on the runway at an Air Force base."

Win couldn't see a thing, as the van had no windows in back. He couldn't even see into the front seat. It was about 15 to 20 minutes before they slowed down and came to a stop. They just sat there with the motor running so the air-conditioning remained on. Even in the spring, a closed van could get pretty hot under the New Mexico sun. Win heard a plane landing, and after a few more minutes, the van started moving again at a slow pace. They came to a stop, the engine was turned off and they got out. The sun was blinding after sitting in the dark. Slowly, Win was able to see and recognize the stigmata of a U.S. Air Force base. They still looked the same after all these years. He was led over to the steps of a white twin-engine jet -- a pretty fancy executive jet for the Feds, he thought. As he climbed the steps, he muttered, "Who woulda thunk my day out fishing would end up like this?"

Chapter 34.

A tall, heavyset man with prominent jowls greeted Win at the top of the steps. He was dressed in a rumpled but stylish brown suit, and was wearing an elegant orange tie. He extended a beefy paw. "You must be Dr. Winston Sage. I'm Dan Tilikso, Chief of the Bureau's Counterintelligence Division. I've heard a lot about you today. Come on in and make yourself comfortable. Please take off that bulletproof vest; it's hot and uncomfortable. We have a nice assortment of cold drinks and snacks behind you, so help yourself."

Win helped himself to a lot of ice and a Diet Coke and found what looked like a club sandwich. "Thanks for the food and drink; I forgot how hungry and thirsty I was."

Tilikso began, "I understand that you claim all this stuff we have in your files about your activities is perfectly innocent, although it stretches the imagination to think so. Is that true?"

"Yes, it really is true."

"Hmm. You've had a lot of people fooled for a long time. You should write a book about your experiences, it sounds like great fiction. So your records are now explained, although I'm still skeptical. How did you get involved in investigating C.Y. Wong?"

Win proceeded to retell his story from the beginning to his near-assassination experience today. He was sure Dan had already heard it.

"That's a complicated story and succinctly described. Bravo, Dr. Sage; your ineptitude is brilliant! So what do you think is the explanation?"

"I think Wong has been an agent for the Chinese Government and may have been passing them nuclear secrets. Either they wanted to reward him financially or he asked for remuneration because he was nearing the end of his physics career. I bet salaries at LANL aren't great and that he hasn't accumulated a very large retirement nest egg. So someone thought up the idea of Wong inheriting a great collection of Warring States ceramics that he could sell off and then have him park the proceeds of the sales in an offshore bank account. Maybe it was that Chinese general that did some private excavations. Probably, to cover up any large shipment of antiques, he had some fake relatives selling pieces to Jessica Harvey in Hong Kong. Wong handled the payment to his relatives for their sales. The Harveys paid Wong in dollars and he ostensibly sent the money off to his relatives. Maybe Jessica got wise to what was going on and went into hiding or she was rubbed out, maybe by the Chinese diplomat that tried to do me in today. I don't think Wong person- ally did her harm."

Tilikso slapped his massive thigh. "That's brilliant detective work! Unfortunately, I think you may be right which means we have a big problem on our hands. First, we need to investigate things at LANL to assess the scope of potential damage Wong could have done. Then we need to see what we can learn about this ceramics trade and who was involved. We need to protect you and prepare you for some further information gathering. I can't tell you much more now because we're still planning our approaches. We also have the issue of what to do with the would-be assassin with a diplomatic passport. We're working on that with our colleagues at the State Department."

Win was munching on his sandwich and listening intently.

Tilikso went on, "Let me outline for you what I think we'll do with your help. First, we need to check your house for bugs, and we have a team of experts on their way here to do that. If we find your house is bugged, we're currently leaning towards leaving the transceivers in place. We then want you and your wife to go home and act like nothing unusual happened today. It'll be hard, but you can do it. I'll brief your wife when we get to the Santa Fe airport, and while you're accompanying our security experts, through your house. We'll place a security force around your home and at the gate and fences of your subdivision. We're considering having a couple of dear old friends of yours visit and stay in your house until we get this whole thing over with. Despite all that, you and your wife should go on and lead your normal lives."

Win shook his head in disbelief. "Do you really expect us to behave as if nothing ever happened today and ignore a whole bunch of listening devices?

"I think it'll be easier than you anticipate."

"Who are these friends of ours that are going to stay with us?"

"They're a charming middle-aged couple who work in our Gs unit. They're easy to tolerate and know how to protect people. I think you'll hit it off just fine with them."

"It sounds as if you're preparing to take over our lives."

"That sums things up in a nutshell. You're about to enter protective custody, but you maintain your identities and live normal lives in your own home. We think you're still in great danger. You're a key witness and can cause great embarrassment to the Chinese. This is not a good time for them to be exposed again as thieves of U.S. defense secrets. Many in our Congress would like just such an excuse to beat up on Chinese exports to the U. S."

"Speaking of the Government, you know, a few years ago the President visited his best friend, who has a home in our subdivision. I bet they installed a bunch of security equipment for his stay in La Tierra Hermosa. Your guys might be able to use some of it."

"Do you mean the President of the United States?"

"Yup."

"Were you living in the subdivision at the time?

"No, our house wasn't finished yet."

"That's useful. Our Secret Service friends have probably already done a lot of the survey work we need to do. That's incredible; POTUS spent some time in your subdivision! Is there anything else you learned in your investigations that you think might be important?"

"Not that I can think of. Oh, wait a minute; I took some photos of the Chinese guy while he was unconscious and of his passport and other IDs and also his car and license plate."

"Did you use your cellphone?"

"No. I'm old fashioned and carry a camera when I fish. Since I try to release trout alive, I document my catches with pictures. It helps to prove I'm not just telling fisherman's tales when I get home. The camera fits nicely into one of the pockets in my fishing vest. I also had some duct tape in another pocket that I used to bind the diplomat's hands together. I also carry a small flask of calvados, but I drank that all after the ambush this morning. Fishing vests are very useful, but they can get awfully heavy if you overload them."

Dan guffawed and said, "Amazing! We should equip all our agents with vests like yours."

"You know they're a lot more stylish than your black suits."

Dan shook his head and asked, "Tom, do you have any further questions for Dr. Sage or anything you'd like to add?"

"No, sir."

"Before we take off for Santa Fe, why don't you have one of your men contact Treasury to see if the Secret Service can help us with some security information for Dr. Sage's subdivision."

Shaw promptly pulled out a small walkie-talkie and gave someone an order to follow up on the Secret Service idea. Tilikso then nodded to an assistant sitting in the rear of the plane who went up to the cockpit to tell the pilot to get going on the short flight to Santa Fe.

"Now Dr. Sage, why don't you kick back and relax on our way to Santa Fe? There are more sandwiches and drinks in back, so help yourself."

Chapter 35.

The flight took only 40 minutes, most of which was spent in takeoff and landing. When they landed at Santa Fe, Win noticed they weren't taxiing over to the passenger terminal but to a distant hanger. The gangway was lowered and Win was asked to remain inside while Tilikso and Shaw got off the plane. He looked out and saw a crowd of about ten people and hoped to see Julia among them, but he realized that Agents Orvis and Loomis were driving his car from Albuquerque and probably hadn't picked her up yet. The group at the foot of the gangway was engaged in serious conversation and retreated into the hangar. Tilikso's female assistant remained on board with Win and said, "Don't worry. We have a lot of details that need to be worked out. Today's events weren't something we anticipated by any stretch of the imagination."

"It's hard not to worry. I was almost killed by a diplomat and I almost killed him"

"Yes, your day would be unnerving for even an experienced agent, although an experienced person wouldn't have gotten into your situation in the first place. But as Dan said, you ultimately performed well and opened up a very important case for us. We're grateful for what you've done and we'll take good care of you. So try to relax."

Win reclined his seat as far as it would go, which was a lot more that the usual commercial, tourist-class seat. He closed his eyes, but couldn't doze off. After about 15 minutes, Win was startled by a voice over a radio the agent on board was wearing. She came over and said, "Dan says we're ready to roll, so let's join them." She indicated to Win to precede her. He noticed that this woman wasn't along as a flight attendant; she had a very large handgun in her right hand. Win got up and climbed down the flight of steps followed by his armed guard. She said, "Go on into the hanger, I'll be right outside the door."

Win went inside, spotted Julia and gave her a big hug. She told him that Dan had already provided the details of his day. "I told you that you never should have gotten involved in this disappearance business," she chided him.

Dan winked at Win and said, "You know, Win has ended up providing an invaluable service to the F.B.I. and our country by his bumbling investigation."

"I would agree on the bumbling part, but I'll reserve judgment on the invaluable service."

"Trust me Ma'am, it's a great service. Now we need to send your husband off to your house with these nice people to do a bit of sweeping and cleaning – electronic sweeping and cleaning, that is. I'd like you to stay here with me. We'll go back on the plane where we can talk some more and I can explain what we plan to do."

They headed out the door, where Julia turned pale as the female agent holding a gun escorted them onto the gangway and Julia realized that this was serious.

The "nice people" started gathering up several large, black canvas bags that they loaded into a van. One of them, a tall woman in blue coveralls, came over to Win to introduce herself. "I'm Pat Ross; I'm the leader of our squad. You'll need to take us to your home and show us the areas the bogus sergeant wandered through. We'll first make sure there's no video surveillance outside your house. Then we'll go inside to sweep for video and then audio devices. Needless to say, there can be no voice communication between us, only hand signals."

The van left the hangar, with Win in the middle of the front seat between Pat and the driver, who looked like he was fresh out of college. Win led them onto Airport Road heading east and then onto the 599 Bypass. He was really looking forward to getting home, despite the bizarre circumstances. The driver was speeding way above the speed limit, and when Win warned him that there was usually a speed trap on this stretch of road, he and Pat just smiled at Win as if he was an idiot.

Win suddenly blurted out, "I forgot the gate opener to get into our subdivision; it's in my car." He looked at his watch and said, "Maybe you should speed a bit more. The gatekeeper mans the gate until 6:30 P.M. and we could just catch him if you keep going at this insane speed."

Pat looked at her watch and said "No problem! But if the gate is closed, one of our guys can figure out how to open it. Let me brief you now on some procedures we'll use. We don't think any video surveillance devices were placed in your house. Ortiz didn't have enough time to install any and they would be too hard to conceal. Nevertheless, our first step is to check for any image collecting devices. After that, assuming we find none, we'll enter your house barefoot and will say absolutely nothing, not even by whispering. All communication will be by gestures. If we do it right, we should look like an accomplished mime troupe. If the phone rings, don't answer it."

Win interrupted, "Whoa --you forgot one big thing, our dogs. They're going to bark their heads off when you all stream in, particularly with your outfits." They were uniformly dressed in black clothes that looked like high-tech gym gear.

"Good point, Sage. No one told us about the dogs."

"I've got an idea, Pat. I can act like I've just come home and found that Julia was out and was probably at one of the neighbors' houses. I can greet the dogs and take them out to their fenced-in kennel. I usually talk to them, so I can say something like: "Hey dogs, where's your mom? I bet she went over to Ann and Herky's house. Maybe I'll stop over and pick her up? That would jibe with my leaving to go back to the airport to join up with Julia. What do you think?"

"Good idea!"

They were approaching La Tierra Hermosa and pulled up to the entry gate. Luckily, Armando was still on duty. Win had Pat roll down her window so he could greet Armando and tell him he was going to the house with some repair people. Armando opened the gate and the van went on to Angus Lane. As they drove up the driveway, Pat reminded Win to keep his mouth shut from here on out, except to talk to his dogs. They parked at the foot of the hill, a distance from the house and the team streamed out and began unloading their gear.

Chapter 36.

Two of the Gs assembled long black poles with black boxes at their ends. They were the advance people, who stealthily went up to the house and began working around the periphery, crouching and waving their wands. It looked ridiculous. Win nearly jumped out of his skin when he saw a pile of rags suddenly emerge from a nearby clump of trees and come towards them. He noticed the rags were camouflage-patterned and enveloping a person with camouflage paint on his or her face, who came up to Pat and began whispering. Win was about to say something when Pat put her finger over her mouth. His pulse was still racing from the sudden emergence of the rag-person.

The two black-clad wand wavers came back after about ten minutes and gave a thumbs-up sign. Pat whispered, "Okay go in now and get your dogs out. Don't forget, you're telling the dogs what you're going to do about your wife. After that, signal us to come in. We want you to point out where Ortiz went and particularly those items you recall seeing him run his hands over. Remember, you're by yourself and you shouldn't be talking to anyone, unless you're in the habit of talking to yourself."

Win headed towards the garage, which was his usual entryway and then realized that his garage-door opener was in the car. So he headed to the glass front door that had a key lock at its base.

He always had a hard time opening it and hoped he could open it easily today. After several tries, he got it open, which triggered a welcoming round of barking.

"Hi ya doggos! How've you been? Poppa's been away fishing all day and it looks like you missed me. Hey, where's your momma? She must have gone over to Ann and Herky's house. Let's go for a walk before I go over to pick momma up." The dogs got all excited at the mention of a walk and Win led them outside. After they did their things, Win locked them in their fenced-in run and went back into the house.

He went to the front door and waved for Pat and her team to come in. First in were the two wand-wavers. They took a few minutes to go around the house interior and then went to the door to signal in the rest of the team who had an arsenal of electronic gear. Win led Pat back to his study and pointed at his desktop phone and at the small rosewood table alongside the red chair on the other side of his desk. She ran some sort of instrument over the phone and took a reading. She disconnected the phone and then removed its plastic face. She smiled and pointed to something inside that Win couldn't discern. She replaced the piece and reconnected the phone. She next got down on the rug and looked under the table, using a flashlight. She was smiling again when she got up and pointed to the table's underside. Win next led her to the dining room table and pointed to it. She again got down on the floor and used her flashlight to examine the table's underside. She indicated with two fingers that there were two devices under that table. In the meantime, the rest of the team was all over the place, poking around and examining everything. Pat signaled to one guy to come over and pointed at the dining room table. She then took him to Win's study and pointed at the phone and little table. This guy was the fingerprint expert and he proceeded to make a mess, sprinkling powder all over the place

He and others were using cameras to take photos of things all over the house. He noticed that a team went up to the guest bed-room, so he followed. They proceeded to remove one of the small listening devices artfully hidden behind a bedside nightstand. They seemed to smother the device with a soft foam block and then used some sort of spatula-like gizmo to remove it and place it in a foam-lined container. The team was a cross between a circus act and the mime troupe Pat had talked about.

More pictures were taken and fingerprints collected. The whole thing probably didn't take more than an hour. Pat suggested to Win by signals that he and the rest of the team should leave. They all trooped out, leaving Win to lock up, although it probably wasn't necessary with the way his house was supposedly being guarded. They trooped down the hill, reloaded their gear, and piled into the van.

It was only after the engine was started that Pat spoke to Win. "Dr. Sage, your house has been thoroughly bugged by Ortiz. Fortunately, the bugging is for sound but not video. Whoever was interested in bugging your house should have a recording device or listening station nearby, and we'll deal with that tomorrow. We were able to retrieve some nice prints, some of which are, hopefully, those of Ortiz. We took one of the bugs for study back at our lab. The listeners should think that one of their devices is simply non-functioning. Taking it from a lightly trafficked area should reinforce this. They would expect you to remove a bug from an important area like your study if you tumbled to them. Back at the airport, we'll need to get fingerprints from you and your wife, so we can sort out the prints we lifted. All I can say is that somebody is very interested in what you have to say. My advice is for you to be very selective in what you say in your house, and to hold any important conversations outdoors. Dan and I will work out a method for your communicating with us should problems arise." Win then noticed that the young-looking driver was on his way to the airport at breakneck speed again

Chapter 37.

It was 12 miles to the Santa Fe Airport, but the hot-rod driver made it in what seemed like only a few minutes. A guard signaled them to drive out on the runway and over to the same hangar as before. Soon after they pulled up, Dan, Julia, and the gun-toting agent got off the executive jet. Dan pow-wowed briefly with Pat and one of her team members and then came over to Win.

"Well, we were right; your place has been bugged. We'll go ahead with our plan to have you and Julia act as if you're totally unaware of the listening devices. This will allow us more time to implement our damage control and endgame plans. I explained to Julia what happened to you today and its importance to national security. She's still blaming you for getting involved in this business, but is coming around to realizing that the outcome is of great importance to our country. Don't discuss it any more with her because of the bugs."

Win interrupted. "How about talking with her in the car on our way home?"

"We checked the car and it looks clean, but I think you're better off playing it safe."

"So where do we discuss confidential things?"

"The two of you go for a nice walk outdoors with your dogs. We have a team of agents patrolling your house and the surrounding land."

"Was one of that team dressed in camouflage rags? Some person in a rag 'dress' came out of the bushes to talk to Pat and scared the bejesus out of me. I've only seen outfits like that in hunting catalogues."

"Oh yes; some of our team members are wearing ghillies to blend into the landscape. We'll also have your old friends Harry and Suzie arriving tomorrow to visit. They'll call tonight and the story line is that they are unexpectedly in New Mexico and have a few days free. They'd like to see you and can you recommend a hotel in Santa Fe? You'll refuse and say they must stay with you. You have a guest bedroom and it would give you more time together to catch up on old times. They'll communicate with you in writing for important stuff. They're highly experienced agents so you can place your trust in them. Now, for emergencies or if you need to talk with me, Tom or Pat, you're to go outside and walk down to the bottom of your driveway and wave a hand. One of our team will come out to help you. They're equipped with communications devices that aren't dependent on cell-phone towers. If we need to speak to you, someone will come up to get you. You're to leave all doors open so they can get in. They won't speak, but will gesture for you to go outside with them. Despite all this, you and Julia are to act as if nothing bad has happened to you, and pretend that you're still leading your normal lives, even down to your continued interest in Jessica Harvey's disappearance. Only, don't discuss Wong or your friends in Hong Kong any more."

"What about going in to town with my new friends to have lunch or visit the galleries?"

"You continue your normal lifestyle, only Harry goes wherever you go and Suzie goes wherever Julia goes. They'll be inseparable visitors who just can't get enough of you."

"Dan, what do I do with phone calls I receive?"

"You'll have to answer them as if you were unaware of the phone tap and as if today never happened. For example, if you got another call from your friend in Hong Kong, don't tell him about developments here. Just say you're upset that he's so worried about your inquiries. You might play dumb and ask him what he thinks is going on and why he's been told to stop asking around about Wong. Just be creative and give out no new information. Any other questions?"

"Not that I can think of. I'm sure that as soon as I get home, I'll have a zillion."

"If you have questions, just hail one of our team outside your house. Now Pat has a few things to cover with you. She's going to remain in Santa Fe and will be in charge of your protection." With that, Dan raised his beefy hand and waved to get Pat's attention. Dan then told Win, "I need to head off to Los Alamos, but will be available if anything important comes up. I plan to stay in the area until we wrap up this nasty business. Try to relax tonight Win, you've had a rough day."

Pat came over and added, "Dr. Sage, when you get home I want you and your wife to behave as if you're totally unaware of the listening devices in the house. You might have noticed that during our sweep of your house, we placed fluorescent-colored stickers at the sites of the transmitters. These are to remind you that there are transmitters there and you should try to stay away from them when you're talking. You're supposed to be unaware of the bugs, but we want to make the listeners' job harder. Remember, your phones are compromised. So you're to walk a fine line between pretending to be ignorant of the bugging and being crafty in what you say and where you say it. I'm sure you'll adapt to the situation quickly."

"Sure. I have all kinds of hidden talents."

"Okay, you're free to go home now. Here are your car keys, but have Julia drive home. You'll have a car tailing you up to your gatehouse. The inside crew will pick up coverage after that. Don't worry; we'll take good care of you. Just don't do anything foolish to make our job more difficult. I'll talk to you in the morning."

Win went to get Julia and they headed off to their car. Once they were buckled in, Julia completely neglected to follow the FBI's advice and exploded. "Win, what on earth did you get us into? I was told you nearly got killed this morning and now we're prisoners of the F.B.I. in our own home. I knew from the beginning that this Harvey business would turn into a disaster. You aren't a detective and you'll never be one! This guy Tilikso is a fat jerk, and he thinks you're some kind of genius who's cracked one of their major spy cases. I think he's nuts."

"Julia, you know that I was going to drop this investigation, and then Michael called and changed everything. I may have stumbled on to a major espionage case, for all the wrong reasons."

"That's great, but I was looking forward to spending a long, pleasant retirement with you and not as a widow."

"There's not much we can do now. We can't back out without putting ourselves in danger. We're in trouble if we go forward and even bigger trouble if we back out."

"That's what I dislike so much about this, Win. We're becoming pawns of the F.B.I."

"I'm really sorry for this mess, Julia."

Julia wasn't appeased by Win's apology and remained silent for the rest of the ride home. When they got to the gate, he used his remote opener and looked back to see a large SUV stop and turn around. The driver gave a thumbs-up sign as he drove off. As bad as the day had been, it felt comforting to be back on familiar turf. Julia drove up to their house and heard the dogs barking in their run. They went inside took off their jackets, and Win went out to bring in the dogs who acting as if they hadn't seen Win and Julia for days, smothered them with wet kisses and left paw prints all over their clothes.

"Okay doggos, that's enough love for now," Win shouted at them. "Hey Julia, how about a margarita?"

The suggestion seemed to improve her mood. "That's a capital idea! We need to go light on the accompaniments as I made us a really fancy supper."

"What did you make?"

"Old-fashioned spaghetti and meatballs."

"One of my favorites!" Julia made a real production of her meatballs, using beef, veal and pork. Win whipped up a batch of margaritas and went heavy on the tequila this time. They'd had a really bad day and needed stiff drinks. After a silent toast, they sat down with the dogs in the den while eyeing the fluorescent chartreuse marker on the cocktail table. It was like having an unwanted guest for dinner. It was going to be hard to relax, let alone function normally, with bugs all over the house. But Win tried feebly to make normal conversation. "How was your visit to Ann and Herky today?"

"Oh, the usual. Ann is big into her new hobby of painting and Herky is his usual obsessive self about physical activity, but they're very sweet people. We're lucky to have them as neighbors."

Win got up. "I'll go clean up and we can have an early dinner."

"That's a good idea. I'll feed the dogs while you get ready."

Chapter 38.

Win passed his study on the way to the bathroom and noticed the voicemail light blinking on the desk telephone. He went into the study and plopped down into his desk chair. He was beat and starting to feel it; the stiff drink didn't help, either. He picked up the phone as if it was radioactive and dialed the number for voicemail. He had two unheard messages. The first was from Armando at the gatehouse about a UPS package for Julia. The second was a female voice that said, "Dr. Sage, this is Nora Corrado. I'm a fellow in forensic pathology at UNM, and Jim Abel suggested I call you. I'm on call for the Office of the Medical Investigator this weekend and we received an interesting specimen this morning – a finger that's probably from a middle-aged woman. It was found on the San Ildefonso Pueblo. Jim said that you knew a middle-aged woman from Santa Fe that disappeared and, as a long shot, he suggested I give you a call. Please call me if you think this could be related to your missing woman. I'm on call all weekend and my beeper number is 505-432-1511. Thanks."

Win had the feeling this was Jessica Harvey's finger. When it rains, it pours. He needed to talk to his new F.B.I. colleagues before returning the call, but that could wait until after dinner.

Julia and Win had a pleasant dinner in the kitchen, away from any fluorescent stickers. They had some Chianti that went perfectly with the pasta, but the bugs in the house and the day's events cast a pall over everything. Win decided to walk the dogs after they finished dinner and had cleared the table. It would give him an excuse to contact one of his 'keepers' so he could get in touch with Tilikso.

Win put leads on the dogs so they wouldn't take off after the guards. He walked down the hill to the low point of their driveway where it took a dogleg turn. He stopped, waved his arm and waited. It was only a few seconds before a tall guy dressed in black, with paint on his face, came out of the trees. "Dr. Sage, I'm Bob St. Croix, part of the detail guarding you. Is there something I can do for you?" The dogs began growling menacingly at him. They clearly didn't like his looks. Maybe it was his painted face.

"Yes. I need to talk to Dan Tilikso or Tom Shaw about something possibly important."

"Can you do something about your dogs?"

"Why don't I finish walking them and take them back to the house? Then I'll hotfoot it down here to talk with one of the brass, if you can reach them."

"Good idea."

Win finished walking the dogs, took them back to the house, and let them in. He then silently closed the door and made his way back down the drive. The guard was waiting, and escorted him into a clump of junipers. He handed Win a military looking phone and said that Dan was on the line.

Win began, "Hello, Dan?"

"How are things going, Win?"

"It's spooky trying to function in your own house when you know that all sounds are being monitored. I'm even afraid to fart."

"Hang in there, Win. It'll get easier and we should have things wrapped up in a few days."

"Look Dan, I received a voicemail today from one of the fellows in forensic pathology who's on call at the Office of the Medical Investigator in Albuquerque. Win reported to Dan what he had heard and added, "I have a hunch it's Jessica's finger."

"Did the fellow give any details about the finger?"

"All she said was that it was found on the San Ildefonso Pueblo and she thought it belonged to a middle-aged woman."

"Where's the Pueblo located?"

"It's just outside Los Alamos."

"Hmm. That's interesting."

"So, do you want me to call her back? If so, when should I call her and on what telephone, and more importantly, what should I say?"

"I need to discuss this with the rest of our team. It's a little after nine, so why don't you call me again at eleven. I don't think you should call her tonight. It's too late, and we don't want your listeners to sense any urgency about your hunch regarding Ms. Harvey. Talk to you later."

Win walked back to the house and let himself in quietly. He found the dogs and gave them their customary post-walk treats. "Hey doggos," he said, "You're both getting fat from lack of exercise. We're going to have to walk you more. Maybe I'll turn you over to Herky; he'll know how to get you fit."

Julia had had a rough day and was getting ready for bed, so Win retreated to his study. He felt violated by the fluorescent-marked bugs in his study. He was feeling sorry for himself when the phone rang. He picked up and answered, "Hello?"

"Is that you Win?" A loud voice on the other end asked. "This is your long lost friend Harry Glamis, and I'm here in Albuquerque."

Win suddenly remembered the "old friends" that Dan had arranged to have visit and baby-sit them. "Harry, it's been a long time since I heard from you. How's Suzie doing?"

"She's doing well. She's here with me at a convention in Albuquerque."

"Are we going to get a chance to see you on this visit?"

"That's what I was calling about. This meeting's proved to be a bust and we were thinking of leaving early to visit Santa Fe. I'd rather see you and Julia than waste my time at a boring meeting. Could you recommend a good hotel for us in Santa Fe?"

"I know a perfect hotel for you, it's called Chez Nous. There's no way we'd let you stay in town when we have a nice, brand new guest bedroom."

"Are you sure it isn't too much of an imposition?"

"Absolutely not! That way, we get to spend more time with you. We have a lot to catch up on."

"Okay then. We have to attend one more breakfast session tomorrow and then we can leave. How long is the drive up to your place?"

"It's about 65 miles from the center of Albuquerque and the driving time is a little over an hour."

"Would it be all right if we got to your place, say, mid-afternoon?"

"That's fine. We're not planning to do much tomorrow." Win proceeded to give him driving instructions and the procedure for getting through their gate, since it was Sunday and the gatehouse attendant wasn't on duty.

"We'll see you tomorrow afternoon, Win. Give Julia my love."

Win sat back and decided that he and Harry made a pretty good improv team, except this wasn't comedy.

Win made himself busy paying bills and reading medical journals until eleven o'clock rolled around, when he told Julia that he was going to walk the dogs and then call it a night. He also told her of the "great surprise" call from Harry and that he and Suzie would be visiting tomorrow and staying with them.

Win put leads on the dogs and led them out of the house. Before he left, he said loudly, "Okay, dogs, we're going to take a longer walk tonight to start working off that excess weight."

He went down to the rendezvous area and signaled St. Croix, who was waiting. This time, the dogs were interested in getting to know him.

"Hi, has Dan called back yet?"

"His assistant is holding and will fetch him as soon as you get on the line."

"How would you like to walk a couple of dogs? It's distracting to hold onto hyperactive dogs when I'm on the phone."

"You know Doc, dog-walking isn't in my job description, but I'll do it anyway."

"Thanks for your gracious dispensation."

He gave Win the phone and Win inquired about Dan's availability.

Dan's assistant said, "Dr. Sage, hold on while I get Dan. He needed to talk to you."

It was a minute or two before Win heard a familiar voice. "This is Dan. I shared your story with our team and they're split on whether the finger story will prove to be relevant. I'm willing to give you the benefit of the doubt. Here's what we came up with regarding getting back to the forensics fellow. First, don't call her back until tomorrow morning and use your office phone. Second, see what you can learn about the finger without appearing to probe too much. Your questions might tip off the listeners that you think this is Jessica's finger. Third, we'd like to know how the finger was dismembered and whether they were able to get a fingerprint. Ask if they're interested in doing any DNA testing to see if this is Harvey's finger. Also, try to find out how they decided the finger belonged to a middle-aged woman and try to get more information on precisely where the finger was found. You could tell her about Harvey's description and her disappearance, but gloss over any connection with her ceramics business or Wong. If the fellow is young and inexperienced she might want to gab with you about all aspects of the case, so encourage her to volunteer as much detail as possible. Just be the patient listener and mentoring faculty member. How does that sound?"

"That sounds fine. Incidentally, I got a call tonight from Harry Glamis. He and his wife Suzie will be staying with us and will arrive tomorrow afternoon."

"That's good. I'm sorry we couldn't get them to you sooner; they're flying in from Europe. Try to get a good night's sleep and I hope you snore loudly to keep your listeners occupied. Give me a follow up after your call to the fellow tomorrow. Ciao."

Win went looking for the guard and the dogs. He saw them way ahead at the end of the driveway. The dogs were clearly in command and taking him for a nice walk. Win ran down to meet them.

"Here's your phone back. It looks like the dogs have taken you for quite a walk.""They're nice dogs, but they do have a mind of their own."

"Well thanks for the dog-sitting. I'm going to head back to the house and turn in for the night. By the way, how many of you are in the detail watching us?"

"There are eight of us here in the vicinity of your house. Don't worry, we have you and your wife covered like a blanket."

"Incidentally, I'm going to need to get in touch with Dan again tomorrow morning."

"No problem!"

"See you in the morning. Okay doggos, let's head home and tuck you in for the night." The dogs led Win up the hill and into the house. He was exhausted and the pulling dogs helped him get home. This had been one of the longest days of Win's life.

Chapter 39.

Julia and Win slept late, or at least as late as the dogs would allow them. At about 8:45 A.M. the dogs started whimpering and when the whimpers brought no response, they began to bark. Win rolled out of bed and shouted, "Okay you demanding dogs, I'm coming."

Win washed up, got dressed, walked the dogs on leads, and picked up the Sunday paper. He decided he'd wait until 10 A.M. before calling the pathology fellow. He didn't want to wake her too early, since he suspected that being on call as a pathology fellow didn't mean getting up early on Sundays. After all, you don't usually make rounds on dead patients or body parts. So he turned on the television to catch the Sunday morning talk shows while making coffee and waiting.

Win was on his second cup of coffee and absorbed in the paper when he realized it was after ten. Julia hadn't stirred yet, so he decided to let her sleep on. As Dan suggested, Win went to his study to use the phone there. He jotted down a list of the questions he'd like to ask Corrado and then dialed her pager number and entered his telephone number as prompted. About 10 minutes later, the phone rang and he grabbed it after one ring so as not to wake Julia.

"Hello, this is Dr. Corrado; you just paged me."

"Yes. This is Dr. Winston Sage. You left me a voicemail yesterday about a human finger and whether it might be related to a missing woman from Santa Fe."

"Oh yes. We had this unusual specimen submitted to us and were puzzled by it. Jim Abel, my boss, thought I should call you about it."

"I'm a new member of the Pathology Department and saw Jim at Grand Rounds and asked him if there were any unidentified bodies that might be my neighbor's wife."

"What can you tell me about this missing person?"

"Her name is Jessica Harvey and she's a 48 year-old Caucasian. She disappeared about a month and a half ago with no trace. She's five-foot-seven and weighs about 130 pounds, and is a natural brunette with blonde-dyed hair. I'm not sure the last information is relevant to your find."

"Well, what we received from the local sheriff's office is an index finger from a person's left hand. It was severed by a heavy, sharp instrument, probably an axe. There was some crushing of the bone on the dorsum, but it was clean cut through the bone."

"What makes you think the finger belongs to a woman?"

"The finger was decomposed and appears to have been nibbled on by an animal, probably a rodent, but it had an attached fingernail. It seemed manicured and had traces of nail polish on it."

"What color nail polish?" Win asked.

"It's a pink – more like a pale, silvery pink color."

Win wrote everything down and asked, "Is there any way of telling the age of the person who lost her finger?"

"We x-rayed the finger and found some evidence of osteoarthritis. That suggests the person was at least middle-aged or did a lot of physical labor using her hands. The nail polish suggests that repetitive physical labor probably wasn't the cause."

"That's interesting. Was there any tissue left to study?"

"Unfortunately, there wasn't enough skin left to get a fingerprint or to assess age-related skin changes. We certainly have enough material available for DNA typing. That's why Jim suggested I call you. He thought you could tell us how we can contact the missing woman's family so we could get a sample of her DNA."

"How do you do that, when she's disappeared?" Win asked, playing dumb.

"Oh, we try to get some cells from a toothbrush or a hairbrush and then we use PCR to amplify the DNA we find."

"That's amazing stuff. Did you want me to try to get the DNA for you?"

"I wasn't thinking of it, but that would probably expedite things."

"I don't want to alarm her husband if it turns out to be someone else's finger."

"I guess you could tell him it's a very long-shot."

"By the way, how was the finger found?"

"The story we got from the sheriff is that the finger was found on the San Ildefonso Pueblo. Two teenage boys were out playing on the rez, when their dog started acting strangely. They went over to see what the problem was and saw the dog digging at the finger. The guys recognized it as a human finger, so they went home and called the police. The police came out and investigated the site and found no other body parts or any instrument that could have been used to amputate the finger. They suspect someone might have been murdered and then dismembered, so they forwarded the specimen to us."

"Is there any way of estimating how long the finger had been out there?"

"That's what I've been assigned to investigate and it's not easy. I would estimate that it wasn't much longer than a month or two."

"Does this sort of thing, I mean finding disarticulated fingers, happen often?"

"Jim's been at this business for a long time, and he's seen only one other case like it. It involved a crazy guy who killed his wife and then decided to cut her up into a lot of little pieces."

"By the way, what should I try to get for you by way of specimens from the missing lady?"

The fellow gave Win detailed instructions for what to obtain and how to collect and package the materials for shipment to the lab in Albuquerque. The OMI facility had regular courier service to and from Santa Fe, the state capital, so they would retrieve the material from Win.

After the call, Win went back to the den and was accosted by the dogs that hadn't had their post-breakfast walk. He'd completely forgotten to walk them and realized that this gave him great cover for going down the hill to contact Dan. "Okay doggos, your poppa forgot to walk you so we'll tale a nice long walk to make up for it," Win said near one of the listening devices. He put leashes on the dogs and headed down the driveway. He stopped at the bottom and waved. A camouflage-dressed person came out of a camouflaged tent that had been assembled in an arroyo. There was a matching camouflaged port-a-john behind it.

"Good morning, Dr. Sage. Did you get a good night's sleep?" It was Pat and not Bob St. Croix, who was probably getting some rest.

"Not really. I kept waking up feeling anxious."

"We did some checking and found the monitoring station for your bugs, which are ultra-high tech. To keep them small and un-noticeable they had to compromise on their range. We thought they would opt for a recorder somewhere in the vicinity of your house, but that's not the case. Instead, they're using a van parked on Buckman Road, adjacent to your subdivision. They got hold of a CenturyLink van so it looks like they're doing some sort of line repairs. That's pretty risky, but gives them excellent reception."

"Who's the 'them' that are involved?"

"It's not going to be anyone from the Chinese diplomatic contingent, but more likely a contractor they hired for the job, like your Sgt. Ortiz probably is. The Chinese would operate with a couple of layers of intermediaries between themselves and the contractors so you couldn't readily trace things back to them. They must be very worried about you to take such big risks. "

"I don't think I'm much to worry about, but I am finding this experience very annoying and frightening. I still can't believe what happened yesterday."

"You worry too much, Win. We're getting everything under control. Let's get Dan on the phone; he's been waiting for you."

She led Win and the two dogs down into the arroyo. The dogs were getting used to the strangers and behaved themselves for a change. Pat got Dan on the phone after a short wait and passed the receiver over to Win, who filled Dan in on what he'd learned from the pathologist about the finger. Dan listened carefully.

"You know, Win," he said, "the woman's finger may have been cut off to prevent anyone from identifying her by fingerprints. We're dealing here with either a madman or someone who really wanted the victim to disappear permanently. Do you think you can get Harvey to give access to his wife's things for DNA identification?"

"I think so. Why wouldn't he?"

"By the way, we're hoping to get everything wrapped up by the end of the week."

"Should I offer to go over to Bill's house to look for sources of his wife's DNA? If so, when should I contact him?"

"Those are good questions Win. I'll hold off answering until after Harry and Suzie arrive and we can discuss strategy. They're going to take you out for dinner tonight. Unfortunately, dinner won't be at one of the posh watering holes in town, but at a non-descript safe house. The food will be takeout pizza or the like. We're on an austerity budget at the Bureau."

"Okay, Julia prefers pepperoni and I prefer sausage. We both prefer thick crusts and Diet Coke for our drinks."

"We're not running a pizzeria, Sage!"

"Too bad."

"Win, would you please put Pat on the line? I need to go over some things with her."

Win got Pat to the phone and took off to finish walking the dogs. He was pleased to find Julia up and about when he got back, and wondered whether they could still salvage some part of their usual Sunday routine.

The rest of Sunday turned out to be pretty routine. Win prepared brunch, preceded by a bloody Mary that made them feel more relaxed, as they unwound from the danger and tension of the previous day. Julia put some music on and Win curled up in his reclining chair with a book and within five minutes was fast asleep and snoring gently, so Julia left him to do some work on a manuscript she was trying to finish. In the mid-afternoon the phone rang, waking Win from his Sunday nap. He answered and was greeted by a loud, excited voice.

"Hey Win, Suzie and I are near the outskirts of Santa Fe on I-25. How long should it take us from here?"

"Oh, about 15 minutes."

"Hey, we thought we'd splurge and take you out for dinner tonight in town. We don't want you and Julia to go through any trouble so we called ahead and made reservations."

"That sounds terrific," Win fibbed, knowing the 'splurge' was a pizza dinner in a modest house in a nondescript neighborhood. "We're anxious to see you after all these years."

Thirty minutes later there was a call from Harry at the subdivision gate. Win buzzed him in and gave him directions to their house. A big tan SUV pulled up at the house, and out popped a heavyset, tall, gray-haired, fiftyish-looking guy and a tall, lean, fiftyish-looking blonde woman.

Win went outside to greet the couple he presumed to be Harry and Suzie. "Well at long last we get to see you two again!"

Julia emerged from the house and exclaimed, "Look who's here; Harry and Suzie! After all these years it's so good to see you."

Win and Julia knew there were no listening devices outside the house but were hamming it up to get into the swing of the charade.

Harry whispered to Win, "You two are overplaying your parts. Why don't you let us in and take us to the guest room."

"You know, you're the first guests to stay with us. Let me get one of those bags for you," Win said as he grabbed a dufflebag. "Follow me." So Win led them to the guest bedroom; it was the one where the Gs had lifted the single listening device planted there.

Win left the two to unpack and clean up. The dogs were excited about having guests and greeted them exuberantly. After about five minutes Harry and Suzie appeared in the living room. "You've got great views from the guest room. How much land do you have, Win? It looks like a huge lot."

"We have a little over 14 acres, so we have lots of privacy."

"Hey, why don't you take us on a tour of your land before it gets dark? Maybe I should refer to it as your 'ranch'; that's a lot of acreage!"

"Okay, but put on some heavy shoes. We have some low growing cacti with very nasty thorns, to say nothing of the occasional rattlesnake."

They went back to the bedroom and emerged a few minutes later with sturdy hiking boots in hand. "Will these do, Win?" Suzie asked.

"They look perfect. I'll leave the dogs behind so we can chat better."

The foursome went outside for a walk and headed down the driveway towards the bend. They stopped and waited, and before long Pat and one of her team members emerged from their almost-invisible lean-to. She and Harry walked off by themselves for a short distance having a serious discussion. After a few minutes, Harry rejoined the group and suggested they walk down to the road. Harry and Suzie walked ahead and started scampering over the hilly terrain adjacent to the road. They seemed to be interested in lines-of-sight to the house. After about ten minutes the "old friends" rejoined Win and Julia.

Harry said, "Your house is on a hillside and pretty exposed from the road. It would be a good idea for you to keep away from windows facing the road."

Suzie piped up, "A skilled marksman could easily climb over the low subdivision fencing, hike over here, climb a hill, and get a clear shot at your house. So, I suggest you stay away from all windows, not just those facing the road."

"We're sure getting circumscribed in our activities," Win said. "We can't speak meaningfully in the house anymore, and now we can't even look out any windows. You know there aren't too many parts of our house that don't have large windows. Do you really think the Chinese would try to shoot me in my house?"

Harry put his arm around Win's shoulder and said, "They tried to kill you once, and you now present more of a danger to them since you've identified your would be assassin."

"The whole damn thing seems unreal. All I did was look for my neighbor's missing wife!"

Harry reassured Win that it was only a few days more that he would have to put up with this restrictive protection. "Now why don't we change and head into town for dinner with Dan Tilikso."

Chapter 40.

They made lots of phony small-talk about how they were looking forward to dinner together, then changed and went outside where Harry suggested they take his SUV and that he drive.

Win sat up front with Harry, giving him directions into town and Harry frequently checking the mirrors. Harry had a map and a GPS finder to get to the safe house after they reached St. Francis Street. It was in a part of town Win hadn't visited before, one with lots of old, small adobe houses that looked like a picture postcard of Santa Fe at the turn of the 20th Century. They pulled into an alleyway alongside the safe house so narrow they could barely open the car doors. Another car immediately pulled in behind them and Dan came out to usher them inside the darkened house. He turned up the lighting once they were all in.

"Looks like the gang's all here," he announced. "It's good to see you, Suzie and Harry; we need your help. We've got a lot of ground to cover tonight, so why don't we eat first." He nodded to Win and said, "We have some pizza in the kitchen, exactly as you ordered, Win, and beer and Diet Coke".

"So you are running a pizzeria," Win retorted.

"Not exactly, as you'll learn after dinner."

After dinner they had coffee and moved to a cozy living room with a latilla ceiling and kiva fireplace. Win noticed that Tom, Pat and the lady with a gun from the airplane had joined them. They sat around a large table covered with a floral plastic tablecloth.

Dan began the meeting: "We're making good progress in sorting out this case. As you know, we've had longstanding suspicions about a spy at Los Alamos, but came up with nothing in the past. Win's suspicion has helped us to focus attention on Wong's work and whether any of it's been leaked. It turns out he's a VIP at the labs and is privy to some of their most critical nuclear secrets. If he's a spy, he's a potential goldmine for the Chinese.

We began by checking out the antique Chinese ceramics part of the story and hit pay dirt. Our Hong Kong agents investigated Wong's father and can confirm Win's theory that the story is a fiction. The agents also confirmed the story about a PRC general's excavation of some ancient tombs. This general happens to be one of the top guys in their intelligence service.

Working on the U.S. side, we found the Harveys' volume of business has recently escalated dramatically from their Chinese ceramics sales. We also sent out a team with search dogs to comb the area where the finger was found and they came up with a dismembered thumb with a remaining nail and traces of polish, but not enough tissue to get a fingerprint; it's likely from the same woman. They found no other body parts. We haven't found any unusually large amounts of money in Wong's financial accounts, and he hasn't reported any foreign bank accounts on his tax returns."

Win interrupted Tilikso: "Remember, I told you that Wong was depositing checks from the Harveys in a Cayman Islands bank account."

"I do, but we need to know which bank he used, and even then, we'll have a hassle getting access to any information," Dan responded. "There are good reasons people like to park hot money there. If we find an account, we could have him on tax evasion charges."

"I've got it," Win exclaimed as he retrieved his beat-up PDA. He found the entry and passed it over to Dan. "Here's the name of the bank and the account number; it was on the back of one of Harvey's checks to Wong. Also, you can figure out the amount of money

Wong received from the East-West Gallery's accounting books, and Bill has been saving cancelled checks to Wong."

"Good job, Win," Dan exclaimed, as he once again slapped his thick thigh. Win was beginning to wonder if Dan had a callus on his thigh from all the slapping. "We're trying to confirm that the ceramics were passed to Wong by the PRC, before he got Jessica to sell them to raise money for himself. Her disappearance could be related to her realization that Wong was using her as a fence. We'll need to get samples of Harvey's DNA to try and match it to the severed fingers, although I still think that's a long-shot. What do you think, Win?"

Win answered, "I bet the fingers are Jessica's. I don't know why; maybe it's the nail polish." He got up and went to the kitchen to fetch a Coke; he needed some caffeine.

Dan went on with his soliloquy: "At this point, we believe it's unlikely Wong himself killed Jessica, let alone hacked her up, assuming the fingers are hers. I wonder if the gent who tried to kill Win yesterday also did Jessica in. The most salient thing is that Wong must be very important to the Chinese for them to use a diplomat to try to kill Win. The bugging of Win's house is another exceptionally risky measure. It's probably not just the loss of access to secrets from Wong that worries them, but our being able to backtrack and find out what he gave them. There's also the concern about a front-page story on Chinese espionage involving our nuclear secrets that must have the PRC intelligence people squirming. Our protectionist lobby would just love such a story to support their attacks on trade and currency exchange with China. In any event, we need to move things along rapidly to keep the Chinese off guard and to investigate all the details so we can roll up Wong and whatever accomplices he might have. We don't think Wong's a flight risk. Those are my thoughts. I'll turn the discussion over to Tom and Pat so they can outline their plans for the next few days."

Tom, who had shed his tie, went first and succinctly described how he planned to get DNA samples from the Harveys' household. Dan nodded and said, "So now let's get to the next issue which is how to keep Win busy, with Harry in tow, while we work out the endgame. Pat, what are your thoughts?"

Pat started by asking, "What are your usual activities Win?"

"Well, I've developed several routines. On Tuesdays I go into town for lunch with my neighbor Herky. We vary where we eat and then Herky goes off to run errands and I usually visit Canyon Road to tour the art galleries. I used my Tuesdays to play detective by bugging Harvey and asking questions about the Harveys at other galleries. Let's see, I also regularly do the Friday evening gallery crawl with my neighbor George DeLeon, who's nuts about art, particularly modern art. Most galleries have their new show openings early on Friday evenings, and people usually go from gallery to gallery. George is addicted to the crawl, and I'm rapidly following suit. I mostly like to 'people watch' at the openings. I also try to get down to the University once a week to keep up with my research team."

Pat said, "We'll need to have you cut down on some activities. For starters, do you really need to go to Albuquerque this week? I don't like long periods of exposure on the highways."

"That's an easy one to defer."

Pat went on. "Keep seeing your friends. It'll give the impression that it's business as usual for you and also won't alert your friends to anything unusual going on. Do you think they'd mind if Harry tagged along? We need to keep him glued to you?"

"I don't think they'd mind at all, so long as Harry can tolerate their idiosyncrasies. They're quite different."

"We wouldn't expect anything less of your friends."

Dan piped up, "Pat, let's stick to business, please. We'll have Win continue his usual forays into town with his buddies. He'll otherwise stay at home. Is that okay Win?"

"That's fine with me."

Dan looked at Win and said, "We have a challenging task coming up for you, Win. We're planning to have you visit Wong and confront him about how you think that the story of his inheritance is bogus and you suspect that he's been spying for the Chinese. We'll have you wearing a wire to record the conversation. We need to get information to do some damage control before we make arrests. You'll go in on your own, but we'll prep you well and we don't think he'll do you harm. We're sure that he and his Chinese controllers consider you a loner and a rank amateur, so he might be more forthcoming with you than with us. It's low probability, but we have nothing to lose since we'll wrap things up shortly after the visit. Are you willing to do this?"

Win thought for a moment and said, "I don't think Wong's capable of doing me harm, at least directly, but I'm not optimistic about getting anything out of him. Assuming he's a spy, he's probably been at it for a long time and I don't think he's going to easily shed the protective armor he's been wearing. But I'm willing to give it a try."

"Good!" Dan responded. "Now let's turn to some loose ends that puzzle us. The story of the Chinese diplomat attempting to shoot you bothers us. Think about it: if he shot you and left you there, it would really complicate the concealment of Wong as a spy. A murder investigation would probably lead to the fact that you were investigating the disappearance of another person, and if he killed you and tried to make you disappear like Jessica Harvey, it would have the same results. Are you sure he was going to shoot you?"

Win looked up at the ceiling and said, "Look, he pointed a very large gun at my face and said 'Goodbye Dr. Sage.' I wasn't hallucinating! My friend Chuck also saw the gun and took it out of the unconscious guy's hand. The gun's hammer was cocked, to boot."

"You know, we never found the gun and he was unconscious when the rescue team arrived."

"Of course you wouldn't find it because I took it. I was afraid he would come to and take a shot at me before I got away."

"Why didn't you tell us that?"

Win grinned at Shaw and said, "Because no one asked me."

"Where's the gun now?"

"In a plastic bag in the back of my car, where I left it when Chuck and I fled the crime scene."

Dan guffawed, slapped his thigh, and said, "You never cease to amaze me, Sage." He then leaned over towards Shaw, who sat there red-faced, and said, "Tom, we need to get the gun over to the nearest crime lab ASAP!" At that, Tom got up and went to the next room to place a call.

Would you tell me what the gun looked like?" Dan asked.

"Sure, it seemed rather big and the guy carried it firmly against his thigh. It had a long attachment to the barrel -- maybe a silencer."

Dan went on to another topic. "I'm still puzzled about Harvey coming to you about his wife's disappearance. He didn't give the police all the information he had, yet he tried to bring you in as another investigator, but since you're inexperienced with crime investigation what does he gain by getting you involved?"

"That's a question I've asked myself," Win answered. "It doesn't make sense. At first I thought he might be trying to deflect attention away from the real reason for her disappearance by getting some-one to focus on possible medical reasons. I possibly represented a safe way for him to pursue his wife's disappearance without fear of going to jail for being an accessory to spying. He's really upset about his wife, so I'm not sure he had a rational strategy for why he got me involved."

Dan nodded and said, "It's getting late and we've covered a lot. You should head home so you can get an early start tomorrow."

Win looked around for Julia and suddenly realized she hadn't said a thing tonight. She was fast asleep, having parked herself with a book in an overstuffed armchair in front of the fireplace that now contained glowing embers. Win shook her gently awake and whis-pered, "It's rise-and-shine time, kiddo. We need to go home. She got up groggily, said goodbyes to everybody and then headed to the car. They were all tired and remained silent on the way home, except for when Win gave the occasional driving directions to Harry.

Chapter 41.

Win got up earlier than usual and was in the kitchen making coffee when Harry came in. "Good morning Harry. I don't know whether you heard the coyotes howling last night. They made a real ruckus and can sound very eerie."

"I was so tired, I didn't hear a thing."

"We have some orange juice in the refrigerator in the pantry. Help yourself and I'll get the coffee going. We didn't have time to do any shopping for your visit, so you'll have to make do with our healthy, but untasty, diet. "

"I wouldn't expect a breakfast of bacon and eggs in the home of two doctors."

"Okay then, I'll make us some egg white omelets, with refried beans and some toast, whole grain of course."

Win turned on the small television in the kitchen to catch up on the news. It also generated extraneous sound to make the unknown listeners' job a bit harder. Win took out a pad and scribbled a note for Harry that read, "I'll wait until 8:00 o'clock to call Bill Harvey. What do you think?"

Harry nodded.

They had a pleasant breakfast while watching the news and reading the paper, but with little conversation, as both felt constrained by the bugs in the house. After a while, Harry tapped his watch to signal that the appointed hour had arrived. Win led Harry to his study and sat down behind his desk. Harry was to listen in to the conversation on an extension phone. He gave Harry a "thumbs up" sign and dialed the number. It seemed like forever before Bill answered.

"Hello." Bill sounded like he'd been sleeping.

"Bill, this is Win Sage. I'm sorry to call you so early, but something has come up in my search for Jessica."

Bill perked up and said cautiously, "I hope it's not bad news."

"I hope not. Do you remember that I'd spoken with the State's Medical Investigator a couple of times about Jessica?"

"Yes and I was encouraged that there were no unidentified bodies in the State." Bill was perking up.

"Well, someone found a finger from a woman a few days ago up in the Jemez Mountains. The MI remembered my story and asked one of his people to contact me on the remote possibility that it could be Jessica's."

"Oh my God, I hope it's not!"

"Well, we need to find that out for you and the quicker the better, so we can put your fears to rest."

"What can we do?"

"What I'd like to do is come over to your house this morning to collect possible sources of Jessica's DNA. Usually things like toothbrushes or hairbrushes are used; they contain tiny amounts of a person's cells. Would that be okay?"

"Sure."

"When can I come by? I have an old friend visiting and he has a complete day of sightseeing planned for us, so the earlier we can do it the better."

"Well how about in an hour; say, 9 o'clock?"

"That would be fine. Remember, there's only a remote possibility that this is related to Jessica."

"Okay, I'll see you later."

Harry gave Win a thumbs-up sign and smiled. Win and Harry went back to the kitchen for refills on coffee and then settled in the den. Win selected a CD and turned on the hi-fi system.

"Harry, let me know if you want anything more for breakfast. Looks like Suzie and Julia aren't up yet."

"What's that you're playing?"

"Oh that's a piece by one of my favorite modern composers, Henryk Gorecki. It's his Symphony Number 3, The Symphony of Sorrowful Songs."

"It sure is sorrowful, and monotonous too. You can use it as a cure for insomnia. Your taste in music hasn't changed much after all these years, Win."

"The more things change, the more things remain the same; it's an old French saying."

"No kidding."

Before they knew it, 9 o'clock was near and Win said that they should head over to Harvey's house. "We'll have to postpone our trip to town, since the women aren't up yet. I'll leave them a note letting them know where we went."

When they got outside Harry said, "You drive, Win; it's OK for you to drive inside your subdivision."

They pulled up to a large, sprawling house built in what's known locally as Pueblo-revival style. They went up to the heavily carved, double, wooden door and rang the bell. Bill, who was still dressed in a bathrobe and hadn't shaved, came to greet them looking disheveled.

"Hi, Bill. This is my old friend Harry Glamis who's visiting. I hope you don't mind my bringing him along."

"No, that's fine. Glad to meet you, Harry. Win, do you think there's a real chance that the finger could belong to Jessie?"

"As I told you earlier, it's a remote possibility, but we have no choice other than to rule out that it's hers. Remember the time the police called you to look at some woman's body? That's the way coroners operate. I thought it might be easier if I helped with this process."

"Thanks, Win. You've been a great help."

Win put his arm around Bill's shoulder and asked where they might find some of Jessica's personal items like her toothbrush and hairbrush. Bill led them back to the master suite. On the way, Win took in the opulent southwestern and Indian décor, as well as some very fine ancient Chinese ceramics.

"Win, this is the master bath. Jessie and I have separate sink areas and this is hers." He pointed to the larger of the two areas.

"Win walked over to Jessica's sink and asked, "Are these her toothbrush and things?"

"Yeah. They're just as she left them."

"Is it all right if I borrow them for the Medical Investigator's Office? They'll return them, of course."

"Sure, why not?"

"Mind if I look around a bit to see if there are any other items that might have some of her DNA on them?"

"Go ahead."

Win examined the sink area and found nothing that he thought was of potential value. He looked next in the small wastebasket by her sink. He saw some used dental floss that could be a source of cells and retrieved it with a pair of tweezers from the counter. He didn't see any signs of nail polish or a manicure kit.

"Bill, does Jessica use nail polish?"

"Yeah, she almost always wears nail polish."

"Did she do her own nails?"

"Not recently. She used to go out once a week or so to get her nails done."

"Do you know where she had them done?"

"No, but Angela, our gallery manager, would know. She goes to the same place."

"Do you remember what color polish Jessica was wearing when she disappeared?"

"I'm not sure, but I think it was some sort of pink. Why do you ask?"

"Since we're dealing with a woman's finger, there could be traces of nail polish on it. Bill, I'm going to borrow Jessica's brushes and comb, as well as some dental floss in the trashcan and some pieces of her dirty laundry in the hamper, if that's O.K."

"Just go ahead. We need to do this and it's a lot easier for me having you handle things."

Win took out several zip-lock bags and loaded them with the items he selected. From the dirty laundry in her hamper he pulled a couple of pairs of panties, a bra and some socks. He picked the bra and socks to shield his selection of the panties, which made him feel like a pervert with a fetish for women's undergarments. He looked over towards Harry for any signals about items he might have overlooked and Harry barely moved his head from side to side to signal, "no."

"Well, Bill, that's all we need to wrap up this horrible business. I hope there's no connection with Jessica. By the way, have you heard anything more from the police?"

"Not a thing, Win. You seem to be the only one who has any interest in finding her. The situation is grim. She's been gone for almost two months now and that's not a good sign. That's why your phone call got me really worried."

"I'm sorry to put you through this. Let me know if I can be of any help."

Bill walked them to the door and let them out. When Win and Harry got in the car, Win asked what he thought.

"This guy is so upset that I couldn't get any feel for how knowledgeable or complicit he really is. His house is very expensively built and he has a lot of fancy-looking art. By the way, you have a knack for improvisation. Well done, Win!"

"You know, what's odd is that he hasn't done his wife's laundry since her disappearance or cleaned her trash. Oh well, how do we get these specimens off to some DNA lab?"

"Well, first you need to call the fellow at the MI's office to let her know you've collected the specimens. To cover your previous phone call, ask her how you can get the specimens to her. Get the instructions and we'll take over. We also need to visit Dan and the crew again at the safe house. So when we go back to your house, we'll talk up our 'sightseeing' trip to town. It should be another interesting day."

Chapter 43.

When they got back to the house, the two women were up and in the midst of preparing a more elaborate breakfast than Win had rustled up. They made lots of invented small talk and hyped up their fictional sightseeing agenda for the day. Win fed the dogs and walked them again on leashes with no sign of any of his watchers. He guessed that now that Harry and Suzie were here, the guards could loosen up a bit on their coverage or else they were dug in and well camouflaged. In any event, he felt secure.

Win went back to his study to use the tapped telephone to call the forensic pathology fellow about his DNA collection. He dialed her pager number and got shunted to a voicemail box. He left a message that he had collected some potential DNA sources from Jessica Harvey and that he would try to reach her later from his cell phone, since he was going out.

They tidied up and headed off to town. Harry again suggested that he drive in his car and Win didn't object. Win really didn't like driving in New Mexico; too many people drove recklessly. On the way in, Julia, who was getting cabin fever, arranged with Suzie to go a local bookstore. She loved to look at magazines and she really didn't want to be involved with this whole mess. So Win directed Harry to the bookstore, where they dropped the two ladies off, and the two men headed off to the safe house. They pulled into the narrow alleyway and went in through the back door. Win carried a brown paper shopping bag with the Jessica Harvey specimens. The "usual suspects" were there, as well as a new guy.

Dan greeted them: "How did things go this morning with Harvey?"

Harry answered first. "I thought it went well. Harvey's a bag of raw nerves and Win maneuvered him nicely without getting him more upset. Win was creative and collected a bunch of possible sources of the wife's DNA. The Harvey house is pretty fancy and they have a lot of expensive looking art."

Win added, "Bill was very cooperative. I suspect he'll be sitting on pins and needles until we get the DNA results. His wife did use nail polish, but didn't do her own nails. He thought she was wearing pink nail polish at the time of her disappearance. Bill didn't know where his wife had her nails done, but thought it was the same place where his manager, Angela, had her nails done. I could phone the gallery and ask Angela for the name of the manicure place or Harry and I could stop in the gallery tomorrow when we go in to town with my friend Herky. I was planning to tour Canyon Road and its galleries as I usually do on Tuesdays. It's your call."

"Let me think about it for a few minutes," Dan responded. He went on, nodding towards the new face in the crowd, "Win, this is Dave Fendji. He's Chief of Security for the Department of Energy. Energy has jurisdiction over the Los Alamos National Labs and the other nuclear labs around the country. Needless to say, he's very interested in our friend Wong. Let's all go into the living room and talk. Would you like anything to drink?"

"Do you have any beer left from our pizza dinner?" Win asked.

Tom Shaw got up and said, "I think so, let me go see. Anyone else for a drink?"

Harry asked for a coke and the others remained quiet. Tom came back in short order with the drinks.

As Win took a long, first swig, Fendji began: "Dr. Sage I really appreciate what you've done in alerting us to Wong as a possible spy. As Dan told you, we've had long-standing suspicions about leakage of top secrets from Los Alamos to the Chinese. We've had no success in finding out what those secrets are or who might be leaking them. As you may know, a couple of years ago we thought we'd found the suspected mole, who was another Chinese-American. It turned out that he may have committed some minor breaches of security, but he wasn't the big-league spy we were after. I understand you've signed an oath of confidentiality so I can share these things with you. Just remember that what you hear from me is highly confidential, and if you ever leak any of it you're heading for the slammer."

Win interrupted, "You know, I don't like being threatened. I did sign a confidentiality agreement, but I also have some common sense and wouldn't go blabbering about this affair. This is serious business for our country and I happen to like the U.S. a lot."

"Sorry if I gave you the wrong impression."

"You sure did," Win muttered under his breath.

"Dan briefed me on you story about Wong, but I have a few more questions to ask you. First, what was your general impression of him and his feelings about LANL?"

"Well, he made a big point about how much he loved his work and how grateful he was to LANL for giving him the opportunity to pursue his love of physics. He even commented, if I recall correctly, that he thought the U.S. was a great country in that it gave immigrants like him incredible career opportunities."

"Which brings me to my next question: did he ever say anything that sounded anti-American or critical of our government?"

"Au contraire! He implied that his father was very bitter about the Communist takeover of China and that he was too."

"I hear you're pretty good with hunches. After talking to Wong twice, did you have any hunches that he was a spy or harbored any resentment of the U.S. or admiration of the Chinese?"

"After my two visits with him, I had none at all, except that I thought Jessica's disappearance was somehow related to the Chinese ceramics Wong helped her obtain. I didn't even have a hunch that he was lying about how he came by his trove of antiques. I did initially have some skepticism about the reasons he gave for helping

Jessica. But my real doubts started when my friends in Hong Kong couldn't confirm the story about his family. Then a call from my friend in Hong Kong to warn me off, clinched my suspicion that Wong was up to no good and was potentially a Chinese spy. But nothing about Wong initially suggested he might be betraying the U.S."

"Did he tell you anything about his work at LANL?"

"Nothing other than that he worked in physics."

"Is there anything else that you can think of about Wong that might be of help to us?"

"Nothing, unfortunately."

Fendji shook his head. "I'm disappointed in you Dr. Sage; I thought you'd figured out more than that."

Win could barely contain himself. "Mr. Benjo, I've been investigating Wong for a few weeks and have identified him as the leading candidate for your LANL mole. How many years have you and your troop of jokers been looking for this spy? As a U.S. citizen, I'm extremely disappointed by your incompetence. You know, Wong has probably been leaking secrets to the Chinese for a long time and no one has had the slightest inkling of it."

Dan intervened, "Win, please cool down. His name is Fendji."

"He's a benjo to me!"

Dan went on: "Look, why don't' we take a break. I have to make a call." Win sat and glowered at Fendji while sipping his beer.

Dan came back smiling and said, "I was just on the phone with our lab guys, who checked out the gun you took from your would-be assassin. Do you remember my questions about whether the Chinese diplomat really was going to shoot you? Well, my hunch turned out to be right. The gun involved is not an ordinary gun, but one fitted with a cylinder over the barrel that was for shooting you with a liquid or gas that was probably a poison of some sort. The gun part was likely necessary to propel compressed gas at you through the cylinder and get the substance injected through your skin without any needle marks. That makes the story a lot more plausible."

"I didn't think my story was implausible. I just described what happened to me and I had a witness."

"Sorry, Win. I should have said your interpretation of what was going to happen to you. You're getting a bit touchy. Maybe you and Harry should take the rest of the day off and drive up to Taos."

"That sounds like a good idea, but first I need to get back to the gun issue. Did you mean that the Chinese guy was not going to shoot me with a bullet, but with some sort of spray?"

"Yes. A lot of assassinations have been committed over recent years by compressed gas devices that shoot a small aerosol of poison with enough force to penetrate the skin, usually leaving no mark. The toxin used is generally very hard to identify and leads to death from what looks like natural causes at autopsy, most often a heart attack. The old Eastern Bloc countries used to be masters at this type of assassination. We'll have to wait and see what the cylinder contains. In any event, it was definitely not a silencer as you thought, except that it would have silenced you!"

"Ha! Ha!" Win retorted. "It looks like I've graduated from playing beanbag to hardball."

"And that's why we're taking your safety so seriously. Harry and Suzie and the rest of the Gs watching over you are some of our best. Remember that for them to perform at their best you have to cooperate with us fully. Got it?"

"Got it, loud and clear! Oh, one other thing: what about finding out about the nail polish from Harvey's gallery manager?"

"That's right, I forgot about it. Why don't you and Harry go by the East-West Gallery tomorrow and ask the manager? It'll be good for Harry to size up the gallery and get a feel for what they sell. Maybe you'll bump into Harvey again and you can find out what he's been up to."

"Sounds good to me," Win responded. "Harry, I guess you need to contact Suzie about the women joining us for our trip north this afternoon. We also could do with some lunch"

Dan saw them to the door, put his arm around Win and whispered to him, "We have only a few more days till we wind this thing down. Just hang in there with us. Ciao."

Chapter 44.

The next morning, Win was at his desk paying some bills when Harry wandered in and said, "Hey, I was going to take a short walk before breakfast. It's a beautiful day and I wouldn't mind taking in some local scenery. Care to join me?" He gestured with his head that they should go outside.

"That sounds like a great idea."

They put on jackets and walked down the driveway away from the house before Harry started to talk. "We need to go over some things and I need to check with Dan as to what's happening. First thing that I need is some information about your friend Herky. We checked him out and he has a clean record. What kind of car does he drive? We don't want our guards to stop him unnecessarily."

"Herky drives an old, beat-up pickup truck. I don't know the make but it's light blue and rusty, but despite the rust, it's now very clean and at least partly shiny. His wife had an issue about the truck's condition, so he gussied it up. Herky is slight in build, has intense blue eyes and is pretty much bald. He's about five foot, ten inches tall."

"Over the next few days, we need to get you measured for some special clothes to conceal a recording device for your meeting with Wong. Think about what sort of clothes you would typically wear to visit him. Also, with your consent, we'll need to make some modifications to your car to protect you. We'll undo them when this business is over and it won't damage the vehicle."

"What kind of modifications?"

"For one thing, we'd like to remove the bench part of your car's rear seat. We might also add some side armored panels inside the car."

"Hey, this isn't Afghanistan. Do you really think someone might attack my car?"

"We don't take chances."

"What's the seat thing about?"

"When you go to visit Wong, we'll have an armed guard concealed in the rear seat area to protect you. Right now, your death would make a lot of people in Beijing happy. There's nothing more dangerous to an intelligence operation than an unskilled amateur who stumbles onto an operation and acts like a bull in a china shop. No pun intended. We're reasonably sure they don't know you're working with us. And lastly, you would make a very credible witness if Wong were tried for espionage."

"They did try to kill me before," Win admitted.

"Before I call Dan, tell me what you were planning to do today with your friend."

"Herky and I have lunch. He gets to choose a different place each week. After lunch, he drops me off at the top of Canyon Road and then goes off to run errands. I usually walk down the Road, stop in different galleries, and I often visit Harvey's gallery. I work my way down and meet Herky at the junction of Canyon Road and Paseo de Peralta. That's my routine in a nutshell."

"Unfortunately, routines can be dangerous if someone is interested in following you. Okay, why don't you go down and get the newspaper while I speak to Dan."

Win got the paper and walked back up to meet Harry, who obviously didn't have a long conversation with Dan. They went in and found the two ladies busy preparing breakfast. Win was getting spoiled; he usually was the one to make breakfast and it was typically a humble repast. Breakfast was quite elaborate now, and they all had a lively, fake conversation. After breakfast, Win went back to his study. Before he knew it, he was startled by the stealthy arrival of Herky who'd padded in wearing his usual felt slippers.

"Hi, Win! You know, your front door was open. Looks like you have visitors. Are you going to be able to join me today?"

"Yeah, I meant to call you to see if it would be okay if my old friend Harry joined us."

"Sure. Now that I've cleaned up the truck there's room for three up front."

"Harry and Suzie are two of our oldest friends. They were at a meeting in Albuquerque that was pretty boring so they left early to spend a few days with us."

"I hope he doesn't mind hot food. I was planning to try a new restaurant that just opened: Hacienda Hots, on Cerrillos Road."

"We'll just have to find out when we get there."

Harry came into the study and Win introduced him to Herky, and then they all headed for Herky's truck in the driveway. Harry insisted Win sit in the center of the front seat and off they went.

Win asked, "Harry, I hope you don't mind hot chili?"

"Not at all; I'm actually a chili lover."

Herky and Harry had a lively conversation, comparing their life histories. Win didn't have any inkling as to the truth of Harry's story, but it sounded mighty believable. It wasn't long before Herky got around to his favorite topic: physical fitness. Herky quizzed Harry thoroughly about what he did to exercise and then gave him his standard lecture on the health benefits of fitness and its life-prolonging effects. Harry was all smiles.

They finally reached the new restaurant, which was a typical Santa Fe ethnic restaurant with Formica tabletops. The food was good but didn't quite live up to its name in hotness, which suited Win just fine. Harry was eloquent in his made-up stories and entertained Herky throughout lunch, skillfully keeping Herky away from his monotonous fixation on the Fountain of Youth, AKA fitness. Win picked up the tab; it was easier that way. He realized that he should have asked for an expense account before he signed his F.B.I.

contract. Nevertheless, they had a pleasant lunch and were in good spirits as they headed off, agreeing that Herky would drop them off at the top of Canyon Road and meet them at the bottom in three hours.

Once they were on their own, Harry instructed Win to walk on the inside and close to the buildings, and to get down if an assault was made on him. Harry pointed out their tails: a couple that was part of the Gs and were perfectly dressed as tourists, except for black running shoes. Win, in turn, briefed Harry on the galleries that they could visit in addition to the East-West Gallery. Harry looked at his watch and suggested they visit Harvey's gallery first. So they headed down the Road for several blocks until they reached the alley on which Bill's gallery was located. Before they turned down the alley, Harry did a complete visual inspection of the area and waited for the watchdog couple to catch up.

"Okay, Harry are you ready to go in?"

"Let's go for it."

"First let me show you their window display. Notice that one window is devoted to Asian stuff, the East part of the Gallery, and the other to Southwestern and Indian stuff, the West part. Those ceramic pieces in the Asian window are mostly from the Han Dynasty, with some from the Warring States Era. They're all about 2,000 years old. These aren't their best pieces and are nothing compared to Wong's pieces."

They went in and triggered the door chime, which made Harry jump almost out of his skin. The pretty manager was there to greet them. Harry went in first so she didn't notice Win. "Welcome to the East-West Gallery," she said. "If you have any questions about anything just let me know."

Harry headed for the Asian side of the gallery with Win close behind him. The gatekeeper tagged along at a distance. Just as she started to ask, "Where are you from?" Win interrupted and said, "I'm from Santa Fe, but he's not."

"Oh it's you, Bill's neighbor," she said with distaste.

"I just found out from Bill that your name is Amanda. Well Amanda, I have a question for you."

"I'm like all ears."

"Where do you like get your nails done? Bill said you and Jessica used the same manicurist."

Amanda looked at Win as if he were some creep with a nail fetish. "Both of us get our nails done by Yolanda at Nefertiti's Nails. It's, like, over in the DeVargas Mall. Why do you need to know?"

"It's something to do with identifying Jessica."

"Did the police find her? I hope she's okay."

"They're not sure yet. Is Bill in today?"

"Yeah. I'm sure he'll be glad to hear the news. Why don't you go back by yourselves."

Harry pulled Win aside and whispered, "Wait here while I go outside and place a call to a friend about a manicurist. I'll be right back."

Less than a minute passed before Harry rejoined Win and they both headed to Bill's office. Bill was on the phone as usual, and indicated to them to sit down. Judging by the part of the conversation they could hear, he was talking to a very indecisive customer. Bill sounded like he was pretty good at selling stuff.

As soon as Bill hung up, he asked, "Any news on the finger and the DNA testing?"

"No, not yet; even with high-tech lab equipment it takes a few days. Have you heard anything more from the police?"

"You know, they haven't contacted me in over two weeks. Jessie's disappearance happened so long ago that I bet they've just dropped it."

Win changed the subject, "I noticed that you still have lots of Chinese ceramic stock."

"That CY is a saint; he's been helping me with newly arrived stock from Hong Kong that Jessie bought a long time back. I really don't know much about pricing them or what vintage they are. CY has been incredibly supportive and a true friend."

"That's nice to hear. Did he handle all the customs, shipping, and foreign currency work for you too?"

"Yes. That stuff isn't easy to do, and the exchange of U.S. to Hong Kong dollars is a bear when you do it from Santa Fe. CY has taken care of it all."

"Oh, is this stuff that Jessica hadn't already paid for?"

"Yeah, she usually pays after the stuff arrives and CY handles payment to the sellers for her."

"I'm sure that eases the burden for you since Jessica disappeared. By the way, how've you been feeling? You look a lot better now than you did the other day."

"It's been rough. Finding out about the finger really got me down."

"Look, Harry and I will leave you alone and mosey on. I wanted him to see your gallery, since we're on a tour of the Road. I'll call you if I hear any more about the DNA testing."

"Thanks, Win. I really appreciate what you're doing."

After they got outside and had walked some distance from the Gallery, Harry piped up, "That was an interesting conversation, and you're a pretty good interrogator. So our friend from up north is still helping them acquire antiques and handling the payment side? It sounds like he's in a hurry to salt away as much money as possible before he retires. The best part of it is that he still thinks no one is on to his racket. By the way, I called one of our team and she's off to see Yolanda at Nefertiti's to ask a few nail polish questions."

Win led Harry and the tailing couple down the Road and into several of the more upscale galleries. Every time Harry saw a price tag on a piece in the galleries, he let out a low whistle. When they passed Honey Chiles gallery, Win turned away and winced. As they walked on, Win suddenly bent down to pick up a quarter. Harry, with cat-like reflexes, covered Win with his body and the two trailing agents came on the run. Win shouted, "Whoa! What's going on?"

Harry stared at Win and asked, "Just what were you doing?"

"I found a quarter for my kettle-bank."

"Well you sure gave me a scare. Let me know when you're going to make a sudden move like that. Okay, what's this kettle bank?"

"I save all my found coins in a piggy-bank and donate them to one of the Salvation Army Christmas kettles before Christmas."

"Oh, I see," Harry said with an incredulous smile. "Let's go meet your fruitcake buddy."

Herky was his usual prompt self, smiling as if he'd just won a triathlon.

"Hi, Herky. What's with the toothy grin?" Win asked.

"I just picked up a gift I had ordered for Ann, and it's a beaut. I had one of the shops get their best Indian jeweler to design a turquoise and silver necklace for our fifth anniversary. I'll show it to you later. Hop in, guys, let's head home.

Herky continued with his lecture to Harry on improving his lifestyle to ensure longevity, oblivious to the fact that his audience looked bored to tears. He got so carried away by his preaching that he forgot to show them the gift for his wife. Harry asked to be dropped off at the entry to Win's driveway claiming he needed more exercise, and Win joined him. Harry needed to check in with Dan, so Win walked on back to the house.

Harry came in and announced that they were going out to dinner, and it was his treat. They discussed various choices and decided on Julia's favorite, Bouche. She called and made a reservation and they decided to get dressed up to celebrate their good old times together.

They had a lively evening of good food and wine with Dan paying for it. They didn't even discuss the Harvey business. On the way out, Win noticed the couple with black running shoes sitting at another table.

Chapter 47.

They all slept soundly that night, despite a loud altercation be-tween several nearby coyotes. Win got up early as usual. He hated getting up early, but all those years of getting up for 7 A.M. meetings as a medical school department chair had changed his brain cir-cuitry. He walked the dogs, got the newspaper and started brewing the coffee. Harry soon joined him.

"Boy, Win, do I have a big head this morning. How many bottles of wine did we have last night?"

"Only two, but we finished them and then had some brandy and calvados too."

"It must be my age then."

"No, it's the altitude. We're 7,000 feet above sea level. The first few weeks here, I would get looped on a single margarita." Because of the bugs, he didn't add: *And that's how I got involved in this whole business – by getting drunk and bragging about my skills at tracing people.*

The women were still sleeping, so Win served juice and coffee and made breakfast. They were listening to one of the TV morning talk shows, and Win had just started on the newspaper when he was startled by the sudden, silent appearance of one of the camouflage-clad guards who signaled them to go outside and quickly. So that's why they wanted all doors unlocked, Win realized.

When they got outside and away from the house, the guard said, "We have an emergency, and we need Dr. Sage to identify an intruder who claims he's a neighbor." Harry drew his gun from the holster on the small of his back and followed Win.

They walked down the driveway to a throng of guards in various costumes, a tractor with a large blade on its front, and Win's neighbor, Ricardo, in the center of it all.

As they approached the crowd, Ricardo saw Win and shouted, "Win, mio amico, who are these pazzi?"

"Ciao, Ricardo," Win answered. "Come sta? What are you up to?"

"Remember you asked me to use my tractor to smooth out your driveway? The Market's closed and I was off today, so I thought I'd tackle your driveway and mine. I was coming up your driveway and one of these pazzi wearing a pile of rags ran right in front of me. I waved him off and he pulled a gun on me. They're nut cases. Do you see how they're dressed? They even have stripes painted on their faces like performers in a bad version of Cats. Santa Maria! What's going on, Win?"

Win turned to Pat and asked, "So what's going on?"

"Well, this guy came barreling up your driveway with his tractor and wouldn't stop. When an agent pulled a gun on him, your friend pulled a knife from his belt. He's wearing a camouflage shirt and hat too. So we apprehended him. He carries no identification and refused to tell us anything other than he's a friend of yours."

"Win signaled to Pat to join him off to the side. "Okay Pat, what do I tell him? How do you explain to a neighbor that you have a band of armed and painted people in bizarre costumes guarding your place and pulling guns on them with minimal provocation?"

"Those are good questions, but first, who is this guy Ricardo?"

"He lives right across the road, which is probably why he doesn't have his driver's license with him. He's a successful venture capitalist and our local Mr. Fixit. He loves gadgets, and that tractor is one of his favorites. By the way, I bet the knife he pulled is from his impressive tool belt. Take a look when we go back; he carries about 20 pounds of tools around his waist. He's also a very nice man."

"Coming back to your questions, why don't you tell him that someone threatened to kidnap you or Julia, and we're here from the F.B.I. to guard you? It sounds like your friend is from Italy, and I think they still have occasional kidnappings for ransom there, so maybe he'll understand. You must tell him that he shouldn't talk to anyone about this incident or it would endanger you further."

"What a cock-and-bull story!"

"It's the best I can do, under the circumstances. I don't know why he wouldn't slow down when we asked him to. What's this potsy stuff that he keeps talking about?"

"Beats me. It's likely an Italian word and one that goes beyond my lexicon of 25 Italian words. Can I talk to my neighbor alone for a couple of minutes?"

"Are you sure he won't harm you?"

"No way! Ricardo wouldn't harm a fly."

"Okay." Pat signaled one of her troops to bring Ricardo over.

Win took Ricardo by the arm and led him away from the motley group. Ricardo put his arm around Win and whispered, "Win, what the heck is going on with you? Are you in trouble?"

"Oh, Ricardo, it's a long story. I'm in trouble. We got a tip that someone was going to kidnap Julia for ransom; you know her family has a lot of money. The F.B.I. handles this kind of thing, and they clearly like to play crazy games. I'm so embarrassed by this. Please don't tell anyone about what happened as it could put Julia in more danger. I'll tell you more when it's all over."

"That's terrible. Is there anything I can do to help?"

"I don't think so. The F.B.I. people think they can handle everything."

"Can I finish your driveway at least?"

"Sure. You're such a good neighbor and I'm sorry to have put you through this. Mille grazie."

"Prego."

Win led Ricardo by the arm back to the group. "Pat, Ricardo would like to finish his work on my driveway and I don't see any reason why he shouldn't."

"Are you sure you want him to do it now?"

"Why not?"

"Okay. We'll clear our people and he can get back to his play."

Win, Pat and Harry headed back to the house and stopped to huddle. Harry was the first to speak. "This event underscores the need to get this operation over with ASAP! I'm going to discuss it with Dan, but I think we need to accelerate the endgame by at least a day. This event shouldn't compromise security, but the next one may not be as easy to deal with."

Pat chimed in, "I agree fully."

Harry looked at Win and said, "Now I know why they have a gate around your development; it's to keep you screwballs locked in. This place is a regular lunatic asylum!"

"Hey, Harry, you haven't even met everybody yet."

Win went back to the house and while it was fresh in his mind, decided to find his Italian-English dictionary to look up "potsy." He found an entry for pazzo, plural pazzi, and learned that it meant "mad, crazy or lunatic": so Ricardo's assessment wasn't far off the mark.

After about 15 minutes, Win decided to go outside to find out what was happening. Ricardo was hard at work leveling the ruts in the driveway, but Harry and Pat were nowhere to be seen. Win walked down further and saw the twosome in the middle of a group of junipers, sitting on camp chairs talking.

Harry noticed Win and said, "I'm glad you're here. We had a conference with Dan, Tom and the others who agree that we should move things along more quickly. We're aiming for a showdown with Wong on Friday, and there's a lot to arrange before then. So, lets go into town for most of the day. It would probably be best if Julia stayed home. We'll need to have you drive your car in for repairs today and leave it overnight. When we're inside you need to talk, for the benefit of our listeners, about the problems with your car and that it needs to be serviced."

"There's nothing wrong with my car, though."

"We need to make some modifications before your visit to Wong. Also, bring along the jacket and shirt you'll wear to go see him. Let's plan on leaving in about an hour."

"That's fine with me. The sooner we get this thing over with, the happier Julia and I will be. By the way, the word pazzi that Ricardo was using to describe your team means lunatics in Italian. So he too thinks this place has become a regular lunatic asylum, but because of your team!" With that remark Win headed back up to get ready for the day in town. He waved to Ricardo as he passed. Yup, Ricardo knows a pazzo when he sees one.

Chapter 48.

It didn't take any persuading to convince Julia to stay home. Win and Harry had a nice conversation about Win's car troubles and then set off to town in separate cars with Harry lagging behind. Win was instructed to leave his car outside the service area at an Exxon gas station on Cerrillos Road. He left his keys in the car and then met Harry at the rear of the service station and off they went to see Dan and the rest of the team at the safe house.

They went in the back door where Dan and Tom greeted them. The crowd was larger and more serious as they took their places at a table set for lunch.

"Win, help yourself," Dan began. "I thought we'd have a working lunch as we have a lot to do. We have some unpleasant news for you. First, the woman's fingers found at San Ildefonso Pueblo are Jessica's. We have a match on the DNA and the nail polish seems to be a match with the stuff we got from her manicurist Yolanda, although that analysis hasn't been completed. Yolanda is pretty certain it was the color she last used on Jessica's nails. We're doing another search of the area where the fingers were found. Nothing has turned up and we're using bloodhounds, in case she was buried in a shallow grave. The clothes you got from the Harvey house are perfect for the dogs to scent. There's still no sign of her car, either. The second piece of bad news is that the weapon you filched from your would-be assassin is an Eastern Bloc device used for shooting a person with a toxic aerosol at high pressure. In your case it was a drug that causes acute cardiac arrhythmias, usually ventricular fibrillation. If the Chinese guy had been successful, it would have appeared that poor old Win Sage was lugging his gear up a hill when he keeled over with a heart attack -- a pretty clever way to get rid of you without raising any suspicions. Probably Sergeant Ortiz would visit your house again to ask some questions about your health status to rule out foul play, and would pull the same house-tour routine on Julia and collect all the bugs he planted. It would have been a neat operation, except for your buddy Chuck and his blessed diarrhea."

"If he succeeded, it would have helped them to have my body discovered and even autopsied. That's slick!"

"Let me go on Win," Dan interrupted. "We now have a complete handle on the information that Wong could possibly have passed along to another country. It's extensive and potentially very damaging to us, and of course, would give the Chinese a big jump-start on expanding their nuclear weapons programs. If he's a spy, as we're certain he is, he's been using an undetectable method for transmitting secrets. We haven't a shred of evidence with which to charge him, let alone convict him of espionage. All we have is that he's benefited from the largesse of the PRC in giving him some very valuable pieces of ancient art. He sold most of these gifts and we don't know where the money for their sale has gone. The Cayman Island bank account has a negligible balance and must have served as a pass-through to another offshore account. Given the minimal balance in the Cayman account, he wouldn't have had to report it on his income tax forms. He could also claim the money was disbursed to the 'dealers' in Hong Kong who sold Jessica the goods. The bottom line is that we don't have the smoking gun with which to charge him with espionage. Talk about slick! It would even be hard for us to convince a jury that the pieces were gifts to Wong from the PRC. The facts that Jessica Harvey was dismembered and that a Chinese guy with a diplomatic passport also tried to kill you are possibly related, but circumstantial. And that's where you come in, Win, our trusty bird-dog, to help flush out Wong. That's why you're so valuable to us and so important for the Chinese to dispose of."

"I'd much rather be important for better reasons. How on earth am I going to flush out Wong, which I take to mean, get him to reveal he's been a spy or run to his masters?"

"You're spot on, as the Brits would say! To get the information, we need you to have another face-to-face meeting with Wong. We have a team of skilled interrogators here who are going to give you a crash course in how you might get old CY to tell you his innermost secrets. We think it's at least worth a try."

Win looked down and shook his head. "Without meaning to denigrate the great expertise you've assembled here, I think it's a waste of time. Wong's a very intelligent and tightly controlled guy. I'm not a magician, and my previous success in getting information on this case has been due more to ineptitude than any skills."

"Nevertheless, we would very much like you to try," Dan said. "There's nothing to be lost at this point and everything to be gained."

"What about my safety?"

"We'll deal with that today. Why don't we break to let Win have a fitting by our tailor?"

"Am I going to get fit for a bespoke suit? I hope it's a Saville Road tailor."

"I'm glad you haven't lost your sense of humor."

A small, bespectacled guy in a well-fitted suit with a tape-measure slung around his neck was waiting for Win in the kitchen. "I hope you brought along some clothes you could wear to a meeting with Wong. We'd like to modify them to provide you with some lightweight body armor. I also need to take some measurements for a hat and an undershirt carrier for your wire."

"I did bring some clothes that Harry had suggested; I'll go get them. So there goes my hope of finally having a bespoke suit!"

"Sorry, but our tailor shop doesn't typically do suits and the ones we make have too many concealed gizmos for comfort."

The tailor took detailed measurements and had Win do all sorts of bending and sitting while he measured him, then told him he'd be done the next day and told him to go back inside. When he did, Dan led him to a seat at the table.

"Win, we first need to go over some details from your meetings with Wong in White Oak. I understand that you met him twice at his home, but nowhere else; is that correct?"

"Yes. I asked if I could see him at his house each time. You know, I'm not sure he'd want to see me again. In fact, he tried to substitute a telephone discussion for my second visit. Also, my previous two meetings with Wong were on Saturday mornings and not during the week as I believe you expect this one to be."

One of the guys at the table, who looked like a Koren cartoon of a disheveled, bearded, scientist piped up, "We'll help you develop a story that will make him drop whatever he's doing to meet with you." Win tried to see if the guy was wearing Birkenstocks or Tevas, but the table was in the way.

"You guys don't know Wong; he's very, very controlled" Win snapped. "I'm willing to give it a try, but I'm a pessimist."

Dan interrupted, "Win this is Art Koparzt. He's a psychiatrist who works with us and is a specialist on interrogating people."

Art chimed in, "Dr. Sage, we're going to try to work with the fact that Wong is so tightly controlled. Make him think you're at your wit's end about the discovery that the fingers were Jessica's, and about to report this whole thing to the F.B.I. Let him know that your friends in Hong Kong couldn't corroborate the story about his father and that one of them called to warn you to stay away from investigating him. Tell him you were almost killed by a guy carrying a Chinese diplomatic passport and then pile onto this by telling him you know about his making deposits into a Cayman bank account. You'll then drop the bombshell that you think he's a spy for the Chinese, because you can't see any other way that all of these pieces could fit together. Now my guess is that even a guy like Wong will be deeply shaken by this revelation. He may be able to remain cool and calm on the surface, but underneath, this tight ball of lies he's constructed over the years is going to start to unravel. He can't completely stonewall you and let you go to the Feds, because he doesn't know how much you know. We want him to panic enough so that he'll try to find out the answer to that for himself. He'll also need to get in touch with his espionage controller, who will of course already know about this conversation since you will have used your tapped phone."

Dan interjected, "It's taken time to get a full surveillance team in place, get court approval for wiretaps, arrange protective coverage for your visit, and the like. Everything's now in place, so if you flush him, we can find out where he runs to hide. We want you to place a call tonight at home from the tapped phone at your desk. Art will be with you when you make the call. By the way, you will insist that the meeting with him be on Friday and during daylight hours. If not, you will go directly to the authorities. You won't take 'no' for an answer on that request. Got it?"

"Gotcha!"

Art took off his glasses, held them up to the light and began cleaning them with a large red bandana. He went on, "Wong is in big time trouble if he's caught red-handed as a spy. We're talking a life sentence and stiff fines, so his family loses out on his ill-gotten money. He's a much-respected member of the Los Alamos and national scientific communities, so there's the issue of 'loss of face,' which I'm sure you know is serious business to an old-fashioned Asian American. Also, he's been living in a very tightly controlled little world, which is suddenly in danger of falling apart. On top of it all, your call will probably be the first to let him know Jessica Harvey is dead. I doubt his Chinese handlers have told him that and there was probably some genuine affection between Wong and Jessica. It's all these confluent factors that make me think he's going to want to see you again."

Win frowned and said, "We'll see."

`Dan picked up, "We have quite a few more details to work out. First off, you will get a call early tonight from one of our agents in Albuquerque who will pose as a forensic pathologist with the

OMI. This person will inform you that the finger is that of Harvey. We'd like you to act quite unnerved by the call. Second, we need Harry and Suzie to tell you, within microphone range, that they'll be heading back to Albuquerque tomorrow night. They've already stayed longer than might appear plausible to your listeners. Third, before you leave, we have two agents here who will give you a quick course on how to protect yourself if attacked. Lastly, you and Art need to work on the scenario for your call to Wong. As Art said, we need you to sound like you've gone bonkers over Jessica's death and you're blaming Wong for it. Talk to yourself in your study. You'll have an early dinner at home; it'll be a takeout meal from the Cowgirl Hall of Fame. They have good barbequed ribs. After dinner, Art will show up at your home and will let himself in. He'll prepare some cue cards for your conversation with Wong. After that, you're on center stage."

Chapter 49.

After picking up the ribs and rehearsing over margaritas on the portal, where it was safe to talk, Harry and Win ate an early quick dinner inside. Shortly after 7 P.M., the phone rang and Win went to his study to take the call. A woman asked if he was Dr. Sage.

"Yes this is he."

"This is Sarah Jamieson; I'm a forensic pathologist at the OMI. I knew you were in the Pathology Department, but never had the chance to meet you. I'm sorry to bother you at home. Jim Abel wanted me to let you know that his hunch was right. We got a complete DNA match of the specimens from the woman in Santa Fe and the mysterious finger that was found on San Ildefonso land. It's a pretty conclusive match."

"Oh my God!" Win blurted out. "I was hoping against this. The missing woman's husband is going to be devastated. He and I were hopeful she might still be alive. Oh, how awful! Have any other body parts turned up from the same place?"

"No. That's what's so strange. We'll definitely let you know if there are any further developments. I'm sorry to bring you this bad news"

"Thanks for letting me know, Sarah. This is crushing news! Well, good night."

"Thanks again for your help, Dr. Sage."

After hanging up, Win said out loud to himself, "Oh my God! She's dead. Poor Bill; I don't want to be the one to tell him about this development. This changes everything. I've got to do something about it!"

Harry walked into the study at that point and winked at Win. "What's going on, Win? You look like you just heard of a death in the family."

"Not my family, but I just heard that the dismembered finger from San Ildefonso is Jessica Harvey's. The DNA specimens we collected at the Harvey home yielded a conclusive match. I don't know what I'm going to do. Unfortunately, I found out some things that scare me. I can't tell you about it, but I may have to go to the F.B.I. to let them know what I uncovered. This is one of the worst things that's ever happened to me. How did I ever get into such a mess? Just leave me alone for a few minutes."

Harry gave Win the thumbs up sign and left the room with a smile on his face. Win sat back, amazed by his previously undiscovered acting talent.

Win got up and said to himself softly, "I'll go feed the dogs and walk them. Maybe some fresh air will be good for me." After feeding the dogs, Win walked them down the driveway and stopped at the bottom where Harry was talking with Pat and Art, the shrink.

Harry came over and put his arm around Win and said "Bravo! That was a great performance. You overdid it a bit, but it sounded believable."

Win shrugged and responded, "I'm not sure we're fooling anyone but ourselves."

Art and Pat joined them. Art looked excited and said, "Win, you did a bang-up acting job and used all the right buzzwords. We have the big performance coming up for you in about an hour and a half. An 8:30 calling time would be optimal. Wong will still be postprandial, hopefully less sharp, and starting to feel ready for bed. We don't want him at his keenest. Why don't we sit and go over the cue cards I've prepared. Pat has a tent set up for us."

"Okay. I need to walk the dogs and get them back into the house. Then I'll leave silently to join you."

Win rejoined Art and the others and they got down to rehearsals. At about 8 o'clock they called it quits and Art recommended that Win go back inside and relax. Win went to his study and poured himself a nip of calvados; it was the best tranquilizer for him. He was concerned that he was over-rehearsed for the call and might not sound convincing. He tried to relax by looking at some of the flies he had tied recently. He still was pretty bad at tying and wished he could get back to his normal life and his mañana list. The whole F.B.I. bit was feeling nightmarish. As he took a long sip of calvados, he muttered, "Who would have thunk I'd wind up in this crazy situation."

It wasn't long before Art arrived silently in the study in his stocking feet. Art quietly got set up across from Win at the desk. He laid out the cue cards on one corner of the desk and had a white-board and marker out ready to add bits to the conversation. He also had a wireless headset to listen in on the conversation. Art was really hyped about this call, and Win was starting to feel his presence was more of a drawback than any help.

He took another long sip of calvados, which got Art upset. He got the board and wrote, "No more drinking! We need you alert."

Win put the glass on the credenza behind him, retrieved Wong's phone number and waited.

At 8:25, Art pointed at his watch and moved his arm in a circular motion to signal that Win should roll. The heck with Art, Win thought as he reached behind to retrieve his calvados and take another long sip. As Win dialed the number, he felt like a robot following programmed instructions. The phone rang for a long time before someone answered.

"Hello?" said the now familiar voice of C.Y. Wong.

"Hello, Dr. Wong. This is Winston Sage in Santa Fe. I'm calling because I just received some very disturbing news that I thought you should know. Jessica Harvey is almost certainly dead. The State Office of the Medical Investigator received a dismembered finger from a woman that was found on San Ildefonso land. They did a DNA match and found it belongs to Jessica. I'm very upset."

Art nodded approvingly at Win and raised his hand with his palm towards Win signaling Win to stop there.

Wong sounded shaken. "That is very disturbing news. Does Bill know about it?"

"I don't know whether the State people notified him. I called you first, because I'm concerned that Jessica's death, or should I say murder, is tied in with something much bigger and I believe you're at the center of this whole nasty business. I'm very angry."

Art again signaled for Win to pause.

Wong was silent for almost a minute before he replied, "I'm not sure I understand what you're saying. You sound like you're taking Jessica's death very hard."

Art signaled for Win to respond and held up one of the cue cards.

"Let me be more explicit, Dr. Wong. I always thought there was something fishy about the story of your collector father, so I checked with some friends in Hong Kong, both of whose fathers were antique collectors in Shanghai before the Communist takeover and then fled to Hong Kong. One owns a major antiques gallery and the other an art gallery in Hong Kong. They checked with their families and wide network of collector friends and no one ever heard of your father. I asked my antiques-gallery friend to ask around about major collectors of Warring States Era pieces. All he could come up with was the story of some important Mainland intelligence general who commissioned the excavation of a couple of Warring States tombs. A short while after that, my friend received a serious warning from the Hong Kong government to lay off asking around about you -- or else. For a while I thought that Jessica got into trouble because she was selling expensive copies and fakes, but this changed my thinking."

Win stopped there, on signal from Art, and waited. After about 30 seconds with no response, Art gave the roll-it sign and Win resumed his script.

"I also found out that the payment checks you received from the Harveys in your name were deposited in a Cayman Islands' bank account. That's not what I'd expect of a government employee. Also, I was almost killed by a Chinese man who was carrying a big gun and a diplomatic passport. I'm very scared and disturbed! Dr. Wong, I think you might be a spy for the Chinese Government, and they've been paying you off with antique ceramics. You're certainly in a position at Los Alamos to trade valuable secrets for old pottery."

Art signaled for another pause and Win waited patiently.

It was almost a full minute before Wong responded. "Dr. Sage, you're clearly very disturbed by Jessica's death, a bit unhinged, and this bizarre story of yours is simply not true."

Art flashed Win a "thumbs up" sign, pointed at another cue card and gave the signal for Win to continue.

"You're right that I'm shaken by what I just found out about Jessica's death. Maybe I should just report all of this to the police or better, to the F.B.I., and let them decide what to do, unless you want to meet before I do anything rash and perhaps make a fool of myself.... "

"I'm not sure what I could say to dissuade you from your fantastic story, but if it would help you, why don't we meet at my place on Friday evening?"

"I can't do that; I have to get this resolved before the weekend in case I need to go to the F.B.I."

"It's really hard for me to get away from my lab during working hours. Can we meet on Saturday morning, like our other meetings?"

"Why don't we forget it? I'll just go directly to the F.B.I. Yeah, that'll be best."

Again, Wong was prompt in his response. "Look, you're clearly very distraught and maybe I can help put your mind at ease. Why don't we meet on Friday at noon at my house? I can get away for a short meeting with you then. Is that all right?"

"Yeah, that'll work for me.

"See you on Friday at noon then. Take care of your health, Dr. Sage."

Win hung up the phone and let out a long, silent sigh of relief.

Art was all smiles as he signaled for them to go outside to talk. He gave Win a big hug as they walked down the driveway to meet with Harry and Pat. Harry was the first to ask how it all went.

Art responded with a big smile, "Win played him like a fiddle. It was beautiful!"

To which Win replied, "And you played me like a puppet!"

Chapter 50.

Win was exhausted again and slept like a rock that night. He and Harry rose early the next morning and were puttering around in the kitchen fixing breakfast when Harry said loudly, in front of one of the bugs, "I called in to my office this morning and unfortunately, I've been playing hooky too long from work. They need me back in St. Louis. So what we plan to do is spend the afternoon here with you and head off to Albuquerque tonight. We'll spend the night at an airport hotel and catch an early flight tomorrow. So we ought to use today to do a bit more sightseeing and have a nice lunch in town."

"That's a great idea. Julia and I are sure going to miss you. It was terrific seeing you again after all these years."

Harry made a sour face at Win's overacting. He got out a pad and wrote a note: "Today, we need both you and Julia out of the house and while you're here, stay away from any windows."

Win nodded in response.

They were soon joined by Julia and Suzie and had a nice breakfast while gabbing away about their fictitious plans for sightseeing. As they drove into town, they picked up two accompanying cars, one in front and one behind. Win started to wonder what they thought might happen, and the possibilities weren't pleasant.

At the safe house they were ushered in through the back door. Win was surprised to see his car parked behind the house. The same crew was there and Dan came up to Win and took him by the arm into the kitchen.

"You did some nice work last night, Win, and the final phase is now rolling. You really flushed out Wong. He took his dog out for a late night walk and used his cell phone to place an interesting call in Chinese, probably to his controller. We were able to eavesdrop and get the number, and we already have his message translated. He sounds panicked, which is exactly what we wanted. So now we need to work on your meeting tomorrow in White Rock. Here's the agenda. We need to get your final fitting done for the outfit you'll wear tomorrow. Art needs to spend some time prepping you for the meeting. We need to show you the changes we made to your car and what they're for. Tom will go over your route for driving to White Rock. Last, we need to spend some time explaining how the transmitter you'll be wearing works and how to maximize its effectiveness. We have a busy day scheduled and we'd like to get you out of here early so you can have a restful night. We need you razor sharp tomorrow. Oh, don't worry about Harry and Suzie being gone. We'll have your house ringed with agents tonight. You've set yourself up nicely as a loose cannon that's about to blow apart one of China's best intelligence coups ever. If I were the Chinese, I would try to take you out ASAP. And we would like nothing better than to apprehend one of their people trying to do it."

"Sounds to me like I'm bait; maybe that's why Wong ended our call by wishing me good health."

"Yes, you're the cheese in the mousetrap."

"Hey Dan, what kind of life insurance coverage do I get as part of my contract?"

"It's actually not bad. Let's get to work so the insurance won't be necessary."

It was a busy day for Win and a very boring day for Julia, who had to hang around.

Win's head was spinning by the end of the day. The plan was for Harry to drive Win and Julia home. Harry and Suzie would pack their bags and make their theatrical goodbyes. Another agent would drive Win's car back as part of their armada and then get a ride to town with Harry. As they were leaving, Dan presented them with an elaborate takeout dinner, from the Cowgirl Hall of Fame again, and a very fancy bottle of wine. Looking at the corpulent Dan, Win could guess that he'd enjoyed more than his share of high fat barbeque. He walked Win to the door with his large arm draped over Win's shoulder and whispered, "Win, you're a champ and we're expecting a major league performance from you. Don't worry; you're going to be smothered with security tonight and tomorrow. You'd be amazed by the logistics of this operation. Have a nice dinner, with a little of your calvados afterwards, and get a good night's sleep. Good luck, mio amico!"

Chapter 51.

It was another beautiful Santa Fe morning, but without Harry and Suzie, who'd left the day before, Win felt naked. The Sangre de Cristo Mountains still had some snow on their crests and the sun made it sparkle. He put the dogs on their leads and headed down the road to get the newspaper. There seemed to be a pile of rags inside every clump of trees.

Pat greeted him at the bottom of the hill. "Good to see you up bright and early! We have a lot of people out here now, so keep your dogs on their leashes. We should start getting you ready at 9:30 and plan on leaving at 10:30."

"Pat, don't you think that's a bit early? The drive to White Oak shouldn't take more than 45 minutes and that's following the speed limits. I usually do it in a lot less time."

"What if you got a flat tire on the way? It's better to get there early and wait."

"Okay, I'll be ready at 9:30."

Win showered, shaved, got dressed and made breakfast. Promptly at 9:30, Pat and two assistants entered the house silently. They decided to use the guest bedroom for Win's preparation since they had removed the only transmitter in that room. They still didn't talk. Win took off his shirt and donned his new electronic undershirt. The wires were connected to batteries in his pants pocket through small holes punched in the inside of the pocket. Pat indicated that they should go outside onto the portal. The guest room had its own door to the portal, which they used to go outside. Pat's assistant whispered some things close to Win's chest while Pat was listening with a headset. They did some volume adjustments and Pat turned the gizmo off to conserve battery power. The dressing continued outside. Pat pointed out that the portal had a tall, concrete, stucco-covered wall, so they were safe from snipers. Pat placed a Pittsburgh Pirates baseball cap on Win's head. It fit perfectly, but weighed a ton. Win whispered to Pat, "What's with this hat? It weighs at least ten pounds."

"It has a customized helmet inside."

"You gotta be joking!"

"This isn't any joke, Win. I just hope we don't have a demonstration today of why."

Win was next fitted with his modified shirt. It too was oddly heavy, and his baseball jacket also weighed an extra five pounds. It occurred to him that Herky would love this outfit; it was like walking around wearing weights. Just think of the extra calories he could burn off! Pat indicated that they should take a walk down the driveway. When they got away from the house she asked, "How does the outfit feel when you move?"

"It feels fine, except for the extra weight."

Pat put her headset on and said, "Let's check the operation of your wire. Say something in your normal conversational voice."

Win recited, "Whan that Aprill with his shoures soote. The droghte of..."

"That's enough please."

Art appeared from a tent in the hollow and greeted Win. "Hi, Win. Do you need a review of what you're to say to Wong?"

"I don't think so. My main worry is that I've been so thoroughly prepped that I'll lose all spontaneity and flexibility."

"Having sat in on your previous performance, I don't think you'll have a problem."

Win and Pat went up to the house, and on the way Pat reviewed how to turn the recording device on and what to do if it didn't work. The gizmo in his undershirt had a full backup system in the event of one system's failure. They went inside, sat in the living room and waited silently.

At 10:20, Pat got up and signaled Win to go outside. Win's car had been moved down the hill and parked at the dogleg in the driveway that concealed the car from the road. Pat had Win get in and see how it felt after the modifications. The heavy board-like material on the inside of the doors didn't bother him, but the new seat covers did. He readjusted the seat's position to compensate for the thick new cover. An agent, all in black, wearing a helmet and body armor, got into the back and settled into a box-like structure that replaced the bench part of the rear seat. This guy was packing: he had what looked like an automatic rifle and a sawed-off shotgun.

Pat gave Win a map and typed out, large-print driving directions to Wong's house. She said, "You should go back to the house and empty your bladder. It's amazing what anxiety can do to urine production"

"That's a good idea. Is there anything you don't think of in planning these operations?"

"My job is to think of everything in advance. There's zero tolerance for errors." Win came back, got in the car and buckled up. The guy in the back lay down on the floor with a black cover over him. Pat tapped her watch and said, "Let's roll! Good luck, Win."

Art piped in. "Win, just stay cool, stick to your script, but don't hesitate to deviate if necessary. Good luck!"

Win drove out through the subdivision gate, glad that Armondo didn't seem to notice the dude in the back. They drove down Camino la Tierra to the 599 Bypass and then to 84/285, going north. The guy in the back was talking on a walkie-talkie and said, "Okay Rat Master, this is Jimbo in the trap-mobile. We're out of the gate and heading onto 84/285. Keep me posted."

Win asked if it was all right to turn on the radio, but his guard politely informed him that it would interfere with operations, so no.

Win responded, "You know, when we opened our Wells Fargo checking account neither my wife nor I ever thought we would actually have someone riding shotgun with us."

"Your sense of humor is becoming legendary in the Bureau. Please spare me. Dr. Sage."

They drove silently for the next ten minutes, until the radio crackled and Jimbo answered. "Rat Master, this is Jimbo."

"Jimbo, we think we have a rat springing for the cheese. He pulled in behind you about a mile ago. It's a tan Chevy Suburban. I can't read the plates from up here. I'll keep you posted. We have two exterminators on his tail."

"Roger."

Win said, "Something tells me that I'm the cheese."

"You're the cheese all right, and this car is the trap to catch the rat. Rat Master is above us in a chopper."

Win tried to drive on as if nothing unusual was happening. As he neared the turn-off to Los Alamos and White Rock, the radio crackled again. "Jimbo, you're three miles from the chokepoint. Do you read me?"

"Roger. Are the exterminators still in position?"

"The answer is affirmative. The big catcher is waiting at the chokepoint now."

"Rat Master we're a go, from our end."

"Roger and good luck."

Win could now see the tan Chevy Suburban in his rear view mirror, catching up. The guy was making no effort to remain out of sight now. Win just kept going. After about five minutes, Jimbo said, "We're going to make a sudden turn to the left about a mile ahead. I want you to increase your speed."

"What's going on?"

"We need to catch a rat or two, before you go on to White Rock. Don't worry; we have a lot of firepower waiting."

Jimbo got on the radio and reported, "Rat Master, this is Jimbo. We're coming up on the chokepoint in about thirty seconds."

"Jimbo, this is Rat Master. Everything's in place. It's a go. Good luck."

Win suddenly realized that Jimbo in the back was using some sort of periscope to look forward without being seen. "Okay, Doc, we'll turn just ahead. Speed up more. Now! Take a sharp left!"

The wheels screeched as Win made the sudden turn at high speed, closely followed by the Suburban. Almost simultaneously, a large van swung across the main road they had been on and a truck pulled from the shoulder onto the road just behind Win. The tan Suburban following Win was instantly blocked off on both ends by the van, now turned sideways in the main road, and the large truck that was stopped just behind Win. The Suburban stopped abruptly and was quickly swarmed by a bunch of camo-clad guys with automatic weapons. Jimbo had Win stop a short distance ahead and then got out and walked back to the Suburban.

The passengers in the big car were not Americans, and one looked like the guy who'd tried to do Win in last week. The two guys were taken out of the car and searched. They had Chinese passports and were carrying an automatic rifle, concealed handguns, and an Eastern European air pistol. One of the FBI agents held up a walkie-talkie he had retrieved from the car and shouted, "We got this before they had a chance to use it."

Jimbo rejoined Win and reported, "I think we got the guy who tried to kill you last weekend. We thought this might happen, and that's why we allocated extra time for your trip. They were hoping to try to get you before you got to Wong. He's their big prize, and they need to keep you as far away from him as possible. Okay, let's turn around and get going again to White Rock." Jimbo got on the radio again. "Rat Master, this is Jimbo."

"Come in, Jimbo. How did it go?"

"Got two rats with black books and heavy duty hardware. We're heading back on the road to our destination."

Win said, "I think I know what you mean by hardware, but what do you mean by black books?"

"Oh, they're diplomatic passports. They have black covers. These two guys are with the Houston PRC Consulate. They were taking one helluva risk to get you. It also shows that they're still unaware you're working with us. You're good, Sage, very good!"

"So what do we do now?"

"We head on to Wong's house in White Rock. You know, we're not out of the woods yet. We have two more take-out setups ahead, just in case they try to interdict us again. So, let's move it and get to White Rock."

"You guys don't take chances; do you?"

"Taking chances is for amateurs."

Jimbo got on the radio again. "Jimbo to Rat Master; we're ready to roll."

"Okay, Jimbo, you're clear and the two Exterminators will pick up behind you. Super-rat is on his way home."

"Who's the cliché maestro that writes you guys' lines? They're epically trite."

"And you were epically in danger. So spare me your humor."

The rest of the trip to White Rock was uneventful, and at 11:50 A.M., Win parked his car across the street from Wong's house. All in all, they hadn't made bad time, given the extra side trip en route.

Chapter 52.

Win was spent from his stunt-driving episode. His instructions were to wait in the car until two minutes before noon and then walk up to Wong's door, wearing his protective garb. He was told there would be heavy-duty protection around Wong's house, but he couldn't detect anything. He asked, "Where's all my protection? Maybe the Gs have substituted garbage cans or fire hydrants for their rag outfits."

"You're not so funny, Dr. Sage. You've got one more minute and then it's show time. Break a leg, as they say in show biz."

"Let's hope a broken leg is the worst that happens to me. Adios, amigo; here I go."

Just as Win was about to exit, the radio crackled. "Hold it Doc, until I learn what this is about." He picked up the radio and said, "This is Jimbo."

"Jimbo, is the Cheese still with you?"

"Yes. He was just about to step out."

"Good. Tell him that Art has a trump card for him to play, if needed. The number that Super-rat dialed Wednesday night was for the cell phone of Sage's black-book friend from last weekend's episode in the Jemez. He's one of the two guys we just picked up. The guy hadn't erased Super-rat's voice mail from Wednesday night. The phone's now in our possession. This tells Wong we have hard evidence of his call and it clearly ties him to the Chinese assassin. It should unnerve him. The card is to be played only if absolutely necessary. Do you read me?"

"Roger. Read you loud and clear." Jimbo turned to Win and asked, "Did you hear that?"

"Yeah. It might turn out to be useful, but we'll see. Adios, again." Win got out and walked slowly to Wong's door. He wondered how many eyes were trained on him and whose side they were on. He rang the doorbell and waited, trying to look very upset. This was his method-acting debut."

Wong was wearing a coat and tie when he answered the door. "Come in, Dr. Sage. How are you feeling?"

"I'm still very badly shaken, but glad you could see me; I really need to talk to you."

"So I gather. Come into the living room." Wong wasn't about to serve Win tea this time. Win waited for Wong to sit and then chose a chair next to him. He needed to stay close to Wong for proper functioning of his wire.

"Dr. Wong, I don't know where to begin. I've been poking around about Jessica's disappearance for two months and I uncovered nothing but a lot of discrepancies and lies. I don't believe you or Bill Harvey has been honest with me. As I told you over the phone, I came to the conclusion early on that Jessica's vanishing had something to do with her success as a dealer in early Chinese ceramics." Win then ran through the same script he had used the night before. Art wanted him to repeat it for psychological impact. Win ended by adding, "You've got to admit, there's a lot of coherence to these theories."

Win paused to study Wong's reaction; Wong was totally impassive, so Win continued. "I shared my ideas with Bill, and soon afterwards, while I was fishing in the Jemez Mountains, a Chinese guy tried to kill me. I was very lucky that he got distracted, which gave me the chance to hit him hard on the head with a heavy walking stick. I thought I'd killed him, but he was unconscious and still breathing. I decided to get away as quickly as possible, because I thought he might die. Before I left, I checked his pockets to see who he was. I got really scared when I found he was carrying a PRC diplomatic passport. I kept checking the newspapers and Internet to see if his death was reported. All I did that would precipitate an attempt to assassinate me was to get involved in investigating Jessica's vanishing and raise questions about you as a spy."

Wong listened carefully and stared at Win icily throughout the whole monologue. He said softly, which made Win move closer to him, "You have a very creative mind, Dr. Sage. The story that I told you about my father is true and well documented. You know, Hong Kong is a big city and Shanghai even bigger. The fact that your friends, who I've probably never heard of either, didn't know of my father means nothing. I don't know what shenanigans your friend in Hong Kong was up to that led to his receiving a reprimand from the Government. Hong Kong is one of the most liberal and open cities in the world, and has hardly changed with the PRC takeover. I don't know what to say about this purported attack you had by a Chinese diplomat. It sounds very far-fetched, and makes me wonder about your mental well-being. You don't look very well and you seem unraveled by Jessica's possible death. I am definitely not a spy and have always been loyal to my adopted country. You would have a very difficult time convincing anyone of the veracity of your concocted story, I'm afraid."

As Win realized that Wong was going to try to stonewall his way out, he played his next card; "I'm not losing my marbles, so I guess I'll just have to make my case with the F.B.I. I think they're the agency that deals with U.S. spies."

Wong remained calm and had a slight smile on his face as he said, "By all means, do so, Dr. Sage. You'll just make a fool of yourself. I don't know why I agreed to meet with you. You've made up your mind that I'm a spy and that Jessica's possible death is related to me. It's preposterous, and I honestly think you're mentally ill."

It was beginning to look like Win was right about Wong clamming up, despite the threats. So he decided he would deviate from the script and play Art's trump card. "Yes, Dr. Wong, I'm crazy;

crazy like a fox. On Wednesday night I spoke to you on the telephone. That conversation was recorded by the F.B.I. and by some uninvited listeners working for the PRC. Later that evening, you took your dog for a walk and made a call on your cell phone to one Xiao Ping, or at least that's the name on his passport, who's a Chinese diplomat based at the Houston Consulate. Your voice mail, in Cantonese, warned him that I was on to you and your activities. Today, on my way here, Xiao Ping tried to kill me. He's the same guy who tried to kill me up in the Jemez last Saturday, and he's failed twice now. He's currently in F.B.I. custody for attempted murder, diplomatic status notwithstanding. He was carrying his cell phone, which the F.B.I. now has in its possession. It seems that poor Xiao, in his haste to do me in, never erased your message to him. You made a good try at stonewalling me, Dr. Wong, but you'd already taken the bait. The sad thing is that you didn't have to call him; an agent of the PRC had bugged my phones and Xiao almost certainly already knew the subject of my call to you. So after all these years of successfully hiding your nefarious activities, you panicked, got sloppy and blew it."

Wong looked stunned. "That's absolute nonsense! It's another story you made up."

It was now time for Win to play the "loss of face" card. "Did I make up the story of your going out to walk your dog Wednesday evening and calling the diplomat Xiao? Several F.B.I. agents observed you and will so testify in court. The F.B.I. now has Xiao's phone with the voice mail on it and the time it was received. The infrared video of you making that call has the time recorded on it as well. These are facts and hard evidence that even a top defense lawyer would have difficulty challenging. By the way, the phone tap was court-ordered. The FBI has other hard evidence as well about many other aspects of your activities. You're done for and in big trouble. You're going to be tried in a court of law, found guilty, and fined very heavily to get the money back. A jury isn't going to take lightly to your making a lot of money spying for a foreign government. At the least, you're going to spend the rest of your life behind bars.

News of your spying and conviction is going to spread through Los Alamos and the whole scientific community. Your family will be disgraced and left poor; they'll probably suffer more than you. So you'll end your highly successful career in jail and in total disgrace."

Wong turned ashen and slumped in his chair. He mumbled, "No. No. This couldn't be happening."

"You know, Dr. Wong, I'm very sorry to have done this to you. I got sucked into the investigation of Jessica's disappearance and just stumbled onto this whole mess. The F.B.I. forced me to do this. I believe you're a good and well-meaning man and I like you. I sense you're actually a very patriotic American and was trying to advance the cause of peace."

This last statement of Win's wasn't just off the wall, like so much of his previous talk. The Feds had done some checks on Wong's student days at Cal and Cal Tech and found he was very active in the campus anti-Viet Nam War and peace movements.

Wong just sat there in a daze, so Win went on: "I feel so badly about Jessica's death and then my playing a part in your professional and personal undoing. I wish I could help you. You're a very talented physicist and an important contributor to our country's defense efforts. You were also very kind to Jessica and gave her a new life as an expert on Chinese ceramics. Bill told me you were like a father to her. She loved you."

Win noticed Wong's eyes were tearing up. He went on, "The F.B.I. told me that my wife and I were in great danger and they would protect us only if I cooperated with them. I really don't like them. It's amazing how these powerful government forces can manipulate you and take control of your life. I had no choice but to cooperate, and that's why I feel so badly for you." Win just sat, looked down at the floor, and was quiet.

After a seemingly endless wait, Wong let out a long sigh and spoke. "Why did it have to end this way? I was also manipulated by a powerful force."

Win interrupted to say, "I thought that was the case."

"I was so young and naïve," Wong went on. "I strongly believed in world peace and still do. I met a group of Chinese scientists at a physics meeting in Singapore. We all were horrified by what was going on in the world, particularly Viet Nam and the Cold War. The U.S. and Russia were bullying the whole world. The effects on Third World countries were devastating. The Chinese scientists had a dream that China could play an important role in mediating the conflict between the two super-powers and become an agent for good in the world. I think you know Chinese history and that China always saw itself as the Middle Kingdom. We talked some more and the upshot was that I would help the Chinese to strengthen themselves militarily, at least in a small way, and gain stature as a diplomatic force. I'm a flag-waving American and didn't think providing some low-level information to the Chinese would do any harm. We're so much ahead of the rest of the world in our nuclear capabilities. I just wanted to help China catch up a bit so that they could have some say at the world's leadership tables. They were and still are such a poor country, with so many mouths to feed that they never would be a real threat to us."

Win nodded and added, "I could see that as a good idea." Art and his shrink team had drilled Win on how to handle this situation.

Wong went on, "So things started out well and I really thought I was doing something important for the cause of world peace. I met with my Chinese colleagues from time to time at scientific meetings and we were very excited by the prospects of close nuclear cooperation between our countries. But it was too good to be true and things changed. Some very nasty people got involved, and they insisted I give them more important secret information or they would expose me as a spy. I would get sent to jail and I would no longer be able to continue with my research. You don't know how much I love my physics research. So I too lost control of my life to evil government forces."

Win spoke up. "I don't know if I told you about my experience doing public health work in Ethiopia. I also wanted to do something small to help the world. The reason I bring this up is because the

Ethiopians have a saying: 'When the elephants play, the grass gets trampled down.' We're both grass to the elephants. It's ironic that we both love ceramics from the Warring States Era. Our elephants are two modern warring states."

Win paused and Wong picked up the conversation again. "I tried very hard to get off this merry-go-round of duplicity I was on. They wouldn't let me. So a few years ago I told them that I was planning to retire and the date was next year, and it was with a heavy heart. I wasn't ready to give up my life's work yet but it was my only way out. As I started to think of retirement, I felt I'd been used and cheated for the past thirty or more years. We didn't save much for retirement, with the kids to educate and taking care of the rest of my family in Hong Kong, so I was planning to work longer. Since the Chinese were using me, I asked for some reward and that's how this whole antiques business with Jessica came about. They couldn't give me money without it being found out, so one of the generals in China, who knew that my family and I were antique collectors, came up with the idea of giving me valuable ceramics under the guise of its being an inheritance from my late father. That's when I happened to meet Jessica and the idea of selling these ceramics through her gallery came to me. . She was naïve, trusting, not the brightest star -- a perfect partner. She wasn't doing anything illegal; she was just selling things for me. It was perfectly harmless for her until she became suspicious about the origins of the pieces. I had nothing to do with the harm that seems to have come to her. I told the PRC people that I could handle Jessica and she wouldn't do them or me any harm. Then she disappeared. I knew they were ruthless and probably killed her. I was right in the middle of this horrible mess and I couldn't get out. Then you came along and made things worse for my Chinese masters and me. I'm sure you were innocently trying to help Bill find Jessica, but you ended up joining me as another pawn in the big powers' game. I'm very tired of this double life I've been leading; in a way, it's a relief that it's over now. I have one other very serious regret. A few years ago, when someone at LANL thought there might be a spy in our midst, my Chinese masters purposely set up my dear friend David Chen. They planted some misinformation and had the finger pointed at him to deflect attention away from me. My peace-loving friends from the PRC turned out to be some pretty vicious people. When they destroyed David's career to protect me, I came to realize they would stop at nothing to advance their cause. I could never begin to apologize to him for destroying his life."

Win seized this opportunity to ask the important question for the F.B.I. of how long Wong had been spying. "It must have been very nerve-wracking and depressing to lead such a double life and see one friend betrayed and another murdered. When did this whole thing begin?"

"It started innocently, just after the Viet Nam War. But about twenty years ago they really put the screws to me and made me step up the level of information I was giving them." He cradled his head in both hands and went on, "I had no choice in the matter. They would destroy me if I didn't cooperate. If I went to the U.S. authorities, I'd be in big trouble, and if I continued to help them I was in big trouble. I was between a rock and a hard place. I was seized by inertia, so I did nothing and continued to help them. I became very bitter about it and that's why I demanded some reward for my dirty work. My motive wasn't greed; I wanted them to pay for the sacrifices I'd made. In retrospect, I was young, stupid, and incredibly naïve when I got involved in this business. But you can't put toothpaste back in the tube once you've squeezed it out. This whole thing's been a nightmare, and I couldn't even tell my wife about it. It'll be devastating to her when she finds out what I've done."

Win answered, "You know, given the circumstances of your story and the way you were blackmailed by the PRC, maybe the authorities won't be so hard on you. I suspect that if you were to cooperate with the U.S. authorities and tell them the details of the whole business, they would probably be lenient with you. I'm willing to help you in any way that I can."

"You're a good man, Dr. Sage, but I'm beyond redemption."

"I don't think so. There's always some hope. Look, I had better get going. I've done enough harm."

"Before you go, I want to give you something." He got up and went to a closet and brought out a large silk brocade covered box with ivory toggle closures that important pieces of pottery typically come in. "I want you to take this. It's a small token of my respect for you. You suffered and earned it and I'll have no need for it in the future."

"No. I can't take a gift from you after what I've done to you."

"You've probably done me a great favor. Please take this to remember me by." He pushed it into Win's arms, led him to the door and said goodbye.

Win couldn't believe the conversation they'd both had. He was dazed and was walking to his car when he was startled by a loud crack that sounded like a gunshot. Before he knew what was happening, Jimbo and two other burly guys pushed him to the ground and shielded him with their bodies. He twisted and managed to protect the box from hitting the ground. After a few seconds, they grabbed Win and rushed him into a nearby van. The van took off with such speed that Win fell to the floor. He was still numb from the meeting with Wong and nobody in the van said anything until they reached their destination about 45 minutes later. Win was still clutching the box when they arrived.

Win was the first to speak. "You guys threw your bodies over me to protect me from bullets. Isn't that what you'd do for the President?"

Jimbo responded, "Dr. Sage, thank God you're not the President! You're a very important witness in this case, and we need you alive and able to testify, nothing more."

Chapter 53.

They stopped at the Santa Fe safe house, where Dan, Art, Harry, Suzie and Pat were all waiting. Before they got started, Pat unbuttoned Win's shirt and retrieved the tape from the recorder he was still wearing. Win took off his coat and shirt and undid the recording device and gave it to Pat. He redressed and sat down at the big table.

Everyone at the table wore big smiles. Dan presided and began, "Win that was an Oscar-winning performance! You're improvisation and quick reactions were incredible! You broke him down and got some very important information. That's the good news! And now for the bad news; a few moments after you left his house, C.Y. Wong put a gun to his head and killed himself. Our agents initially thought a sniper had taken a shot at you. Suicide was something Art and his people were always worried about. Although we would have liked to know what he gave the Chinese, we also dreaded having to charge him with espionage and bring him to trial. We could have kept some of it under wraps, but the media would have had a field day with us. You know, 'there goes the incompetent F.B.I. again' type stories. So this is actually a great outcome for us."

Art jumped in to the conversation. "Win you followed our strategy pretty well and were doing fine. I don't understand why you played the trump card so early."

"Because he was stonewalling and I was getting nowhere," Win snapped back. "I could see the resistance in his face and body language. He didn't know how much I knew. I had to let him know what I really had on him. I think my knowledge of his recorded message in Cantonese really got to him."

"What do you think made him commit suicide?" Art asked.

"I think it was the realization that he was about to be totally disgraced. He'd never told his wife what he'd been doing and she would soon find out. He got in too deep and the Chinese would never let him off the hook, so he's been feeling helpless for a long time. There was no other way out for him. Sadly, he really thought he was doing a good deed for mankind."

"I believe you're right, but we'll never have definitive answers now," Art said. "By the way, who told you that Wong's conversation was in Cantonese?"

Win thought for a moment and said, "I think Dan told me."

Dan piped up, "I didn't. I told you Wong's cell phone message was in Chinese. I didn't even think of any dialect."

"You know, Wong grew up in Hong Kong where most people speak Cantonese, so I must have assumed it. Also, it probably would have been safer for him to talk to a foreign agent in Cantonese than in Mandarin; it's less commonly spoken nowadays."

Art stared at Win and said, "That's an amazing intuition. You're lucky you were right and it probably had an impact on Wong. You've got a future in this kind of work Win!"

"No thanks Art. I've had my fill of detective work and the nasty business of espionage. I just want to get back to my doddering dotage."

Dan asked, "Where did you get the story about our videotaping his telephone call in the dark? That's nonsense."

Win shrugged. "I made it up, but I think it had some effect."

Dan shook his head and quipped, "You really winged it Win, and you were lucky. By the way, what's in that box that you left Wong's house with?"

"I don't know. As I was leaving he insisted that I take it as a gift 'out of respect for me', whatever that means. Let me take a look."

"No. Hold it," Harry shouted. How do we know it isn't booby-trapped?"

Win got up and brought the box over to a table. "I very much doubt it's booby-trapped." Win opened it and carefully took out an exquisite Warring States Era ceramic ceremonial bowl. "Wow." he exclaimed, "This is spectacular!"

Dan interjected, "It's yours to keep. He owned it and gave it to you and we have that conversation recorded. We don't need it as evidence."

Win was flabbergasted. "I can't keep a piece like this; it should go to a place like the Freer Gallery or another U.S. museum. The American people paid a stiff price for this piece and they should own it."

Dan agreed. "That's certainly true. Wong had access to a lot of top-secret knowledge and was a leader in our fusion program. He also had a very long time over which to give secrets away. Unfortunately, this is one of the worst security failures in the Bureau's history. A lot of our security guys were asleep at the wheel. Heads are going to roll in DOE and maybe even in our Bureau and at high levels. The damage has been done, so it's better with Wong gone. We can probably make some more radical and effective changes in security at Los Alamos and elsewhere without a trial and a media feeding-frenzy and then a bunch of grandstanding, indignant politicians holding hearings and trying to call the shots. One item we'll never know is how he passed information to the Chinese for so long without being detected. That's something we badly needed to know and in retrospect, we should have had you ask about." Dan sighed and continued, "It's fascinating to me that in this case and so many others, a secret agent's undoing is greed or lust. Old Wong was getting away with murder until he wanted to be paid for his efforts. He started as an ideologic spy and became a mercenary. We never would have found him out if not for his Chinese art caper. We owe you Win. Just think, if you hadn't tumbled to Wong, he would have retired a rich man next year and we wouldn't have any clue that we were robbed of a lot of top nuclear secrets."

Win was curious, "What happens to Comrade Xiao now? I'm sure he killed poor Jessica and he tried to kill me twice."

Dan smiled. "Oh yes, the marvels of diplomacy kick in now. Xiao's certainly a murderer and he's going to walk. We'll declare him persona non grata and send him packing home. He carries a diplomatic passport and is immune from a lot of things, but not murder. Neither the Chinese nor we would want Xiao to be charged with murder in the U.S. They don't want the political repercussions of a front-page story of Chinese nuclear espionage and murder by one of their diplomats. We don't want to be exposed for our incompetence again. Fortunately, they would be a lot more damaged by such a trial than we would and that presents some opportunities for us. We'll exact a high price from them for letting Xiao go. I can't go into it, but it will be a lot more substantial than having them simply release a few prisoners of conscience. Probably the Chinese will expel a few of our diplomats to save face. Xiao will get his comeuppance; he's blown as an undercover agent and since he screwed up big-time, he'll be disgraced and sent off to prison, if he's lucky. Someday one of our diplomats might get caught in a similar position, although our guys are more likely to be framed, and we'll need to get this person out of whatever country he's in. They'll owe us a big 'Get Out of Jail Free' card. This is a cold-blooded business and there are rarely happy endings. Also, never forget, there are no such things as 'justice' or 'fairness' in diplomacy."

"And I thought academic medicine was nasty!" Win muttered while shaking his head.

Dan frowned. "Can't you ever be serious?"

"I am serious, and pretty angry about letting this creature go scot-free. I don't have the temperament for your business."

Dan smiled slyly at Win and said, "Actually you do. Just think about your performance today with Dr. Wong."

Win exhaled loudly and asked, "O.K. So what happens to me now?"

"Well, you're not free to go just yet. You're still in danger of being silenced by the Chinese, since you could serve as a witness against your twice-failed, would-be assassin. We're still negotiating the price of the release of Xiao and the other diplomatic thug we rounded up today. One condition of the Chinese prisoners' release is that the PRC is never to do you harm again. They'll keep their word on this, I can assure you. We have ways of enforcing such deals."

"You know Dan, it would be nice if we could also get the PRC off my friend Michael's back as another part of the deal."

"That's a good point. Your friend's panicked phone call to you really broke this case open. Yes, we owe him that. I'll see what the guys over at State can do."

"What about Dr. David Chen? That poor guy was deliberately set up to deflect attention away from the real culprit, Wong. You guys harassed him but never could bring specific charges against him, not surprisingly. How about reinstating and clearing him?"

Dan answered, "We couldn't do that without revealing that Wong was the true LANL mole and we won't do that. The damage has already been done with Chen; as Wong said, we can't put the toothpaste back in the tube. We'll just have to let it ride. Sorry about that."

"Don't you people care about the terrible harm you've done to this innocent man?"

Dan shook his head slowly and responded, "Win, there are very big stakes involved here. As we say in this business, the mission is more important than the individual. We can't reveal Wong's espionage for many reasons. Chen's misfortune can't derail our larger needs. We care about the security of our great country very much, and that supersedes caring about any single person. It's a tough business Win."

Win snapped back, "You guys sound like you're straight out of the movie Dr. Strangelove with your high-sounding platitudes. At least you're not trying to preserve the purity of our bodily fluids like the deranged general in the movie."

"Look, I'm sure we'll gradually ease our restrictions on Chen. You know, on things like limiting his travel or access to his papers and files. We'll do these gradually so as not to raise eyebrows. I suspect that within a year or so, he'll start to feel fully unrestricted. That's the best we can do under the circumstances."

Win shook his head. "I could never be one of you noble protectors of this great country. I have a conscience and a sense of justice."

"Win, we have a serious responsibility and often have to make hard choices. It's not easy for us either. You're very smart and courageous, but you can't let emotions get in the way. Things will eventually work out for poor Chen. Enough said."

"Hogwash! But you're right, enough's been said and you know where I stand."

Art, the shrink, quickly intervened with some small talk about minor details of the operation wrap-up to defuse the tension between Dan and Win.

On the way out, Dan came up to Win, put his arm around him, and said softly, "Win, I understand all you've been through and how tensions can build after a very nerve-wracking, high-risk operation. I'm truly sorry if I've offended you in any way. We'll talk some more after you get some rest."

"I just don't like the ruthless way you people operate. I have one more request; I'd like you to get this man's telephone number for me," Win said, as he scribbled a name on a piece of paper. "I'd like to call him, anonymously of course, from a payphone, if I can still find one, and ease his mind. It's important for me to bring some sort of closure to this case."

Dan raised his eyebrows, sighed, and said, "Okay, I trust you know what you're doing. Just don't say too much and keep things untraceable and unattributable." He changed the subject and continued, "We rolled up the mobile listening post just outside your subdivision this morning. They're from a contract outfit based in Texas and are in big trouble for running an illegal wiretap. So you can now talk freely at home. We'll send a team in tomorrow morning to remove all the listening devices."

"Thanks. Now Julia can give me a piece of her mind about this crazy interlude with no holds barred. She hasn't been a happy camper about this."

"We'll have to explain to her again just how invaluable your help has been and how important this case is for the country."

"I think she understands that. She just didn't want to have a very patriotic, invaluable and dead husband."

"We'll try to help you on this."

Win felt compelled to ask the next question. "Dan, what happens to Bill Harvey now?"

"That's uncertain. We'll interrogate him extensively, of course. A lot depends on what he knows and what he tells us. I suspect he had a good idea of what Wong was up to. If so, we'll have to charge him with something; you don't get off scot-free when you abet espionage. Charging him with being an accessory to espionage isn't an option since officially there wasn't any espionage. He wasn't a fence; the merchandise wasn't stolen. Incidentally, we never found any more of Jessica Harvey's body, despite extensive efforts, and nothing of her car either. Xiao or whoever did her in was very careful and clever." Dan got up and said, "We need to get you home now. Our team will remain around your house until the State Department people finish their negotiations with the PRC. Tonight, I'm going to take you and Julia out to a fancy dinner at Alphonso's. It's to thank you, and as sad as the day turned out to be, to celebrate a very good outcome. Oh, by the way, your car is back in your garage, without the temporary modifications. See you later."

Win suddenly remembered a piece of unfinished business and looked back to see what kind of shoes Art was wearing. Art was wearing ordinary running shoes -- no Birkenstocks, no Tevas. Win shook his head and headed outside.

Win was surprised to see his old friend Harry waiting to drive him home. "Now that we're winding down the operation, I can surface again. You did a nice job today old buddy. Sorry about the outcome. You can't let yourself feel guilty about Wong's suicide. He cooked his own goose the minute he started giving away secrets, no matter how small initially. Suzie and I are going to join you for dinner tonight at Alphonso's, so let's get you home to clean up. You can take off the armored clothing now and kick back." Win had forgotten that he'd put the heavy shirt and jacket back on.

Chapter 54.

Win went in by himself. Julia came to greet him, gave him a big hug and said, "I'm glad you're home safe and sound. Dan told me you were going to do something important today and that you could be in harm's way. He said it's OK to talk in the house now. Is this whole thing over?"

"Not exactly." Ever since one of the car rental companies began running its series of "not exactly" ads, Win found himself using the phrase a lot and he always cringed when he did.

"Oh come on Win, you're kidding."

"There's still a chance the Chinese would like to see me, how shall I put it, terminated."

"You've been hanging around with Dan and his friends too long."

"Did Dan tell you Wong killed himself after my meeting with him?"

"No. How horrible! Was he really a spy for the Chinese?"

"I'm afraid so. He never told his wife about it. I suspect the prospect of his wife, family, and colleagues finding out he'd been spying for the Chinese and of being tried and going to jail, or worse, pushed him to suicide."

"I almost feel sorry for him. Did he say why he became a spy?"

"Naïveté and gullibility. He was a peacenik during his college days at the Peoples Republic of Berkeley. In a convoluted way, he thought by helping to strengthen the Chinese militarily he could advance the cause of world peace. Once the Chinese had their hooks into him they demanded more and more secrets from him and he was cooked."

"What about Jessica?"

"The only thing they found of her are those two fingers. She's certainly dead. She probably had no idea that her unbelievably good luck in having Wong as her mentor would lead to her destruction. I believe she didn't know that Wong was a spy, and when she finally tumbled to things not adding up, she became a big liability to the Chinese.

"Win, you got sucked into this horrible mess as an innocent too.

"Remember the old East African saying? We're all just grass to the elephants. In superpower games, individuals matter for little. And I don't think our country is any better than others."

Win was finding the unraveling of the whole saga depressing. There was no triumph or justice, just loss. He shrugged and said, "Well, we need a little hedonism for a change. Dan's springing us to dinner tonight at Alphonso's. So we'll skip a guacarita time, even though I need one badly. I'm going to wash up. He'll pick us up at 8:00."

"He must be feeling guilty."

"Julia, the Dans of this world don't even know what feeling guilty is! Tonight they'll high-five us and celebrate our great success. Never mind that two people are dead and I could have been a third. Their celebration will be about getting the LANL mole out of the facility, having him dead, and avoiding a messy and embarrassing trial. It's all about protecting their rear ends. Their incompetence over thirty years in not detecting the mole will be forgotten and some functionaries at LANL and the Energy Department will be scapegoats. There's no accountability or justice in their twisted world, only survival."

They cleaned up and got ready without speaking any more. At 8 sharp there was honking from a car waiting out front. It was a typical, nondescript, F.B.I. van with a smiling Harry behind the wheel. Julia and Win got in to join Suzie and Dan and off they went to Canyon Road. Win didn't notice another van pull in behind them as they left.

Dan was at his most charming as a host and the dinner and wines were lavish. At the end of the meal, Dan stood up, raised a snifter of cognac and said, "Here's to Winston Sage for a job well done and for an excellent outcome." He and Julia had almost forgotten about poor Wong and Jessica as the wines mellowed them. It suddenly occurred to Win that this was a wake for Wong with a twist. His body wasn't present and they weren't celebrating his life; they were celebrating his death.

On the way out, Dan came over and put his heavy arm around Win, passed him a small piece of paper with a phone number on it, and said, "Use this with great circumspection. Win, thank you for service above and beyond. The Bureau and I are very grateful for what you've done."

Chapter 55.

Win slept very late the next morning. It was a glorious Santa Fe day with a refreshing briskness about it. He went out and walked the dogs on leads, since Pat and her people were still around. As he got to the bottom of the driveway, Pat and one of her assistants came out to greet him.

"Good morning Win, how are you feeling after yesterday?"

"A bit washed out, but relieved."

"We need to clean out the listening devices from your place this morning. When would be a good time?"

"Would 9:30 be all right?"

"Sounds good to me. You know, those transmitters in your house are really state-of-the-art. They're a new Chinese design and our techies can't wait to get more to study."

"Pat, do you have any idea when your friends at the State Department will wrap up negotiations with the Chinese and this whole thing will be over?"

"My guess is it'll be sometime today, or tomorrow at the latest. We're as anxious to get this business over with as you are."

It wasn't long after breakfast that Pat and her crew came in to clean up the bugs. Win trailed along to watch. It was amazing how many transmitters Ortiz had planted and how cleverly he had placed them.

Pat muttered to Win, "Your friend Ortiz was very good at his work."

"Did you ever find him?"

"Not yet. We got some good fingerprints on him so we know who he is. He does a lot of private detective work and is based in Austin. He's skipped, but we'll catch him sooner or later. Illegal wiretapping will cost him his license at the least. You know, these transmitters are self-adhesive and Ortiz's popping them in his mouth was probably to use his teeth to peel off their backing."

"Would it be all right if Julia and I went into town this afternoon? We need to do some grocery shopping, and it would be nice to make the rounds of some of our favorite galleries. We've been cooped up."

"Sorry Win. My orders are to keep you home until I hear otherwise from Dan. We're almost at the end and it's not worth taking the risk of exposing you now. So just bear with us a little longer."

"Well, at least Julia and I can hold normal conversations now."

It took the crew about an hour to get all the bugs out and clean up the glue left behind on the furniture. They thanked Julia and Win for their cooperation and took off for their sentry posts.

"Julia, we're still caged birds and can't go anywhere until the diplomats finish their negotiations with the Chinese."

"When will this thing ever end? It just goes on and on."

"Pat seems to think it'll end today or tomorrow, at the latest."

So Win and Julia went back to their normal routines. They had a nice dinner with a bottle of wine and watched a movie, though neither of them could feel relaxed with the resolution of the case still hanging.

It wasn't until early the next morning that they heard anything more from the F.B.I. Win was awakened at about 8:30 by the doorbell chiming. It was Pat holding their Sunday paper.

"I've got some great news, Win. The case is over! The negotiations with the Chinese went well and they won't try to harm you again. So we're packing up our stuff and we'll be leaving this morning. Thank you for being so tolerant of our taking over your lives.

Oh, Dan wanted me to tell you that your friend in Hong Kong now has a clean slate with the Government there and Subject X, whoever that is, is now being covertly cleared." She gave Win a hug and said, "Take care Win. You did a great job. Just remember not to say anything about this whole episode to anybody. It's in your best interest to stay mum. Ciao!"

Chapter 56.

Win went inside and found Julia busy in the kitchen. He shouted to her, "It's all over!"

"Do you mean the Wong affair?"

"Yeah. Pat just came up to tell me it's all wrapped up and they're leaving us alone finally. We're no longer in danger. We got so swept up in this nasty business that going back to a normal life is going to seem strange and lonely for a while."

"So what shall we do today? I would actually like to do nothing and putter around the house without any watchdogs."

"I need to run into town for some groceries and to make a phone call."

"That's fine, but why do you need to make a call in town, Win?"

"I need to make an anonymous call from a pay phone. It's part of the wrap-up of this crazy case. If I remember correctly, there's an old-style, payphone in the lobby of the Eldorado Hotel."

"I thought your career as a detective was over."

"It is. This is a humanitarian call. I need to do one good deed after all the trouble I've stirred up."

Win gathered up a bunch of coins before he left. He drove into town and pulled into the Sandoval Parking Garage across from the Eldorado. He found a parking space, put on a large-brimmed hat and crossed the street to the hotel. He pulled the brim down, went into the lobby and found the pay phone booth near the restrooms. He retrieved the piece of paper with a phone number that Dan had given him at Alphonso's, and proceeded to dial the number. The mechanical operator asked him to deposit 95 cents. The phone rang five times before someone answered. It was an older-sounding woman's voice that said "Hello."

Win started his spiel, "Is this Mrs. David Chen?"

"Yes. Who's calling?"

"I'm a friend of C.Y. Wong. I'm afraid you don't know me."

She interrupted, "How did you get our phone number? It's unlisted."

"From the U.S. Government."

"C.Y. Wong just died, I heard."

"That's why I'm calling. I wish to speak to your husband."

"Who are you and what's this all about? I don't want to have anything to do with the Government."

"I don't work for the U.S. or any other Government and I need to remain anonymous. I'm calling about the trouble your husband had with the security people at LANL a few years back. I was with C.Y. Wong at his home just before he died, and he asked me to tell your husband something very important. I'm sure your husband will want to hear what Wong said. Hear me out; don't hang up please."

"You're not one of those nasty reporters, are you?"

"No, ma'am; I'm not. Please connect me with your husband. I will ask him nothing; only tell him some things he needs to know for peace of mind. Look, he can always hang up on me if he doesn't care to hear what I have to tell him"

She thought about it and said, "Well you sound honest. Just don't hurt him and no questions. Let me get him."

As Win was waiting, the operator asked for deposit of another 95 cents. Dr. Chen finally came to the phone and asked, "Who's this and what's this about?"

"I can't tell you who I am, but I was with C.Y. Wong just before he committed suicide at his home in White Rock on Friday."

"I heard he'd died, but I didn't know it was a suicide. Was he ill?"

"No. Wong was a spy for the People's Republic of China and had just been found out. I was with him in his home when he was confronted with the charges. He confessed and told me that one of his greatest regrets was that Chinese Government agents had directed attention to you as a possible spy to protect him from being discovered. You became a decoy. You were his friend, and you were thrown to the dogs to protect him."

There was a long silence before Chen responded, "So CY was the LANL mole! He sure had me fooled."

"Yes, he was the mole! Look, this call will never have occurred and you can't trace me. News about Wong being a spy will never surface. The U.S. Government will never harass you again about being a spy or disloyal to the U.S. Trust me on this. You'll find that the government will ease restrictions on your travel, ease any limits on access to your files and things like that. They'll do it gradually though. All you may find out about this in the newspapers is that some people at LANL and DOE will get fired and maybe that some Chinese diplomats get expelled."

"Why are you telling me this?"

"To set the record straight and put your mind at ease. I think CY will rest easier in his troubled grave with you knowing this. The U.S. Government will never admit it made a glaring error in charging you wrongly. They can't correct things publicly without revealing a lot of embarrassing information about Wong. But now you know that they know you're completely innocent. Goodbye." Win hung up abruptly and quickly exited the hotel. He hoped this information would ease some of the hurt of Chen's disgrace and not exacerbate it. He then wondered why he did this. It wasn't at Wong's request; he never really made one.

Win pondered this as he hotfooted it over to the garage and got into his car. He felt he needed to get as far away from that phone as possible. He could hardly imagine how much it must have hurt Chen to be framed and falsely accused of another man's crimes and how Chen and his wife will feel now. Although they could never make a real case against him, Chen's career was ruined. He was another innocent caught in this elephants' fight.

That evening after dinner, it occurred to Win that Chen wasn't the only one who needed some balm. He decided to send an e-mail to his friend Michael in Hong Kong. He wrote:

> Dear Michael,
>
> I need to bring you up to date on that awful business of your being warned by the Hong Kong Government for making inquiries about C.Y. Wong and his father. It turned out that Wong was engaged in some serious criminal activity that the U.S. and PRC Governments were investigating. He's now been arrested and the investigation is over. My friends in the U.S. Government spoke with the Hong Kong and PRC Governments and you are officially forgiven for making inquiries about the Wong family. You will find that your record is now wiped completely clean of this whole business. I'm very sorry to have caused you this trouble and getting you so upset. At the least, I owe you a fancy dinner in Hong Kong to make amends.
>
> Julia sends her love,
> Warm regards,
> Win

Win was developing quite a knack for gilding the facts. The brief association with Dan and his crowd had rubbed off on him.

Chapter 57.

Win slept late again the next morning. The experiences of the preceding days were taking their toll on him and he was exhausted. Win had some juice before he started down the driveway with the dogs to get the paper. On the way back, he was seized by curiosity as to whether the Wong saga had made it to the newspaper. He stopped and started to read the paper and found nothing at all in the news section. He headed on up the road and let the dogs in. As he was waiting for coffee to brew, he went through the paper again.

He found an obituary for Wong with a relatively large article. Win read it carefully and realized it was artfully written. It made no mention of the cause of Wong's death; it only stated that he died suddenly of unknown causes. From the description of his career, it sounded as if he was a real big shot at LANL. He was described as a very popular figure and a true loss to the laboratories and the nation, with no hint of the true story. A funeral service was to be held tomorrow at the White Rock Presbyterian Church at 10:00 A.M.

Win scanned further and found an obituary, with a much smaller story, for Jessica. She was described as the co-owner of a successful gallery on Canyon Road that specialized in Asian and Southwestern arts and as an expert on ancient Chinese ceramics, particularly wares of the Warring States Era. The cause of death wasn't stated. A memorial service was scheduled for tomorrow at 3:00 P.M. at the Santa Fe Unitarian Church.

Win thought about it and decided he would go to both funerals to pay his respects. He felt instrumental in Wong's death and though he'd never met Jessica, he felt he knew her. He still felt sorry for Bill. Although Bill was probably a three-dollar bill, he had suffered greatly and who knows what kind of closure he's come to with only fragments of Jessica's body found. What a horrible set of outcomes, Win thought. He would call Herky to cancel his usual Tuesday afternoon jaunt into town tomorrow.

***

Win was not looking forward to this Tuesday. He disliked funerals and would go to two today. After walking the dogs, he sat down to see what was in today's paper about the Wong-Harvey case. Again, there was nothing in the news sections about Wong or Harvey. In the "North" section of the paper he did find something of interest. There was a small article with the headline: "Chief of Security at LANL Resigns". It went on to state that the local LANL Security Chief and his Deputy resigned yesterday and that it was part of a national reorganization of the Department of Energy's Security Division. David Fendji, Chief of the Security Division at DOE in Washington. D.C. also resigned He found nothing else of relevance. He had breakfast and chose a black blazer and black trousers to wear. He wasn't sure whether to wear a tie. People hardly ever wore ties in New Mexico, but he was going to funerals, so he compromised and put on a silver bola that Julia had given him as a housewarming present. He looked up the location of the White Rock church on–line and then checked on the location of the church for Jessica's funeral service.

Win got to the church in White Rock promptly at 10:00 and took a seat at the rear. There was a large crowd with nobody he knew. He noticed a black-clad, elderly Asian woman sitting in the front row. She was flanked by two younger Asian women, also in black, who were holding the hands of men whom he guessed were their significant others. They were well composed although clearly sad. Win wondered whether they ever learned that Wong was a spy and committed suicide because he was found out. Win suddenly felt very conspicuous because he was the one who fingered Wong. Win suspected that Wong never had time to compose a suicide note to his loved ones. After all, he heard the shot only seconds after he left the house. He guessed the F.B.I. wouldn't tell them anything either.

The service was long with eulogies by some famous physicists and one of Wong's LANL colleagues; all were highly laudatory and touching. The wife and daughters sobbed throughout the service and Win couldn't look in their direction. As soon as the service was over, he rushed for the exit.

The ride back to Santa Fe was depressing. It really upset him to see the aftermath of his amateur detective work. He realized that Wong's death didn't help the U.S. Government very much. If Win hadn't stumbled onto Wong's plot, Wong would have retired next year and the F.B.I. would know just as little then as they do now about what secrets he had passed to the Chinese and they couldn't take the secrets back. Yes, it spared the Government the embarrassment of a public trial, but just look at the misery of Wong's family. Win wondered about the fate of the house-full of valuable antiques Wong left behind. He guessed the Government would just leave them there. They wouldn't run the risk of revealing how they were obtained. So Wong's family should be well off as a small consolation. Tilikso never told Win the fate of Wong's overseas accounts.

There was a much smaller crowd at Jessica Harvey's memorial service in Santa Fe. Win again took a seat at the rear of the chapel. He recognized a few faces in the audience, and fortunately, Honey Chile Boudreaux wasn't there. Bill Harvey was seated in the front row and was wearing a black, Western dress suit and a black string tie. He looked very sad and had taken his seat as if he were a zombie. Poor Jessica had her dreams answered when C.Y. Wong walked into her gallery, but Win was sure she never suspected she would end up as the fence for a nuclear spy – and lose her life in the process.

Win stared at poor Bill and wondered what he really knew about Wong. Was he an unfortunate sad sack or did he just look the other way for financial gain? Win noticed two odd things: there was no coffin or urn present; and a cop in uniform was sitting next to Bill. The first wasn't surprising -- Jessica's body was never found. The presence of the cop was interesting and suggested the F.B.I. did get something on him. The service was mercifully short and the eulogy was given by one of her daughters who broke down several times. As she spoke, Win wondered whether he would have liked Jessica.

Win walked over to Bill, who looked surprised to see him, and said, "Hi Bill, I'm so sorry about Jessica's death. How are you doing?" The policeman stuck at Bill's side.

Bill sobbed as he said, "I lost Jessie and now I'm in trouble with the Feds."

"Bill, there are some things I need to ask you." Win asked the cop if it would be all right if he and Bill went over to the corner of the chapel to discuss a private matter for a few minutes. Win continued, "Do you know that Wong is dead and that he was a spy for the Chinese?"

"I heard that CY died, but his being a spy is news to me."

Win scowled as he said, "Come on Bill, you knew he was a spy and was using Jessie as his fence to sell Chinese ceramics that his spymasters used to pay him off. Didn't Jessie tell you of her suspicions about him?"

He looked away. "Yes, she did," he said softly.

"Why didn't you or Jessie go to the FBI about it?"

"I was protecting her. I didn't want to get her into trouble. She knew nothing about CY being a possible spy when she first got involved with him."

Win fixed Bill with an icy stare and said, "Bill, getting her into trouble would have been a helluva lot better than getting her killed. You might have prevented her murder."

Bill started to sob.

"I have one last question: why did you come to me to help find Jessie? I'm not a detective."

"I was really mixed up and scared. I was desperate for any straw I could grasp to find Jessie. I thought there could be medical reasons for her disappearance. Maybe I wanted to direct attention away from the Wong business. I don't know; I was on pills and out of my gourd, I guess."

"I don't envy you having to live with your conscience." Win shook his head and said, "Goodbye Bill."

At supper that night, Win said little other than that he shouldn't have gone to the funerals. Julia kissed him, patted him on the hand and said, "It probably was good for you. You need to come to closure on this horrible business and you can't blame yourself for what happened. Everyone's fate was sealed before you ever got involved."

"It's depressing when you tally everything; Wong's dead, Jessica's dead, the F.B.I. never learned what or how Wong gave information to the Chinese, the spying's hushed up, some token firings of LANL and DOE personnel were made, the Chinese assassin walks, and David Chen never gets his name cleared. Wong would have gotten away with his espionage and still be alive if I didn't get involved and I'll feel conflicted over that for a long time. He would have retired next year, so relatively little extra damage could have been done. So what did all my efforts and those of the F.B.I. really accomplish? Not much! I'll go to my study and maybe have a touch of calvados."

"That'll be good for you."

Win settled down in his study and poured himself a good measure of calvados; he was on his third bottle now. He remained curious about whether anything about the case ever got into the media and turned on his computer. He searched for "C.Y. Wong + Los Alamos" which led him to the local paper's obituary plus one in the New York Times. He was curious to see what the Times had to say about Wong's cause of death. It was the same as the Santa Fe newspaper. He found no other news stories. Win next searched for information on the Chinese diplomat. He keyed in "Chinese diplomat + Houston + persona non grata" and was surprised to find something on the first try. It was an article from today's Houston Chronicle with the headline, "Two Chinese Diplomats at Houston

Consulate Expelled". He read on and saw that it was about his two friends from Friday. Win next tried "spy + Los Alamos National Laboratory" and got several items, but they were all old and related to poor Dr. Chen. He next tried "William Harvey + East-West Gallery", and found an article in today's Albuquerque Herald. The headline read, "Santa Fe Gallery Owner Charged With Tax Evasion." It was Bill; so that explained the cop at the funeral. Win didn't have the heart to go on, so he turned the computer off.

He had one more thing to do to wrap up this incredible saga. He went to the closet and brought out the Warring States bowl Wong had given him just before he committed suicide. Win sat down on the floor with the precious pot. The bowl was very rare, and the last thing he wanted to do was accidentally knock it off his desk. He carefully removed the piece from its silk-covered, cushioned box. It was a stupendous, large ceramic bowl on three massive, horn-like feet. As best he could tell, it was worth well into six figures. He gently picked it up and examined it closely. He realized he couldn't live with himself if he saw it every day. This piece had blood all over it. It was buried long ago with some dead person and resulted, indirectly, in the deaths of two other people two millennia later. The U.S. had paid dearly for this pot and it should be in some U.S. public museum. Tomorrow he'd write to the Freer Gallery and the Asian Art Museum in San Francisco.

It suddenly dawned on Win that he couldn't donate it to any museum without a clean provenance for the piece. He probably couldn't sell it openly either. No wonder the FBI wanted him to keep it. Did Win now have to invent a phony inheritance story like Wong? It depressed Win that he could be stuck with this piece as a lasting reminder of the terrible story of Wong and the Harveys. He repacked the bowl carefully and felt like washing his hands after handling it. He went back to his desk and slowly finished his calvados. It was time to walk the dogs.

Win roused the dogs and led them down the driveway. The dogs went off looking for F.B.I. agents, but they'd all left. Win climbed his favorite hillock and looked out over their land and at the star-packed sky. Out of the blue, he recalled some lines from a Keats sonnet he'd studied in college decades ago. "Then felt I like some watcher of the skies," and something like standing "Silent upon a peak in Darien." He remembered the sonnet had something to do with the wonder people felt when making discoveries. Win hadn't discovered a damn thing other than how cynical and ruthless governments can be. He sighed and shrugged. This recollection was probably just another early sign of senility.

He'd forgotten how much he loved the desert landscape. He had gotten so absorbed in playing two-bit detective and F.B.I. pseudo-agent that he forgot his late-night communions with nature. He realized it was over and time to get back to a normal life, but could it ever be normal again? Win never even remotely envisioned retirement would be like this.

He called out, "Let's go doggos! If you don't come in the coyotes will get you." The dogs ambled up to Win and he led them towards the house.

As the procession wended its way up the hill, Win muttered, "Doggos, it looks like your Poppa sure got caught between two big-time warring states. What a helluva way to start a new life in Santa Fe!

The End

About the Author

SEYMOUR GRUFFERMAN, MD, DrPH, is an octogenarian epidemiologist who began his medical career as a pediatrician and went on to obtain three degrees in epidemiology from Harvard. After serving in the Air Force in Japan during the Vietnam War, he taught at the Gondar Public Health College in Ethiopia. He returned to the US for further training and spent the rest of his career in academic medicine, teaching and doing research at Duke University, the University of Pittsburgh and the University of New Mexico Schools of Medicine. His research was on cancer clusters and the causes of childhood and hematologic cancers. He is retired and enjoys living with his wife and dog in the hills outside Santa Fe, New Mexico. This is the first novel in a Winston Sage trilogy.

CPSIA information can be obtained
at www.ICGtesting.com
Printed in the USA
FFHW01n2305061018
48706540-52751FF